Because
Shit
Happened

Because Shit Happened

HARSH SNEHANSHU

RANDOM HOUSE INDIA

Published by Random House India in 2013
1

Copyright © Harsh Snehanshu 2013

Random House Publishers India Private Limited
Windsor IT Park, 7th Floor, Tower-B
A-1, Sector 125, Noida-201 301, UP

Random House Group Limited
20 Vauxhall Bridge Road
London SW1V 2SA
United Kingdom

978 81 8400 348 2

This book is loosely based on the author's own life. However, all conversations, characters, events, and happenings have been completely fictionalized and any resemblance to any person, living or dead, is purely coincidental. All views and opinions expressed in this book are the author's own.

Typeset in Adobe Caslon Pro by SwaRadha Typesetting

Printed and bound in India by Replika Press Private Limited

To my parents,
Sudha and S.S. Pathak,
for believing and
investing their trust in me

Contents

Author's Note

Before I proceed, it's important to forewarn you that this book is not just a guide to a start-up. It's also a real life story of two ambitious entrepreneurs who failed miserably. Entrepreneurs, as you might know, are crazy beings. They get excited when faced with a challenge and God forbid, if they find something that poses a challenge to others, their madness turns into an epidemic and inducts many more. With time, we have been made to believe that entrepreneurs are tough as steel, capable of bearing pain, facing countless struggles, and taking everything in their stride for the sake of their ideas. But only an entrepreneur can tell you that there are times when he gets scared, when he wishes to cry, and when he wishes to be enveloped in his mother's arms, away from the gruelling world. This book touches upon that aspect—the emotional side—of entrepreneurship, where all your relationships stand the test of time as you fight the world on your own.

This book would not have been possible without the turn of events at a critical juncture in my life. I thank all those who have been a part of my entrepreneurial journey, however short lived it may have been. Some of you might not like the fact that the story is being brought up now. But as a writer and a former entrepreneur, I feel this book had to be written so it could be of help to all the budding entrepreneurs and guide them to not repeat the same mistakes that I made. I am still not a successful entrepreneur and so I can't really tell what it takes to become successful, but I definitely know what it does NOT take to become one. Hope you enjoy the disastrous journey I'm making you partake.

Knowing when to lose is more important than knowing how to win.

Prologue

Patna, Bihar

When I was twelve, I had a very serious conversation with my mother. I wanted to know the answer to a question that had been bothering me for the past few days.

'Mom, will you and Daddy ever leave me?' I asked her.

'Yes, if we find a more obedient boy than you, then we definitely would,' she said, her serious face increasing my worries with each passing minute. Then she suddenly broke into a huge smile and I knew there was nothing to worry about. She was only kidding!

'Mom, seriously, please answer me,' I persisted.

'No, Amol. We will never leave you,' she assured me.

But my curiosity was still not satiated and my question was not going to be bogged down by a simple yes or no.

'Never ever?' I asked once again.

'No parent will ever leave his or her child, no matter what happens. Never ever,' she said. Her eyes twinkled this time.

I smiled, took my cricket bat, and went outside to play gully cricket, imbibing her statement as the universal truth that was never going to change. The question never haunted me again. Well, not for ten years.

A decade later, when I became a parent to my baby—my start-up—the question resurfaced and drilled an irreparable hole in my heart. After raising my start-up from birth for two whole years, I left it. Yes, I left my child. And I never bothered to look back. Never ever.

The Spark

May 25, 2009
Glasgow, UK

Shades of blue painted my laptop screen. Like always, my eyes were glued to the screen. I re-read the address bar for the umpteenth time that day. It said www.facebook.com.

> Sign up, connect and share with the people in your life.
> It's free and always will be.

I read the above lines twice. It was my first encounter with a mission statement of a company. And I was touched by its simplicity. I logged in, completely awestruck.

There was a dark blue bar on top which contained the logo of Facebook written in lowercase. No flashy fonts, no flashy colors. There was a notification box at the bottom right (yes, it used to be there in 2009!), something known as a News Feed in the centre, a few sponsored ads on the right, and my profile on the left. After assimilating whatever I saw, I came to a realization. That I frigging hated the damn website! Everyone could read my updates, which was so unlike the social network with the funny name that I was addicted to—

Orkut. Whatever I wrote on my wall was visible to everybody. And whatever I was writing on my friend's wall was visible to all our mutual friends. It seemed so sickening! All the privacy was suddenly turned into news for people who had absolutely no connection with it in the first place, thus the name 'News Feed'.

I cursed the friends who spammed me with numerous mails asking me to join the damn site. Harassed, I wrote my first status.

I hate Facebook. It's boring, disorganized, and does not respect privacy at all.

And I closed the tab.

'Hello sugar.'

Priya loved it when I called her sugar. She was the woman I was madly in love with. Back in India, she was counting the days left for my return to the country.

'Hi boyfriend', she said in her typically excited tone.

It had been almost one month since I last saw her face. I had come to Glasgow, Scotland, on a three-month summer internship program, and I still had two months to go. Almost everybody at IIT, just by virtue of being an IITian, aspired to get a sponsored internship in the second year, where one hoped of working less and travelling more. I was one of those lucky ones who got a fully sponsored, 'academically stimulating' research internship at the Optics group of the University of Glasgow.

'Have you heard of this thing called Facebook?' I asked her.

'Huh, so my boyfriend gets the time from his busy schedule to call his oh-so-awesome girlfriend from the other end of the globe and the first thing he wants to know is whether I know about a frikkin social networking site! Aren't you already too addicted to that Orkut thing of yours?' she retaliated. Being one of those rare species who preferred the real world more than its virtual counterpart, she completely despised the concept of an online social network. Orkut had been her mortal enemy for getting more attention from me lately.

'Wow, so you have heard of it! I thought you were technically imbecile,' I remarked.

'I always keep myself updated with the arrival of my competitors, especially when I have loyal friends like you who send me an invite to join it,' she replied sharply, which, as I thought in my head, would have definitely been followed by a wink.

'Smart. You would be glad to know that I don't like her,' I said.

'Her? Who is she?'

'Your rival, Facebook. I just posted my first update a couple of minutes ago.'

'Yes, I saw that. I even 'liked' it along with three other people.'

'Really? Which three?'

'Pratik, Ravi, and another girl—Mary. Who is she?' Priya asked curiously.

'Well, she's just a woman I have had the pleasure of spending a few nights with,' I joked, hoping to fuel her anger even further. In the meanwhile, I unconsciously logged into the website that had sent me to hate trips an hour ago.

'Is she blind?'

'No, she is dumb like you. I'm going now; have to check my notifications,' I said, my mouse pointer inadvertently moving towards the bottom right corner where number 3 popped up in a red voice-box. The hatred at first sight was immediately vaporized.

'Hello, come again? You just told me you hated it,' she said.

I was too engrossed in what was displaying on my computer screen to pay any heed to her, and so disconnected the call.

A moment later, number 3 changed to 4, with a wall post from Priya complimenting me: 'You are the biggest jerk on this planet.'

I liked the post. And unknowingly, I started to like Facebook as well.

Two days later, Orkut was history and Facebook became the next grand love affair of my life. Already an avid blogger, I could not find a better place to showcase my opinions, get friends and readers to read them, involve them in a discussion, and more than anything else, get appreciated for it in the form of 'likes'. Such was my obsession with likes that I started coming up with something outrageously witty, or at times, profound or philosophical, just in hope of getting likes. Facebook became a mini-blog for me.

To Priya, I became a bigger jerk with each passing day since she would come to know about my well-being more via Facebook than through my awaited international calls—

although the website did provide her with a medium to keep a constant tab on me.

It allowed her check my pictures in picturesque Scotland, including snaps of my fair-skinned female friends, three of whom seemed quite hot to her, as I could tell from her comments on the pictures.

On one of my only pictures with Mary, Priya made sure I would not be saved from embarrassment, commenting: 'Why is that gadhi keeping her hand on your shoulders?' which prompted Mary to follow-up with a question for me: 'Hey Amol, what does gadhi mean?' After two minutes of thinking for an apt answer, I replied: 'It's a Hindi word meaning "beautiful girl".' Mary instantly replied saying, '@Priya—Even you are a gadhi honey!' If Facebook had an option to like comments back then, I would have definitely clicked it.

In the next seven days, I had posted over 25 status updates. More than 3 statuses a day. All of them were original, witty, or profound one-liners and could easily be classified as popular judging by the number of likes they managed to get, helping me outshine every other friend in my list. I wouldn't be wrong in calling myself a Facebook addict. And the only fuel to ignite this addiction was likes, their number, and the happiness that followed.

However there was one problem. Though now Facebook works on the concept of a 'timeline', back then it sucked at archiving data. The chronological organization of the posts meant that my favorite one-liners, if they got too old, couldn't be traced back immediately. I needed to click on older posts and go on and on to collect data. Even with the new timeline, I need to remember the exact date when I posted a particular quote to check it.

This posed a grave problem for me. And, this was the moment that gave me a sense of a great opportunity. I thought how Facebook was making people exercise their creativity but was unable to archive it properly. Moreover, there was no way that creativity could be monetized. Being a prolific blogger, I valued my creativity and didn't like seeing it go to waste. I searched for websites where my one-liners could mint money for me; and if not the money, then at least the recognition that I was the creator.

I came across Twitter which was a fledgling website back then but was focussed more on updates and interactions than just quotes. Then there were micro-blogging websites, but none that concentrated on monetization or even giving some recognition to the inventor of the one-liner. I came across quotes websites, all of which archived famous peoples' quotes. There was no room for the common man. Oddly enough, a lot of them listed many anonymous quotes. This infuriated me further as I realized that some common man who would have come up with that quote hadn't been credited for it and was now forgotten. His name was probably buried along with an epitaph stating: 'Here lived the man who would be remembered by nobody in future'.

Can't common people get a chance to get famous? Can't they be quoted? Can't their words become immortal? Why is fame a prerequisite immortalize creativity? Thoughts like these clouded my mind.

Suddenly, I smelled a very viable business opportunity. I was going to do what no one had attempted so far. You see, I had to. The seed was implanted in my brain and I had to make a tree sprout out of it—come what may.

As I explored further, I realized that the time was apt. Thanks to Facebook (and later on, Twitter), common people had started writing one-liners, but there was no avenue where they could be archived or monetized or even recognized. Why would you need to quote Shakespeare, when you yourselves could come up with something apt to suit an occasion? What you say matters. *You deserve to be quoted.* Your quote matters. YourQuote. I checked the domain. The address was available. *yourquote.in.* It didn't even take me a minute to confirm the booking. However, there was a little problem. I didn't know how to 'code', that is, how to develop a website.

I thought that until I figured out a way to get the damn website made, I would run it as a blog. I was already an avid blogger, and knew it inside out. Within minutes, I started a blog and put down all my quotes in it.

I logged in my Facebook account to share the link of the blog with friends. On top of my News Feed was my friend Pratik's update which struck me with its witty humour.

The root of all sins is…less than 1.

I googled the quote to check whether it was original or copied. It was an original one. I liked his post and immediately, I called him asking him to become the co-author of the blog. I didn't share with him the bigger picture. He complied, published a bunch of his quotes on the blog. We had two authors now, including me, as I began hunting for more.

An hour later, I pinged my friend Vikram—one of my closest school friends—on Google Talk. He was on the other side of the globe, pursuing Computer Science in Punjab. He could tell from how thrilled I seemed that I was onto something new. Five minutes into the chat, I inducted him on board as the web developer for the website. He liked the idea but asked for some more time, around four to five months, to prepare himself for the task at hand. Having just passed his second year, he still wasn't adept in programming to undertake the project of developing a social network. I gladly gave him the time he asked for, assuring him that I needed time to ideate as well.

I couldn't sleep that night. I was dreaming with eyes wide open.

Late at night, Shardul, my co-intern from IIT whom I was sharing the room with, returned piss drunk state and dropped off to sleep. I didn't need alcohol to remain intoxicated for the rest of my college life.

Sharing the Idea

I was intoxicated by an idea. And you know what happens when you are intoxicated? You start talking a lot.

I wanted to talk to someone in person. Though Shardul, my roommate in Glasgow, was very well-acquainted with the entrepreneurial world, I hesitated to share my idea with him. I feared he would mock me or the idea. I felt he was much more aware than me, more well-read, and exposed to the start-up domain as he headed the Entrepreneurship Development Cell at IIT Delhi.

So I figured the person to talk to about my deam was Pratik—the creative, sharp, and trustworthy friend from my alma mater—who was interning in Glasgow itself, at the University of Strathclyde. I explained my vision to him over the phone. He liked the idea and we decided that I would visit his place in George Square the next day so we could discuss it further. Neither of us had any idea about starting up, technology, finance, marketing, or organizational structure. But, we still called our session the next day an 'Entrepreneurial Meeting'.

We decided to continue with the meeting at my place instead. Despite having no idea of how we were going to take the project forward, our meeting went on for two hours, and we kept thinking of ways to raise the seed capital, an initial amount required to start the project. Ultimately, I came up with an ingenuous plan. We would print our one-liners on T-shirts and sell them as soon as we got back to India. I told Pratik that Vikram, being a Computer Science guy, would handle the technology end of it. Pratik and I would handle the creative, outreach, manufacturing, and team-building part. We figured that selling T-shirts was no small feat and could transform into a big business as our friends Rishabh and Akshay were already selling T-shirts in the college campus and were making big money out of it. We had even heard that they received 30,000 rupees for each order by selling around 300 T-shirts at a 100 rupees each. Our inexperience made us think that after creating a team of around four to five people, we could make over 30 lakh a month by delivering roughly 100 orders a month. The momentous figure stoked our fantasy and we day-dreamt for the rest of the day.

Little did we realize that 100 orders a month was a friggin' impossible situation in such a fragmented market, with myriad players in the field already active before us.

I returned with a wide grin on my face, as though I had been awarded the Entrepreneur of the Year award for just discussing a unique idea. Pratik stayed at my lodge for the night. While Pratik caught up with Shardul, I decided to say hi to my long-ignored girlfriend, who I had not called for almost three days. Yes, I was going into the lion's den to be eaten alive.

'Hi Sugar,' I uttered, anticipating an outburst.

'Jerk! You are such a jerk. I hate you, I hate you, I hate you,' she shrieked. BINGO.

'Why, what happened?'

'You don't care about me. All you care about is yourself. Three days and no call, no chats. You had time to update your Facebook status, you had time to upload photos, but you didn't have time for me.'

'I'm so sorry honey. I got caught up with a business idea,' I said, trying to impress her. She was pursuing an undergraduate Economics Honors degree from the University of Delhi. I thought that it might interest her, but I was wrong.

'Whatever. I'm not talking to you,' she said and disconnected her phone.

'Sorry,' I cried, only to hear the disconnecting beep sound.

I heaved a sigh of relief.

I noticed that both Shardul and Pratik were staring in my direction, grinning.

'See the happiness on his face after putting the phone down. Bloody dog!' Shardul remarked.

Pratik chuckled. I wanted to smear their faces with the coal ash from the hearth in our room. I looked away, vexed. I retorted by updating my status on FB, writing yet another one-liner:

Happiness requires two things. A friend to laugh with and a friend to laugh at.

Both of them liked it within minutes, in a way soothing my bruised ego. But someone else didn't like it. There lay a comment saying, 'Jerk! Call me, or I'll kill you.'

Just because it was cheaper to call from the UK to India than the other way instead, I was blamed for all the lack of communication that happened between the two of us.

'Sugar,' I said when I called her next, faking a doting voice and this time, I went out of the room to not let the duo disturb me.

'Why couldn't you call me back? Don't you miss me?'

'No.'

'You are so rude. I'm breaking up with you.'

'Hey, no need to do that. I don't miss you because you are here with me. You are the wallpaper of my heart.'

'Aww, that was sweet. Now stop being so cheesy.'

Yes, sugar.'

'By the way, your recent update was nice. Where did you copy it from?'

'It was original. I'm a writer. I don't need to copy, dumbass.'

'Wow, I have trapped a talented guy, Mr Sabharwal, isn't it?' That was another layer of butter on my ego, thankfully, from someone who had already buttered my heart.

'Absolutely.'

'Jerk, now you need to say something in my appreciation. It's my turn to feel happy.'

'Umm, you are…beautiful and intelligent.' I carefully chose the last word, for it has the power to flatter any dumb girl.

'You are such a bad writer with no imagination, no creativity, and no vocabulary.'

I was glad that she wasn't dumb at least. It made me feel good since she was *my* girlfriend.

'You are the song on my lips, you are the tears in my eyes, you are the smile on my face, you are the throbbing of my heart,' I uttered in a go.

'Finally, some appreciation.'

'It's not over yet. It goes like—you are the pimple on my hip, you are the wax in my ears, you are the gas in my belly, you are the lice in my hair.'

'Jackass, I hate you. Bye,' she said and hung up once again. I returned laughing. Pratik and Shardul were watching *Basic Instinct*. I joined them on the couch and watched Sharon Stone and her never-ending legs perform...

The next day was amazing. We saw a surge of traffic on our blog. There were over fifteen comments, all of them appreciative. People liked our one-liners. And it dawned on me why the idea was being appreciated. Others were more confident about their one-liner writing potential—than suppose their art, or poetry or story—because it didn't take more than five seconds to come up with it, making it easy for the contributor, as well as for the reader who didn't need more than five seconds to go through one such witty quote.

I had the idea. I had a few friends interested in the idea. The only thing that was left was how to get started, but the question that bothered me was about the right time. An idea was not enough, an idea about how and when we should go about it was the need of the hour.

The next one month in Glasgow went off smoothly, as I finished my work diligently as well as travelled across the beautiful country with Shardul, Pratik, and Rajiv.

Meanwhile, I had also managed to write a novel on my blog and it was going to be published in August, with just two months remaining. It was an erroneous love story of contrasting couples—much like Priya and I—except that

13

the story was totally imagined, written just to popularize my blog. What actually happened was that it became so popular as a blog that publishers saw the huge potential in it when I approached them. So, I was also going to become an author by pure chance.

Much of the time that was left from my internship, beside my numerous fights with Priya and chilling with my batchmates, was spent in proofreading, editing, and cover designing for my upcoming book. When I received the edited copy from the publisher, I sent it to two of my friends —Pallavi and Rishabh for proofreading. Pallavi was my very dear friend from school who had introduced me to Priya and paved the way for our relationship, while Rishabh was one of my coolest friends IIT—the one who sold tees and who I had inducted into blogging.

I was very particular about whom I should send my work to before it got published. I didn't want unwanted criticism that would have led to my wings being cut even before take-off, that's why I chose my proofreaders with care. The reason I decided on Rishabh and Pallavi was because we shared immense mutual respect and admiration, which ensured that even criticism that was going to come my way would be gentle and honest.

Pallavi's reply was short and simple. She liked it, she found it unbelievable that a so-called nerdy guy (read: me) had written such a humorous book, while Rishabh had become a huge fan of my work.

I let the idea remain as a blog for some time, until I came back and published my novel.

The Stepping Stone

September, 2009

Months passed by. The foreign-returned Indian in me was busy sharing stories of the UK with all my friends and relatives. The YourQuote blog became dormant, updated only monthly now. My book had got published on my birthday. I was enraptured by my newfound fame. New friend requests, new appreciation mails, new readers, new likes.

But one thing that didn't change was my habit of writing one-liners. I started writing more of them. The new readers brought in a flood of likes to keep my habit going and after two months of publishing my novel and letting my blog remain dormant, I began considering setting it up pretty seriously. It all started with this mail from one of my readers named Urvashi:

You know what, I see some status update from you, I read it, I like it. And then I'm I like, 'God, he must be thinking I am such an irritating person who is almost stalking him.'

Then, I decide I won't like or comment on your next update. But how can I help myself when the next update is even more awesome than the previous one?

I have been quoting your one-liners in my profile so
much that all my friends know you too by now.

Reading her mail, I realized that it was high time to flush out
the comfort zone from my life. The more I kept delaying the
launch of the website, the more I missed out on.

The new semester was a little hectic and it became really
difficult to involve Pratik into any brainstorming sessions.
Moreover, Pratik had gotten involved with the Dramatics
society and had almost no time left for anything else. Most
IITians preferred to do everything at night and sleep during
the day. No wonder, I would find Pratik's door always shut
as he would spend tireless nights practising for street plays.
In those moments, it dawned on me that the idea was my
calling: it being my child, it had to be me and me alone to lay
the foundation stone.

But was I ready?

I haven't shared anything about my personality yet, I guess.
All that you would have learnt about me till now is that I was
a creative and somewhat, emotional guy. Well, that's certainly
true, but there was one more side to me. I was a wimp. A person
with no self-confidence for face-to-face encounters. I had to
fight an inner tug-of-war to even get the courage to speak with
my network operator, leave aside the dreaded thought of dealing
with rowdy T-shirt manufacturers, the astute businessmen of
Delhi, or any such person for that matter.

For the next one month, I let my ambition struggle for
oxygen in the evacuated chamber of my diffidence. Until one
day, Rishabh, the friend who marketed T-shirts in college
campuses earlier, walked into my room.

November, 2009

'Bro, one of my female friends read your novel.'

'Wow, what's her name?'

'You might know her. Anjali Yadav.'

'Yes, heard her name from Pratik. She is in the Dramatics Club, right?'

'Yes,' he said.

'What did she say about my book?' I asked, curious. Who doesn't like female attention?

'She read it in one go. She didn't say much, just complimented your sense of humour.'

'That's flattering enough. So how do you two know each other?'

'Nothing. She commented on my blog after which I added her.'

'Awesome. So, writing makes one famous, isn't it?' I complimented.

'Indeed, all thanks to you, bro. It was you who told me: "Everyone can write, not everyone can sit to write".'

I was flattered. A person who credits his friend at the moment of his glory truly values one's friendship. Rishabh was that special friend. The real purpose why he had come had been to ask me to register for a course on Entrepreneurial Management, which he was interested in after his brief stint with the T-shirt business. But he didn't know that I was more inclined to take that course and had already registered for it. Besides, as I was more regular, more sincere in classes, he needed me to mark his proxies while he spent his nights playing LAN games.

'It's been long time since you updated your blog, YourQuote. I was seriously missing your one-liners,' said

Rishabh. His words seemed flattering since all those one-liners first made it to my Facebook wall and he liked most of them.

'I'll update,' I said thoughtfully.

Should I mention the idea to him? The thought hit my head. He seemed enterprising, actually much more enterprising than Pratik, and moreover, he was the Secretary of the Student Activity Council (SAC), a student body that managed and organized cultural activities around the campus, and was thus well connected to a lot of students.

The initial kick of sharing the idea encountered a sudden drag when Pratik's advice echoed in my mind—'Don't disclose this idea to anyone, we'll pursue it together.' I thought of asking Pratik first; after all I'd given him my word, despite the fact that his lack of participation or enthusiasm lately had reflected poorly on his reliability to the project in my mind. I bid Rishabh a cordial goodbye. In any case, I had figured that Rishabh was a more reliable friend and would be willing to help at all times.

Hurriedly, I went towards Pratik's room. It was four in the evening and Pratik had just woken up from sleep. I initiated the talk saying, 'Brother, you need to listen to me. What course have you registered for in the next semester?'

'Introduction to Dramatics. Nair ma'am will be taking the course. All of us in the dramatics society are taking it,' he said enthusiastically. His energy had flushed out his lethargy by then.

'Remember we had to start the venture? I'm taking the course on Entrepreneurial Management. Want to join in with me?'

'I have already registered for the dramatics course.'

'But you can deregister as well, can't you?' I persisted.

'You join the entrepreneurial course, you tell me the bits and bytes of it. You are behaving as if you want to start-up now, in college itself,' he said in an irate tone. I had got my answer. He wasn't ready. He wasn't willing. Was I?

'Thanks,' I returned, thinking.

It was time to charter my own plane and bury my limitations by finding a partner with complementary skills, someone who filled in for my shortcomings. I wanted someone outgoing, persuasive, and patient. It didn't take me long to figure who I wanted. Rishabh. My belief was strengthened because the two of us shared great mutual respect and trust. Besides, Rishabh was single at the time which meant he would remain focussed, no matter what happened.

I went to Rishabh's room and knocked at the door. He was busy playing the game Counter Strike (CS). On seeing me, he paused the game and asked, 'What happened?' which stunned me as pausing Counter Strike in the middle of play was considered blasphemous to the divine game for any avid gamer .

'Yes, I wanted to talk to you...' I mumbled.

Rishabh shut his laptop and came over to meet me. It was a highly unanticipated gesture. Dumbstruck, I asked him for an explanation when he ranted, 'Bloody CS! It sucks up most of my time. What should I do?'

'I just have the right thing for you,' I said. But once again, I was encapsulated by the fear of sharing *my* idea with another person. The guilt of avenging Pratik's flat refusal by involving someone else clouded my mind and made me superstitious that things might go wrong. I played a gimmick on Rishabh.

'Watch porn instead,' I said with a goofy smile.

'Asshole, you wasted my game,' he grunted.

As the major examinations were approaching, I postponed the discussions on YourQuote for another one or two months, before affirming Pratik's final stand. I waited for Pratik to take an interest on his own. But he seemed least bothered.

By next month, I was least bothered about him as well.

January, 2010

It's difficult facing the chilly winter mornings of Delhi just when you have risen from the cozy comforts of your home. However, as it happened, the lectures on Entrepreneurial Management were early morning classes that were held in the farthest lecture theater of the campus at 8 am. As Rishabh and I, already fifteen minutes late, tried to enter the first of many such classes to come stealthily through the back door, the plump old veteran Prof. Karmakar, stopped us short. He looked serious.

Both of us stood with downcast eyes, busy as if discerning the chemical composition of the floor on which we stood. We feared being reprimanded. Three guys entered after us and were summoned by him once again.

'Now, since you guys are late, think of a business idea that can prevent students from coming late.'

Most of us were sleepy and couldn't think creatively after a ten minutes' walk in the chilly winter morning. We remained quiet.

'Come on, until you guys answer, I won't let you sit,' the Professor said with a cunning smile. I was glad that he wasn't as serious as he looked. As my eyes forayed across the class, I realized that even the sex ratio was better than most of the other courses that semester. The sudden happiness fondled my creative instincts and I replied, 'A video lectures website. No student would ever be late to class if there was such a website, simply because nobody would need to come,' I uttered, sending the class rolling in the aisles, including Prof. Karmakar who signalled us to sit with a smile.

My witty answer didn't have any takers except for the professor who explained, 'What this sleepy guy just said is indeed a good idea. In fact, there is a start-up in the US working on the same by the name of Khan Academy—one of the most sought after online educational organization of the world.'

I felt elated. I would have felt more elated had he not called me a 'sleepy guy'. Nevertheless, it was nice to see a few pretty faces smiling with a sense of ridicule at me, which I mistook for admiration.

The professor, on the first day itself, cited examples of various start-ups by our alumni while they were still in college and had now made big. At the end of the class, the professor invited us to ask questions. While the other students were getting ready to leave, I—shedding my wimpy self for a higher calling—raised my right hand. You know the kind of nasty look a fellow student gives you when you remind the teacher of the previous day's homework? I received plenty of those. Rishabh, who was seated next to me, said, 'Amol, I will never forgive you for this', but I didn't care.

'Yes, sleepy guy. You are awake now. Ask,' said professor.

'Sir, when is the right time to start-up?'

'Whenever you feel ready.'

Disgusted, angry, and irate looks were thrown at me like rotten tomatoes. I could even hear a girl sitting behind me say, 'This *novel* guy thinks himself to be too smart,' which surprisingly made me happy and more willing to continue, for it made me feel better about myself. People now addressed me as the novel guy!

'I feel I'm ready for a start-up, sir. So what should I do?' I said impulsively.

'Take the leap then,' he said, turning off the projector and walking out of the room before I could prod him any further.

Rishabh passed me a quizzical you-still-want-more? look. I shrugged and walked away.

'What do you want to start a venture on?' Rishabh asked me on the way back.

The soothing 10 o'clock winter sun had just risen from its slumber and shown its face, coming out of the blanket of clouds. As the gentle heat of the sun tickled my brown skin, I reflected on my time in Glasgow, where rain didn't leave us a chance to catch a glimpse of sun for days on end and we would be enveloped in darkness even at noon.

'Light is incomplete without its absence,' I said out of the blue.

'What the fuck!' he said.

'I wanted to post this on YourQuote.'

'It's a good one, but why do you suddenly want to post it on your blog?'

'Not blog. I want to start a website. Where common people can archive their one-liners, get famous, and in the long run, earn incentives. Imagine, tomorrow people quoting you, instead of the likes of Gandhi or Bill Gates.'

'The idea sounds good. But I can't see it as a viable business prospect. How are you planning on making money from it?'

'You are going to help me achieve that, my friend.'

'Me? How?'

'T-shirts. The best original quotes, especially the witty ones, go on a T-shirt.'

'What if the quotes are philosophical, like a quote on life?'

'They go on other merchandize like a coffee mug or a poster.'

'I'll think about it and let you know.'

'If you can come on board, we'll be three people. My friend Vikram, you, and me.'

'What about Pratik?' he asked, concerned. He knew that Pratik and Vikram had been my co-authors of the YourQuote blog from day 1.

'He's not interested.'

'Has he told you that?' Rishabh asked.

'Yes,' I lied. 'He's busy with dramatics, he won't get time.'

'Fine, I'll let you know.'

⊏⫣

I was happy things were finally falling into place. I had talked to the right person. As I reached my hostel, I called Vikram. It was the first time I was calling him in the new year. I greeted him and straightaway came to the point.

'Just wanted to tell you that I'm pretty kicked up about YourQuote and I'm probably going to start it soon.'

'That's...great, brother,' Vikram faltered in his speech.

'You're going to make the website. I hope in the last few months you have learned whatever you wanted to,' I said authoritatively, taking the liberty to do so since he was my friend.

'Bro, I'm really sorry but I don't think I can be of any help. I need to learn a lot more. Currently, I can just do basic HTML and CSS, no coding as such,' Vikram said in a frank manner. But, I felt betrayed, as though I had been given false hope. I didn't say a thing, just learned my first lesson: In a start-up, never take anybody's words for granted.

From three to two. Disappointment clouded my mind while I waited for Rishabh to respond. When I pestered him for an answer, he explained the delay saying he didn't get time to discuss it with his elder brother who was pursuing an MBA. However, often after classes, I would see him strolling and chit-chatting with his new friend Anjali Yadav.

I neither had the courage nor the skill set to go solo. I didn't mention anything about Vikram's betrayal to Rishabh, fearing that one man's choice might affect the other man's decision.

A few days later, Vikram called and shared with me the real reason why he could not uphold his promise. Four months before, he had fallen in love with someone in his college and didn't get time to learn how to develop a dynamic website. I smiled and congratulated him. I actually felt happy for him.

'It's difficult,' I uttered to Priya, lost in my own thoughts.

We were sitting at Giani's ice cream parlour on Bungalow Road, Delhi University. It was January 14 and she had just come back from her home. She was wearing a black jacket, one we had bought together last winter, inside which she wore a white top that I'd brought for her from Glasgow. Our left hands were wrapped around each other, while our right hands were waging a spoon war against each other to scoop out the Belgian Dark Chocolate ice cream. She won.

'What, this game of ice creams?' she asked with a winning smile on her pretty face. Had I not been lost, I would have wanted to kiss her on the cheeks. That level of public display of affection was doable in the North Campus—it's another thing that it meant getting slapped from her, since she despised PDA.

'Building a founding team,' I said in a contemplative tone.

'What are you talking about?'

'Start-up. YourQuote.'

'What—the blog thing?'

'No, I want to start a website on it. I've told you about it.'

'Yes, you have. But why now?'

'I just want to. I have also booked the domain yourquote. in.'

'Yes, I'm proud of you for that,' she said. Though she didn't pay much heed to what I was saying, she was still supportive. Love is not only blind, but also deaf. I could choose to be irritated but you know, it's really difficult to get angry at a pretty girl, especially if she happens to be your girlfriend who you are seeing after almost a month.

'See, I'm the creative guy of the company. Rishabh, hopefully, would agree and handle the marketing and operational end. There's no tech guy as of now.'

'What happened to…what's that friend of yours in Chandigarh?'

'Vikram? He's fallen in love,' I said, as though love was a dreaded disease like HIV.

'Wow, that's so nice—your friends are getting lucky,' she remarked.

'Either make me lucky, or else…'

'What…here? I know a better place,' she said with a wink. We entered a three-storeyed apparel showroom at the corner of Kamla Nagar market that had an elevator. It was the perfect spot for a quick make out session. We jumped inside it, a little bit of grabbing, a little bit of tussle followed, and as the doors opened, we were wiping our faces with our handkerchiefs, standing at two opposite ends. Thankfully, nobody saw us. Except the camera, which I saw hung over the corner of the elevator but ignored.

We rushed out as soon as possible, before anyone at the reception could tell what we had just done.

'So, it's only you and Pratik, right?'

'No, it's just me at the moment. I'm waiting for Rishabh to respond,' I answered.

'Why? What happened to Pratik?'

'We broke up—rather he broke up. He's busy with dramatics, he says.'

'Okay, I think Rishabh would anyway be better. He's already handled operations before. And you are already the king of Facebook, with all those cheesy I-love-you-Amol fans who would become your website's users, and being an IITian, you'll certainly find someone to manage tech domain too,' she said placing her confidence in me and immediately winning my heart.

Firstly, she sounded interested and moreover, she made me realize that I was wrong. She knew and understood the situation. The greatest support an entrepreneur can get is when someone from one's family reaffirms their faith. Priya, in our steady one and a half years' relationship, had become more than family to me.

'Have I ever told you that I love you?'

'No, but several others have,' she winked and ran away towards the other side of the road, while I stood behind a car, silently adoring her raw beauty from a distance. I considered myself the luckiest man on Earth.

When I returned to the hostel, I was informed by a fellow hosteller that Rishabh had been looking for me. I excitedly went towards Rishab's room. I thought I was indeed going to strike lucky that day.

'Rishabh, what's up?' I asked anxiously.

'Sorry bro, I can't be a part of it,' he said.

'What?' It was loud, resentful, and expressed my anguish.

'Amol, I talked to my brother who told me to first get into a job, save some money, and then think about a start-up, else the money will be a big issue.'

'Rishu, come on. It's an online venture—it requires very little investment. You know with T-shirts you have made as much as 50,000 rupees per order. Think about it, we don't need much money.'

'Bhai, you don't know the hassles I had to face. Manufacturers don't work on deadlines. They delay, make excuses, and in the end it'll be us—the middlemen—who will face the misery of being abused by customers.'

'But what if we can find one reliable manufacturer who works with us efficiently? With my reader base and your junior circle of friends, both of us can create—hell—get entry to every college, publicize the website, and route our T-shirts through our select ambassadors in colleges.'

'Only if things were as easy as you make them sound.'

'Only if you were not so cynical,' I retorted.

'I am not being cynical. I am just being practical.'

'Let's first try it, then opine,' I replied.

'I have already tried it.'

'With just one manufacturer. Let's find new ones. Let me google.'

'Don't Google, JustDial.'

JustDial, India's phone search engine, came to our rescue. Within moments, we had the numbers of over fifteen dealers in the South Delhi region.

'I am not sure about it. My parents don't like all this,' Rishabh said.

'Your brother is an MBA. Ask him to convince them.'

There was silence. We didn't speak for a while.

'You know why people do an MBA? To earn themselves a good job. It's ironical that they are called Masters of Business Administration when in fact most of them study to get administered by those who actually administer business,' Rishabh yelled, in frustration.

I chose not to fiddle in his family issues, it being his personal matter anyway. My family was yet to be informed about what I was up to and that kept me quite content for the time being.

'Rishu, relax. Chill year. Let it remain unofficial. Don't tell them,' I advised.

He was unwilling. I chose to let him go with the belief that if God wanted, Rishabh would return someday.

Two months passed by. Nothing substantial happened in the period.

'Rishabh is no more in the scene. He has backed out as I already told you,' I was cribbing to Priya, she being the only confidante during the putting-the-first-brick sequence.

'So what? You have got an entire IIT at your disposal. Reach out, talk to others.'

'Yes, but I don't know any other marketing guy.'

'Have you found a tech guy yet?'

'Nope.'

'What the hell is wrong with you, Amol? You are cribbing just because you are not working,' Priya chided. She just knew what suited the occasion more—a reprimand or a token of appreciation.

'What do you mean?'

'You find a tech guy and get the damn thing started.'

I knew she was right. I was letting my inhibitions in reaching out and befriending strangers affect my own dream. I was cutting my own feathers before my first flight.

'Thanks. Bye. Gotta go,' I uttered.

'What happened so suddenly?'

'I'm going to find a tech guy,' I said.

'Sometimes, I feel that I put my wishes at bay by suggesting you to do the right thing.'

'That's why I love you—for all the sacrifices you make for me.'

'Have you ever made any sacrifices for me?' she asked in a serious tone.

'Yes, I sacrifice something every night, for you,' I joked.

'Jerk,' she replied and went off.

It was time to test my negotiation skills—the skills that I had never ever utilized in my entire life. I had to pitch my idea to all of my batchmates. None of them were scary, none of them were unapproachable, yet I could hear my heart thumping in fear.

Was I afraid of sharing my idea? No, not at all. After talking about it confidently with three friends, who acknowledged the plausibility of the idea but didn't come on board, I apprehended something—ideas are not stolen, ambition is.

My heart was still thumping. It was the fear of confrontation, the fear of being rejected, the fear of getting critically analyzed by my analytical batchmates. But, with the belief that my enormous passion would ease the process, I began. I was very clear that I would just share my idea with them, talk a little bit about my ambitious plans for it, and ask for their help.

'Hi Sarthak. Are you free?' I said entering the room of one of the best coders in my hostel. He was an AIR Rank 34, a CS sophomore, an International Mathematics Olympiad Silver Medalist, and had a perfect 10 GPA along with a dozen other achievements to his credit. His words used to hold such authority over my batchmates that if anyone affirmed that Sarthak had said something, it was considered an irrefutable fact. I chose him first, not because I saw a technical partner in him, but to get connected to someone he recommended. His recommendations carried so much weight that the person he would send me to would also take me seriously.

'Hi Amol, how have you been doing? I have seen updates about your novel. Looks like it's going well. Congrats!' he commented courteously as I got seated on his neatly done bed. The bed sheet had a giant Earth printed on it, with the moon crouching down. I shifted a bit to observe what was printed on the area just beneath me. I realized I was sitting on a goddamn space station!

'Wow, you sleep in space buddy,' I joked. 'Where did you get this bed sheet from?'

'My uncle got it for me from NASA,' he said.

'Wow,' I complimented.

'So, how come the famous author of our batch is here?' he flattered me.

'Oh dude, leave all that crap. I have an idea. A business idea. I am looking for a tech guy,' I said.

I explained the entire idea to him. He seemed boggled. He didn't expect an author to become an entrepreneur, it seemed. At first, he started pointing out flaws in the model. I took all his criticism in my stride and offered explanations to all of them, except one—how would I ensure that a one-liner isn't copied?

As the discussion went ahead, I could see him getting interested, but alas, he had to maintain his perfect 10 all throughout and he couldn't be a part of it. He referred me to five other guys, all of whom were good coders, interested in web designing, he said.

Just when I was about to go, he asked me, 'Why don't you learn coding? You have an enormous passion for your idea. It would be great if you take out a month or two and do it on your own.'

I was astonished to hear that. I wasn't a coder. All I had ever coded was those rectilinear doodles on the primitive language LOGO, way back in school. I had almost failed when they tried to teach me the simple programming language C in the first semester.

'In a start-up, it's impossible to do everything on your own. It's all about outsourcing, finding a team,' I said.

'For a product start-up, the founder needs to understand codes very keenly.'

'I'll see. Thanks.'

I made a swift exit from the space station.

The next five meetings with the guys Sarthak suggested turned out to be hazy. Two of them said that they would 'see'—implying they would never see—two openly told me that they were not good enough for the job, while one said 'he liked the idea', which I took as hey- I-like-it-but-from-a-distance.

Dejected, I came back and saw the door to my friend Rajiv's room ajar. Rajiv Boddeda, one of my dear friends, hailed from Vishakhapatnam. He was in the same department as me, Engineering Physics, and had also interned at Glasgow at the time when I was there. He was one of those guys whose smile—full of innocence and humility—could brighten your day. Thankfully, he was all alone, unlike other times when all the South Indians of our batch used to flock his room and share gossip in their mother tongue.

I had shared my idea with him once before during our time in Glasgow. He liked the concept but we couldn't discuss it further.

'Hey Bodu, how are you?' Bodu was the nickname I had given him.

I discussed about YourQuote with him in detail this time. He seemed intrigued.

'Where would you get the investment from?'

'No idea. For the initial bit, the advance from my novel would work. I have around 80,000 rupees in my bank account.'

'Wow, you are rich,' Bodu complimented.

'Bro, I haven't yet found a developer. Do you know someone?'

'My elder brother Suresh has started a company named Brilliant Pals. They develop websites. I can connect you to him.'

'Amazing!'

'Okay.'

'Connect me with him right now!' I yelled in excitement. Things were working finally.

For the next two hours, I was on the phone with Rajiv's brother, Suresh. He stayed in Vizag and unfortunately didn't understand English or Hindi at all. Nevertheless, he was as polite and helpful as his brother. He said he would put up a static website on the domain yourquote.in by the next week. I was to send him the layout and text.

I waited desperately for Suresh to come up with something. Meanwhile, I just thought of updating Pratik about the development at my end. Pratik, relieving my conscience, told me that he had indeed become immensely involved with the dramatics club and was always on tours to perform street plays across the colleges in the Delhi-NCR region. When I told him that I was starting-up, he wasn't shocked—which somehow redeemed me of my guilt of having kept him in the dark.

On the other hand, it meant the search for the marketing guy was still on. I tried talking to a few guys, but as you know, engineers are reticent and laid back. Every time I passed near Rishabh's door, I felt like knocking and begging him to join in. He made for the perfect partner, for we shared great chemistry. But then his irregularity in Entrepreneurial Management classes of late showed his disinterest, which in turn provoked my disinterest too.

⌁

February, 2010

In the meantime, there was something else that was cooking in my life. Much like 2009, when I got a chance to go to Glasgow, I had applied to several universities for internship in 2010 even. After two months of waiting, I finally received a mail from a professor from the University of Bordeaux offering me a fully sponsored two months' internship in France, during the summer of 2010.

Bordeaux is a vintage French town, situated in southern France near the France-Spain border, and is famous for the Bordeaux wine, besides some spectacular nude beaches. Moreover, I would get a Schengen visa which would allow me to travel all across Europe. A Euro trip was on my cards. The sheer thought of it sent me into an ecstatic trance. I called my parents to share the good news with them. They were joyous as it was my first academic achievement since my Glasgow internship.

I announced the internship offer to each and every friend of mine, though they were more excited about the nude beaches that came free with it and turned green with envy. As I knocked on Rishabh's door to share the good news, he had something else to tell me:

'Amol, I needed to talk to you. I was just about to come to your room.'

'I was...' I was interrupted.

'Have a seat,' he said excitedly, 'I'm in.'

'What? Where? What are you talking about?'

'I'm in for YourQuote.'

At first, I could not believe it. How did he change his mind so suddenly?

'What happened? How come such a drastic decision?'

'I just consulted my senior. You know what my CV looks like. I've got a 6.4 GPA and there is just one position of responsibility of secretary, SAC, that I have which, frankly speaking, isn't of much value. Starting up a venture would brighten my chances of cracking into good companies,' said Rishabh.

'You want to get into a start-up for getting yourself a job?' I asked.

'Yes. That's what you want to do too, right?'

'I don't know. I want to do it because...I want to do it,' I said in a contemplative tone.

'You seem unclear about it. It's good that I'm clear then. So what will be my designation and share of equity in the company?'

My mind went blank. I had not given much thought to it at all. My mind raced with all kinds of possibilities—from I becoming the Founder and CEO taking a major portion of equity, to being co-founder with equal designation and equity. I fast forwarded my mind into an imaginable future. The thought of Rishabh taking orders from me seemed repulsive. I thought I would feel really awkward ordering Rishabh, my batchmate, my dear friend, about anything. I thought that the motivation to work would be equal if both equity and designation were divided equally between us.

'Co-founder, Director. 33 percent each.'

'That's great. So, your friend Vikram would be working from Chandigarh, right?'

'No, he's backed out. I have found a more experienced person. Suresh Boddeda, Rajiv's elder brother. I have even talked to him.'

'You have given him 33 percent as well?'

I hadn't, but I lied about it to avoid the uncomfortable equity talk.

'Great! Let's get done with this semester and we'll rock the hell out of *our* YourQuote in the summer holidays. I know so many guys in the campus that we would be able to set up a big team out here with ease,' Rishabh exclaimed. I had not failed to notice the 'our' that he had put before YourQuote. It came as a pleasant surprise to see him so involved.

'I have an internship at my father's company in Lucknow. So most of the time I'll be free,' Rishabh explained. I suddenly realized that there was a problem. I had forgotten about the internship in France which I'd got after sending around almost five hundred applications across the globe. I just couldn't miss it, now that I'd announced it to everyone in my family and my hostel. It just meant losing credibility.

'I'll be in France. I just got an internship there, so we'll try and manage things over the net,' I said, though my voice did not sound convincing at all.

'Uh, okay. Should we postpone it till you come back?'

'No. We can't delay anymore. We'll have to manage somehow,' I said as I left his room, contemplating on what to do next.

I was in a fix. I knew that if I went abroad for an internship, I wouldn't be able to do anything significant. I had to be here in India if the start-up were to see fruition during the vacation itself. Otherwise it would get delayed by another semester for we would not be able to involve students till the next big vacation.

The thought of calling my parents or talking to my friends or even Priya wasn't going to help as France was too lucrative to let go and they would definitely convince me to not let go of the opportunity. As I entered my room, I found Rajiv waiting there for me.

'Hi buddy, what's up?' I asked, faking excitement in my voice.

'I have got something for you. I just saw this poster stuck on the board in the campus,' he said and handed me the poster of xIncubator—India's premier start-up incubator of IIM-A. I was not aware of the concept of a start-up incubator, so Rajiv, who had googled it on his laptop by then, explained that incubators offered seed money (5-10 lakh rupees), office space, and mentorship to promising ideas and prepared them for getting funding. The whole concept seemed really intriguing to me and I immediately grabbed hold of the poster and read through the details. The deadline for the application was just five hours later.

I thanked Rajiv and called Rishabh to my room. As Rishabh went through the poster, he questioned me, 'The result comes out on May 20 after which they call us to IIM-A for a ten days' workshop. How are you going to attend if you're going to France?'

'Simple. I won't go,' I said in an impulse. Little did I know that this was what I had wanted. I wasn't made for engineering. Two months in France would anyway not add to my career as much as making it to xIncubator would have. Whenever you are stuck between two choices, both lucrative, choose the one that brings you closer to the future that you have imagined for yourself every day.

As both of them sat next to me, I opened my laptop and subsequently, Photoshop. Five minutes later, as I doodled my heart out, the company's logo was finalized. Next step was writing the business plan. None of us had any idea about it. But it was the task that brought synergy to all our energies. We spent the next hour discussing and answering the various questions that were put up on the xIncubator website. Though Rajiv wasn't the co-founder, he represented his brother's side and offered us keen advice. When they left, satisfied, the idea was left to me, its real father, to type out the answers until I was content with them to click on the 'submit' button.

I submitted our answers just three minutes before the mentioned deadline. The wheels had been set rolling. There was a wide grin on my face as I looked at myself in the mirror. After stupidly smiling at myself for a few minutes, I carried out an important task. I mailed the professor in France who had offered me the internship, saying I wouldn't be able to make it because of some personal reasons, and referred Rajiv to him instead. The professor replied within minutes, irritably mentioning that it was unprofessional on my part and even rejected Rajiv's reference. I could just mumble a sorry to both of them.

A bit lost, I looked at my cell phone, which was stranded in the silent mode at the other corner of the bed. It had seven missed calls. All of them being Priya's. Unprepared, I lazily dialed her number.

'Do you have any idea what happened today?' Priya screamed at me.

'I had a baby, that's all I know,' I said.

'Jerk, I almost fell from stairs in the college.'

'Oh, did it hurt?'

'No and yes.'

'What do you mean?'

'No, because it didn't; yes, because all my seniors laughed at me.'

'Ha! Ha!' I wasn't the nicest boyfriend out there.

'Go to hell!'

'I'll go there tomorrow, okay? C'ya outside Vishwavidyalaya station.'

I intentionally didn't tell her about the team completion or xIncubator because she, much like my parents, had boasted about my France internship to all her friends and if she had come to know that I wasn't going, she would have been disappointed.

⌁

The next day I met Priya and informed her about my backout from the France offer. She was shocked, but when I assured her that it meant that I could get an internship in DRDO, near her PG, and could spend the entire vacation being near her instead, she was more than happy. It was just a matter of changing her perspective with the basic art of persuasion that would be of immense help to me in the time to come.

She made me call up my mother who shocked me saying she knew I had backed out.

'I was so worried how you were going to manage things all alone, that too in a place where people don't even know English. I was inwardly praying for you to not go and see,

Saibaba has heard my wish. We'll go to Shirdi in the summers to thank him, okay?' my mother said.

'Okay, Jai Sainath,' I said and disconnected the call with a smile.

Two weeks later, Suresh stood up to his words and launched our basic website, with a bright colorful logo shining at the top, an about page, a careers page, and our introductions on the team page—something that I was very proud of. I had called my mother that day and asked her to check the website. Though she didn't have the faintest idea about what yourquote.in was there for, she congratulated me by saying, 'Wow, someone has put your name there and added Co-founder & Director after it.'

I could not be happier.

Apparently, what we didn't realize was that Suresh had started a web development company called Brilliant Pals and we didn't pay him for the work. So he had gone to seek other work instead, and owing to his talent, there was no dearth of it—he got work for which clients actually paid him, unlike penniless entrepreneurs like us. As two days passed by and we failed to hear from him, we panicked. We went to meet one of the best developers of our college, nicknamed Bhallaji, who later got recruited by Facebook. He was pursuing Civil Engineering yet he was a better web developer than most of the CS guys out there.

'Bhallaji, we need your help,' Rishabh began his persuasion. We had found him sitting in the canteen. We told him about our idea and about Suresh as well. The first thing he did was google Suresh on the net and he was appalled to find no significant links or websites having his signature, which meant that he was a novice in web development as were we in entrepreneurship. Upon realizing the evident hole, Rishabh went ahead and asked Bhallaji to join us, which he politely refused, as he was working with another start-up which has now become a major restaurant listing website.

We realized that a long distance relationship with Suresh wouldn't be possible. And we had to break up from our own side. My side, specifically, as I'd been the one dealing with him.

'It has been two weeks and he has been holding us up. What should we do? Get Suresh out of the scene?' I asked Rishabh.

'What would happen to the equity then?' Rishabh asked. Apparently, his primary concern was equity.

'We will divide it fifty-fifty,' I said naturally.

'Yes, we should. I'll get in touch with Animesh. He's in first year CS, a very bright guy.'

'Perfect!'

Since I was dealing with Suresh, I had been given the daunting task of getting rid of him. Awkwardly, I called Suresh. He picked up the call.

'Suresh, I'm sorry, it's not working out,' I said.

'What? The website is working pretty fine,' he said. The cultural and linguistic gap between us was too big to make understanding easy.

'I'm talking about our coordination. We are facing trouble in communicating our thoughts on design and all, and also, in understanding what's going on in your mind.'

'Amol, it's okay. I know perfect English, I can explain things again,' Suresh replied. He mistook my call for an apology for the communication gap—the majority of which was from his end.

'I know, I know. I mean that we have to find a…' I began and realized that I missed the tact there. I immediately modified my statement to, 'I mean that it would be great if you can shift to New Delhi. We three could work together then.'

I knew I had hit the bull's eye. He explained his situation saying he couldn't leave his hometown for two not-yet-graduates pursuing some completely new idea. I sympathized and immediately paid for the expenses from Suresh's side to Rajiv so as to not affect our friendship in any way. Now we were back to square one, with no developers on our side. The search continued…

April, 2010

Noon. The pleasant morning sun had just transformed into a big ball of fire. In Delhi, spring departs even before it has fully arrived. I was sleepily returning from one of the most boring lectures I'd ever attended when my cell phone buzzed. It was an unknown number. I have a strange fascination for unknown numbers; whenever one flashes on my cellphone, it sends my heart pounding.

It was a girl on the other end of the line.

'Hello, am I speaking to Mr Sabharwal?'

'Yes,' I answered excitedly. It was the first time my name had been taken with so much courtesy.

It was a call from the xIncubator team of IIM-Ahmedabad. They had asked us to reach Gurgaon the next day and give our elevator pitch to their panel as a part of the shortlisting process. I jumped with delight and ran like a lunatic with dishevelled hair and a big smile to Rishabh's room.

'We are going to...' I said, panting, 'Gurgaon tomorrow. xIncubator guys called us.'

'Awesome!' Rishabh yelled, a little unconcerned though.

We decided that we would divide the work. I was to prepare the ideas, concept, and plan of action slides, while Rishabh would take care of the T-shirt revenue forecasts based on his experience. I had to work on the slides that night, and since Rishabh had the next morning off, he chose to work during that time by waking up at 6. By 1 o'clock at night, I was almost done. I sent the ppt to Rishabh and went to sleep.

Our presentation in Gurgaon was scheduled for 10 am. We had called a cab at 9 am, which cost us five hundred rupees—the first extravagant expenditure for our venture—the next day. I got up at 8, went to brush my teeth, and chose to see what my able partner was up to. The door was locked from inside, the fan was on, the lights were off. He was still asleep! I panicked. I hammered on the door and woke him up. In that one moment, I got the glimpse of future—he would never be punctual.

As I got dressed in formal clothes for the first time in my college life, my mind had lost its serenity. I couldn't believe the ease with which Rishabh had taken the entire matter. Thanks to the distance to Gurgaon, we had forty five minutes in hand, and fortunately when we reached our destination, we were ready for the show.

'Who among you is Amol, the author?' said Praneet, one of the organizers.

'That's me. Hi,' I introduced myself.

We engaged in a discussion on our way to the conference room, which had two investors already seated. Seeing Rishabh less involved, I introduced him to the panel. We hadn't decided who was to present the plan till the very last minute. Just before the presentation, Rishabh had asked me to present it. I couldn't decipher whether it was nervousness or lack of preparation from his end and I charted my own course. Though I was nervous, my passion for my idea helped me speak up. I passed the baton to Rishabh to talk about the sales forecast which he faltered through. His voice showed that his heart wasn't in it.

We completed the nervewraking Q & A session as I answered most of the questions with my fledgling knowledge about entrepreneurship. Rishabh bumped in with his views in between. They seemed concerned about whether we would go ahead full-time with the venture or not. We tried to answer them to the best of our ability. But we couldn't tell if our answers had impressed them or not.

Just as we were about to leave, Praneet said to us, 'Guys, you are the sellers of T-shirts with quirky quotes. Next time, wear your brand instead of these boring shirts!'

We smiled.

⌦

'How do you think it went?' said Rishabh as soon as we came out of the conference room.

'Good, maybe...frankly, I don't know,' I said.

'I doubt if we will make it. Did you see the look on that investor's face? He didn't know what Twitter was,' Rishabh retaliated.

As we returned to the campus, we decided to go to the wind tunnel, one of the most prominent hangout spots for IITians. My eyes drifted towards a girl with medium height, dark complexion, oily hair, and a wide grin, who was running towards us. The only fact that comforted me was that she wasn't smiling at me. As she neared, I observed that she had a burn mark on her neck.

'How was it? How was it?' she boomed in her shrill voice, and jumped across the hallway towards us. She looked at Rishabh while speaking, and subsequently at me. There was a naivety, a rare innocence in her personality, a characteristic that was lacking in other girls in my college. Her demeanour was not very feminine, which showed that she had been raised along with brothers and she was also slightly boyish herself, her speech embellished with too many 'yaars'.

'Hi, I'm Anjali,' she said to me in a rather shy tone. *Anjali Yadav, the one who liked my novel; the one who was a part of Pratik's dramatics society; the one with whom Rishabh had been spending a lot of time recently*, I thought.

'Hi, Rishabh keeps talking about you,' I said shaking hands with her. Her bashfulness disappeared like smoke in thin air.

'Yes, I'm awesome, I know. How was the presentation?' she asked again, this time to both of us.

'Good,' Rishabh assured her. I wondered whether he really meant it since he had told me otherwise just a while ago.

'Great. Let's go outside and eat something,' she said grabbing Rishabh by the hand.

'Amol, do you want to join us?' Rishabh asked. The tone of his voice told me that he was just saying it out of compulsion, not his will. I asked him to carry on without me and chose to call on someone who had been waiting for me.

⌐⊂⊐

The next day, after classes, we took out some time to brainstorm. Just during the middle of the discussion, Rishabh asked me, 'Would you mind if I involve Anjali in our discussion too? She is very creative and can give great inputs.'

Looking back in hindsight, I feel I should have said no. It was two directors talking, two founders discussing, and any third person, no matter how creative or fruitful he or she is, should have been shut out. But back at that time, unaware of professional etiquette and rules of the organizational game, I had said yes. Rishabh immediately turned back and called out to her to give her the news. I was surprised to find that she was sitting right behind him.

Little did I know that when she became a part of our discussion, she was going to become part of every discussion that was to happen thereafter. Her entry into our discussion was her entry into our venture. Though I must also add that she was creative, had some really whacky ideas, which sometimes didn't fit in the business side of things, but occasionally outshined others.

A week passed by and as Anjali seeped into the top tier of our organization, I started getting more worried. Rishabh had been spending more and more time with her, which alarmed me.

'Dude, is there something cooking between Anjali and you?' We were sitting in our hostel mess. The question made him cough.

'Do you want water?'

'No. The answer to both your questions,' he said irritably.

'Okay. There was no need to feel offended about it,' I mumbled.

'I'm not offended. It's just that we are really good friends.'

'You have been spending too much time with her lately,' I said, without any prior thinking.

'Yes, we have been discussing about YourQuote all throughout.'

'Okay, that's cool,' I said, despite knowing that it was not cool. It was our venture. All the discussions about the venture should be done with me being present. But I didn't say a thing to him.

⌁

'You sound sad. What happened honey?' I had called up Priya to tell her about Anjali.

'You know the reason why I haven't involved you in the venture?' I told Priya.

'Yes, because you don't want someone to replace Rishabh in your discussions about the venture. You have told me that several times. Don't spoil your mood because of it.'

I hung up a few minutes later, relieved I had Priya to share my thoughts with.

⌁

Last week of April, 2010

April passed by in the wink of an eye. Though Rishabh and I tried our best to find a developer, we could not find anyone in campus. Exams were nearing and no one was ready to take part with novice entrepreneurs like us at the helm. Tired, helpless, and desperately waiting for xIncubator to set our wheels in motion, we decided to pay heed to academics for the time being. We disengaged ourselves from our entrepreneurial avatars and began preparing for the exams.

I was happy to observe that Rishabh had reduced his interactions with Anjali. On one of the days when we were studying together, I probed.

'Hey, I am seeing you at the hostel quite often these days. Has there been a problem between you and Anjali?' I asked.

'Yeah, I'm getting worried. Last week, Anjali's roommate told me that she cries every night for me. It is just friendship between us as far as I'm concerned, but it turns out that she has fallen in love with me. That's why I have stopped thinking about her altogether.'

'Why does it make you worried?' I asked.

'Come on, I am not eager to go out with her. I had made it clear to her that I, having already been through three relationships, want to now only date a super-hot bombshell. That is enough of a hint not to come near me, isn't it? After all, I have my own personal choices,' he said.

'Is it all about the looks?'

'No, it isn't...' he fumbled, failing to complete his sentence.

'Hmmm, moreover she is too young,' he uttered after a lot of thinking. 'She is just in her first year, straight out of school from a small town in UP.'

'Hmmm,' I said.

Till the time Rishabh kept a safe distance from her, I was happy. But destiny wanted otherwise.

⌁

The exams were over by May 6. Unlike our pursuits, we both landed up with an average grade B in Entrepreneurial Management. Frustrated, I had put up a status: 'Don't judge a book by its cover and a man by his grades', which fetched a 100 likes to soothe my disappointment.

As soon as we got free from our classes, Rishabh scheduled a meeting with a few of his juniors who worked with him in SAC. I introduced the concept of YourQuote to them. They all liked it. We included three of the juniors into the team: Animesh Bansal, Bhaskar Jain, and Shweta Khandelwal. All of them had just passed their first year and were spending two months at IIT to finish a summer project in Computer Science which didn't require too much effort from them.

Our team had become bigger. We were six people from IIT and two from NIFT. Rishabh included his ex-girlfriend Bhavika from Jesus & Mary College, who was for some reason still interested in him. Bhavika was already working with a prominent automobiles company as a marketing executive, and going by her credentials, we made her the Marketing Lead with the task of fetching T-shirt orders from colleges. Our little recruitment drive spread like wildfire in the campus and we started seeing more and more juniors willing to be a part of it. Another junior from IIT, Armaan, who was a reader of my novel, joined us after he got to know that it was my venture.

By May 10, we were a team of ten people. We called it the Core Team, with C and T in capitals, and we organized our first meeting where we created the timeline to put things into perspective. Keeping in mind May 20, when xIncubator's result would come out, we had targeted to launch the website by June 5. In the meanwhile, I was going to manage the technical development along with social media; Rishabh, along with Bhavika, Armaan, and Anjali, was to take care of the marketing division.

Just as I was about to finish the presentation, Rishabh introduced a new member to all of us. Shikha Gupta—a straight faced girl with heavy spectacles and ill-fitted clothes. While we cracked a few jokes on her and laughed like dogs, she remained unfazed. It seemed as though she had been coercively dragged into the gathering.

I signalled Rishabh to ask her to speak. She had somehow spoiled the cohesiveness of the gang. Rishabh shrugged, expressing that he had no idea about why Shikha was so silent. She was a year junior to us, had just started designing, and used to paint earlier. She joined as an assistant designer, under our Chief Designer Ruchi, who was from NIFT. Once the introductions were over, we hit the discotheque. The toughest phase of building a team was finally over and we were glad to realize that all it took was the deadly exams to end. It was time to party. Though Shikha was not interested, Rishabh took her to a side and persuaded her to come along.

We went to Vasant Vihar, which was quite near to our institute. To promote interaction, mixing, and friendship, we broke into groups of two with people we knew the least in the group. I was clubbed with Anjali, Armaan was clubbed with Bhavika, and Rishabh with the lost and confused Shikha. We proceeded to Vasant Vihar in different autos.

We partied all day long, but it cost us 5,000 rupees.

'Damn, we wasted a lot of money,' I said while returning.

'It's an investment, don't you see?' Rishabh said.

'We haven't even started earning with the venture.'

'We will, very soon,' he assured me.

⌁

We finally started with web development. We used a Content Management System (CMS) named Drupal to make the basic version. Out of the three junior developers, Animesh, was the best. He was diligent, sincere, and really quick. Though I didn't have any interest when it came to coding, but since I had a mental picture of the website ready, I chose to guide them.

On May 12, as a token of their involvement, we printed fifty business cards for each of our team members and handed them over. I still remember the pride on their faces when the first held their cards with flashy designations like Marketing Executive, Chief Developer, Strategy Lead etc.

Rishabh and my cards carried our pre-decided designations: Co-founder-Director. We had got something to boast about. I had stuck the business card on my hostel room door, while Rishabh chose to keep his cards hidden in his pocket wallet. There was another development taking shape during the after examination phase—Rishabh had once again started spending a lot of time with Anjali, which bugged me to no end, since most of the times when I would to go to have a quick brainstorming session in his room at night, he would never be around. I changed my designation on Facebook from Student at IIT Delhi to Co-founder, Director at yourquote.in.

On May 13, 2010, I created the page called yourquote.in, just to enable us to add it as our employers. Little did I know that this page would become our face to the world. I didn't post anything for the first few days, as I had no idea what to post. I just added a description which said:

YourQuote is a networking-cum-crowdsourcing website intended to tap surges of creativity in common people by creating a network of people who are good with words (especially one-liners), providing them with customizable space to record and host their creativity, and giving them an opportunity to get incentives for the same by branding for clients, merchandizing, and other avenues.

As soon as I added it as an employer, it created some curiosity among my friends and readers. They all started asking me about it, about my future plans with it, and so on.

The newly found attention seemed mesmerizing. The pride of being an entrepreneur captivated me. It gave me a better opinion of myself, better than even being a writer did.

On May 15, I joined my internship in a renowned government defence organization that was to take most of my time for the following two months. The only good thing about the internship was that Pratik was my co-intern and the office was in Lucknow Road. Priya's PG was at a five-minute walking distance from the organization.

Every day after the internship, our trio—Priya, Pratik, and I—would attack all the famous eating points in Kamla Nagar, the bustling market of North Campus. Right from the delicious momos at the end of the lane, to Momo Point and QD's in the side alleys, to Udupi—we raided all of them. The best part of the evening food raid was standing in front of book-stalls and seeing my books displayed on the stalls. If I saw any girl browsing through my book, I would suddenly appear and say, 'Hey, I'm the author of that book you are holding.' While some girls went gaga, others exhibited controlled indifference.

Priya was done with her semester and had no internship at hand. On May 17, she left for home, promising that she would be back soon and making me promise to not call her all throughout, thanks to her conservative Jat parents who would have grounded her if they found out that she even had a guy friend, forget a boyfriend.

'Is there something going on between Anjali and Rishabh?' Pratik asked me in college.

'No. Why do you ask?'

'She leaves our dramatics team outings for him. I have never seen her do that in the past, since dramatics had always been a priority for her.'

'I have no idea. Rishabh didn't tell me anything about it. All I know is that they are good friends.'

'Good friends don't stick to each other so much,' Pratik retorted.

I had no clue. I came back to the hostel and was glad to find that Rishabh was in his room. But I soon found out that he was there just to share some bad news.

'You know what? One of my school friends, Atul Mehta from IIT Kanpur, had also cracked xIncubator. He has already made it through,' Rishabh said nervously.

'What? How's that possible? They were to announce the results on May 20,' I said in shock.

'That's what I asked him. He said they had already informed the ones who were sure shot winners.'

'Which means that we are not?'

'Obviously. I told you that we were not good,' Rishabh pointed out. I had never felt this low before. I had left my goddamned foreign internship for this.

'Hmm, let's wait till the 20th and see,' I said.

'Yes, let's wait, but I seriously doubt us making it.'

Only I know how I passed the next two days. There were sleepless nights accompanied by long strolls in the cricket ground, thinking about the forthcoming rejection. My ambitions had never felt so frightened thinking about the future. I had always been a man of the present. Consciously, restlessly, and doubtfully, I waited.

May 20

'You jerk! Where the hell have you been? Why didn't you pick up my call?' she whispered.

'Umm, I was sleeping, I bunked my internship today. Where are you? Why are you speaking in such a low voice?'

'Silly, I'm in the loo.'

'If you are in the loo, then do the things that you went there for. Why are you calling while attending to nature's call? Yuck. Can't you do one thing in peace?' I sleepily yelled.

'Dumbass. I am not attending to anything. My Mom's home. I just called to ask about xIncubator. Today is 20th; the result was about to come today. Have you forgotten?'

'Damn! Sorry, I need to check. Hold on.'

'I have to rush out. I'll come online in a while. Let me know then,' she said.

'Sure,' I sprang up from my bed and rushed to my laptop. Never before had I been so swift in getting out of bed.

Refresh. Refresh. Refresh. There were just three mails—all three of them being praise mails from readers of my first book. For the first time, they didn't make me happy. I was infuriated, saddened, and as I waited, Rishabh walked into my room. He was brushing his teeth.

'We are done,' he exclaimed upon seeing my morose face. His words were muddled by the toothbrush. He went to the washroom, spat, and returned with a clearer voice, saying, 'No mail, right?'

'No. Maybe, we are done. Shouldn't they at least send a rejection mail?' I asked.

'They should, but I don't know whether they will today itself.'

'Hmm.'

'I was thinking maybe we should start with this after placements are over. If we don't get selected by xIncubator, we would have nothing great to boast about in our resumes. We are already in IIT-Delhi, other IIMs don't have such a reputed program, and competitions held by other institutes don't have so much prestige.'

'Hmmm, maybe you are right. What should we do? Call it off?'

'Yes, I guess so. Continuing would be an unwise choice given the circumstances.'

'I'm glad that we haven't made any public announcements yet. The posters have still not been put up,' I rejoiced.

'Hmm,' he said and went out.

Was it really over? I thought. There was no response inside my head. It stood still as if waiting for a ghastly storm to strike. I waited for the mail the entire day while Rishabh chose to spend that time with Anjali. Interestingly, I didn't feel bad about that anymore. I had accepted defeat. I also got angry with Priya during our online chat session when she messaged me saying 'Don't worry'. I found that very insincere because in my place, not worrying wasn't possible. I had spent more than a year on that very idea—I couldn't let it fall off. It couldn't end it in a snap.

The mail didn't come. Nor did any call. It was over. It needed another sleepless night to bring me face to face with what had happened.

May 21

I lazily got up at eight o'clock the next morning. Languidly, I slogged ahead to the loo, put a thin layer of toothpaste on the dry bristles and brushed as slow as possible, not letting my teeth wake up from their slumber. My eyes remained closed for most of the time, partly in sleep and partly in dreams. There was somebody in the washroom who broke my concentration spell with his terrible singing. Wary of letting my sleepy mood get destroyed, I rushed back to my room with the brush held between my molars and as customary, I turned on my laptop and logged into my mailbox.

Two heavy streaks of tears dropped down my eyes and kissed my toothpaste-laced lips. I started sobbing. It was the mail that I thought would never arrive in my mailbox.

```
Hi Amol,
Congratulations!
Thanks for your patience during the xIncubator
process. We really enjoyed interacting with you and
believe that we can help you in your endeavour to make
YourQuote into a growing concern and a big company!
   Sanjay has decided to fund you for xIncubator
program and I will send you the term sheet on his
behalf by 24th. Feel free to call us in case of any
doubts.
   Meanwhile, we will get back to you on the next steps
(apart from getting back to us on the agreement) by
tomorrow.
Thanks,
Praneet
```

Crying, I ran into the corridor to find Rishabh. He was

sleeping. I banged on his door with my fist. Upon hearing the noise, three other batchmates came out of their rooms but Rishabh was still asleep. After two minutes of continuous vociferation, Rishabh finally opened the door and I embraced him tightly. He drowsily asked me what had happened.

I screamed, 'Rebirth! We cracked xIncubator.'

We both howled like wild foxes and our smiles outgrew our faces. It was a new beginning for us, it relinquished our faith, it pushed us into believing that our journey meant to be on the road for a longer time.

I came back to my room and informed my parents who had little idea about what entrepreneurship was all about. But I tried, nevertheless.

'Dad, pranam. I have won a contest in IIM-Ahmedabad. They have invited us for a ten days' workshop in management.'

'Amazing. I'm really proud of you.'

'Yes, it's indeed one of my best achievements.'

'Will it help you secure a better job?' my father asked.

I thought for a while, and answered, 'Yes.'

'Great. I'll distribute sweets in my office. Do go to a temple and offer sweets.'

Gratitude is best experienced when it can be credited to someone who deserves more attention than our egos. Despite my parents being extremely religious, I visited temples only when I was forced into accompanying them. But it was the first time I went to the Hanuman Mandir just outside the campus by myself and offered half a kilo of laddoos.

We announced with a great pride on Facebook about our selection at one of India's most prestigious internet start-up incubation programs and the news took our seniors and batchmates by storm. Congratulatory messages flooded our

News Feed. Even Priya, upon reading the good news on Facebook, called me and chatted with me for half an hour pretending to be talking to a female friend of hers with lots of 'Kya kar rahi ho?' and 'Kab ja rahi ho?' so her parents wouldn't suspect a thing.

It was while talking to her that I got an idea. We could take four team members to IIM-A and I thought that I might include Priya into the list, thereby assuring us a mini-honeymoon at India's best management institute. She tried to convince her parents for the next three hours but when they came to know that there were boys in the group as well, they refused.

'Had it been only girls going, they would have asked you to back off then too, saying it's unsafe. I know your parents, they are...' I messaged her online at night.

'No need to curse them. Howsoever they may be, at least they are mine.'

'I am not cursing them. All I'm saying is that they are typical orthodox parents. I wonder whether they will let us marry someday or go for an honour killing.'

'Come on, it's time to celebrate. Don't spoil your mood thinking about the future. Your present is so bright. I'm sure that my parents will agree if you carry on like this,' she said boosting my morale. Her words of encouragement meant a lot to me because she was the only person who wouldn't flatter me without any reason.

In the evening, after giving a treat to our small team, I came back and dropped down on my bed with a happy smile. The world knew about something called yourquote. in but didn't know what we did. Our development was still under process and the website didn't carry anything other than a timer which showed '15 days to launch', an about page which hardly interested anyone to read further, a team page carrying the photos, and a two line introduction of both of us.

I opened my laptop thinking that I would ask Animesh to mention the fact that we had cracked the prestigious xIncubator program on the website. As I logged into my blogger account, there were notifications about two comments on the YourQuote blog announcement status we had put up, one of which anonymously said—'It's foolish of you guys starting up a venture on such a shitty idea. If it could have been a feasible idea, it would already have been done.' I felt choked. My blood boiled and I started posting something vile in return but chose not to.

Letting go of my anguish, I read the other comment, which said, 'It has been months since you guys updated the blog. Eagerly waiting for the next set. You guys are good! Even I want to post my one-liners on your blog. Keep it coming.'

It sparked a smile on my face. I replied in a go, 'Check YourQuote.in, we are arriving in a month. Till then, we have an operational fan page with the same name. Until the website is up, post there.'

And, thus I posted the first post on the fan page—the yourquote of the Day:

'Some people will hate you because you are doing what you love. Make sure you don't love them more.' Amol Sabharwal

It was perhaps for the first time in the world that a common man was quoted in public. The 500+ likes on the fan page assured me that I was indeed on the right path and the very first post received around 50 likes—nearly ten percent interaction.

What happened thereafter was etched in our venture's history. Floored by the likes, the noise that we created in the social media, our fan page had become our loudspeaker to announce to the world our arrival. We invited people to pour down their one-liners on our fan page. If they received 10+ likes we would feature them as YourQuote of the Day. I introduced other categories like Midnight Thought that featured a philosophical thought at night, Sarcastic Quote of the Day, Slapstick Quote of the Day, and so on.

People flooded the fan page. We crossed 1000 likes within the next day itself. As people had to get 10+ likes to get featured, the people who posted their quote brought their friends to fetch some likes. The entire fan page had been 'gamified', meaning, there were incentives to participate, there was a viral element that brought in more users. By the 23rd, we had 1500 people on our page.

When I went for my internship the next day, I felt very awkward to find Pratik congratulating me for yourquote.in. Before he could send me on any further guilt trips, I changed the topic to Anjali and Rishabh and the awkwardness fizzled down a bit.

May 22

Early morning, I received Praneet's mail in my mailbox. It carried a four page term sheet with words that were way beyond my vocabulary. While Rishabh and I went through the term sheet over three times, we were unable to comprehend it completely. One clause, however, was particularly puzzling. It said that for five percent of the equity, Sanjay—the investor—was giving us 2.5 lakh rupees as loan for one year. If we succeeded in our execution, he would invest further. If we didn't, we would have to return to him the 2.5 lakhs along with three percent interest. And there was a catch; we would be invited for the ten days' workshop at IIM-A only if we agreed to sign the agreement. We had no idea what to do next.

Unaware about legalities about the business, I forwarded the agreement to my uncle who was a prominent lawyer at Supreme Court. He called me back in the evening and explained that the term sheet was completely one-sided. He advised me against it, as they were not even doing equity investment, but instead giving us a debenture. My uncle went to the extent of saying that 2.5 lakh rupees was so small an amount that he or our parents could lend us that much money without interest instead.

'Right now in the initial phase, your job is to build your product/service and increase your valuation so that you can get a better deal later for the same percentage of equity,' my uncle advised me.

It was time to call Praneet for an elaborate discussion. When I told him that the term sheet seemed one-sided and we just wanted to come over for the workshop without accepting investment, he politely asked us to get lost, as it was only meant for those who accepted the investment. I felt disappointed by Praneet's hypocrisy. At first they had said that the purpose of their endeavour was to promote entrepreneurs, but they were actually promoting investors.

After the call, Praneet sent a message that didn't go well with us. It said, 'YourQuote didn't even feature in our Top 10. However, Sanjay was keen on you guys and your idea.

That's why we had selected you. Personally speaking, I doubt this idea has any scope.'

It was the last thing we heard from him. Rishabh and I dejectedly looked at each other. We had announced everywhere that we were going for ten days to IIM-A but all in vain. But, soon disappointment turned into something else. Determination.

The next thing that I did was I posted one of my quotes on the fan page as the YourQuote of the Day:

The best motivational line that I've ever heard is— 'You can't do it.' —Amol Sabharwal.

It fetched 25 likes within two minutes. Rishabh and I didn't speak to each other for a long time after Praneet's call.

'We would get certificates about our selection, don't worry,' I jokingly assured Rishabhafter a half an hour gap.

'Damn Praneet and those certificates. I will make them see what we are capable of,' he said angrily. The anger was born out of insult, born out of belittlement of one's dreams.

We both had a definite resolve to continue. What xIncubator did for us was that it gave us the push at the critical juncture when we had decided to let go of our efforts. It gave us the push to forge ahead, fight with all our zeal, and prove someone wrong. And there is no better inspiration that that.

YourQuote was alive and we were certain that it would remain alive till its founders were alive.

Affairs Aplenty

We had shifted gears. Meeting hours had become elongated, documentation of points had moved from a paragraph to a dozen pages, the web development hours had increased from five to ten, and the fan page was seeing unprecedented activity. People now knew what YourQuote was all about. Along with these things, Anjali was back in Rishabh's life. While I was busy with the web development team to create the skeleton model for the website, they were roaming around in campus late at nights. I know it's unfair of me to keep an eye on them like a detective, but since both of them had become a part of our company and were accountable for its activities, I had to observe.

On May 28, Rishabh, Anjali, and I were sitting at the Wind Tunnel at around 1 o' clock at night when Rishabh's cellphone buzzed. It was Shikha at the other end. The same Shikha, who during our first meeting had acted like a dumb statue, had now outgrown her earlier self. She laughed often, loved to be a part of our team hang-outs, and realized that the element of fun was missing in her life. All thanks to Rishabh and his ability to induce fun in the environment.

'What happened?' Anjali interrogated Rishabh.

'Nothing. She wants to meet me.'

'At this hour?' I questioned.

'Yeah, I don't know,' Rishabh shrugged and bid farewell to us saying that he would be back within half an hour. I observed Anjali's face. She didn't look pleased.

'Is everything okay?' I asked Anjali.

'I hate Shikha. She has been spending quite a lot of time with Rishabh,' Anjali said with wife-like authority. I just nodded.

An awkward lull followed and I asked Anjali if she wanted to join me for a coffee break at the nearby Nescafe which remained open till three in the morning. Rishabh and Shikha were already seated there. Three smiles and a frown passed.

'Do you know she even has a boyfriend?' Anjali said on our way back to the Wind-T.

'No, I didn't know that.'

'He is presently in France on an exchange program,' she said.

'Okay,' I said. I didn't opine about Shikha. I had hardly talked to her to form opinions on her. The only opinion that I had formed till then was that she was well-endowed.

Half an hour later, Rishabh and Shikha joined us at the Wind T. Rishabh said that Shikha was really frustrated and wanted to take her mind off irritable things. Shikha complimented Rishabh for lightening her mood with his great sense of humour. It made both Anjali and me cringe. While I was envious of Rishabh's popularity with well-endowed girls, Anjali was still angry about the half an hour with Rishabh that Shikha took away from her.

'So, what were you frustrated about?' I asked.

'Nothing,' Rishabh answered. 'Let's play dumb charades. It's been a long time since we chilled out a bit.'

When Rishabh asked Anjali to team up with him, she refused and said bitterly, 'You team up with your 1 o'clock friend,' and teamed up with me. The game went for over an hour and in the process, I made everyone, especially Shikha, laugh a lot, which boosted my confidence. As a consolation prize to Anjali, we won the game.

Since Priya had gone home, all my nights were completely free. Earlier, the time between 11 pm-1 am used to be hers. Now, I was free to do anything of my choice.

May 31

It was the day of our team party. After ten days of consistent work, a respite from work was necessary. We were five people: Armaan, Animesh, Shikha, Rishabh, and I. Anjali could not join us as she had another party held by the Dramatics Society to attend. She had gotten a decree from her Dramatics Society friends that if she skipped Dramatic Society get togethers for the sake of YourQuote, they would stop speaking to her. We had earned ourselves a bad name in the dramatics society, as Anjali preferred us over them, despite being associated with them for nearly two years. It was quite late when they realized that it was not because of YourQuote, but Rishabh, that she preferred us more.

The five of us assembled at the institute gate. Shikha stuck to Rishabh all throughout, sometimes clinging to his sleeves and at other times, clasping his hands. It seemed that the last half an hour late night chat with Rishabh had casted a deep impression in her mind. When we had to board an auto, Shikha grabbed the opportunity and said, 'You three go in the auto. Rishabh and I will come in the other one.' We followed her command.

Since the matter involved my partner, I chose to keep mum about it in front of other team members, even though my gossip-loving self wanted to talk about it. We reached DLF Promenade Vasant Vihar, one of Delhi's few luxury malls. Rishabh and Shikha arrived around half an hour late, citing not being able to find an auto as the reason. The three of us, Armaan, Animesh, and I, observed everything but preferred to remain mum. It was the Director who was involved, they couldn't dare say anything against him and nor could I for fear of letting his respect dwindle among the team members losing him.

We decided to watch a movie and, as expected, Shikha asked Rishabh to sit next to her. I sat next to Rishabh on his left. In the stark darkness, my eyes veered to at his seat. Her hands were wrapped with Rishabh's.

The movie began and though the movie seemed interesting at first, a really irritating song made my ears flinch in pain and I turned sideways to see Shikha resting her head on Rishabh's shoulders. Stunned, envious, and distracted, I couldn't concentrate for the rest of the movie, until the intermission brought some light into the surroundings.

During the interval, Rishabh asked me to accompany him to the loo. I followed. He seemed nervous.

'Buddy, things are really weird.'

'What happened?' I pretended to not know about anything that was going on.

'She looks desperate. She has been holding my hands all through the movie. I don't know what is the matter with her.'

'Oh, I thought there was something already going on between you two.'

'No man, come on. Ever since I listened to her story that night, she had been behaving like a nymphomaniac.'

He gave me the lowdown on her. Her boyfriend Kartik had been treating her with contempt and had completely suffocated her freedom. Now that he was abroad, she realized that she didn't love him anymore. Rishabh was nervous and asked me a difficult question.

'Should I go ahead with her?'

'Is it an ethical question to ask?'

'Not from the point of view of her already having a boyfriend, but from the point of view of her being our employee.'

'I don't know. If you get committed, then it won't be a problem. Just a fling might cause a problem.'

'I like her. And now she seems ready too. God knows what she is going to do in the second half.'

'Ha, ha!' I faked laughter adorned with envy. I was in a relationship but who doesn't want attention. Physical attention, especially.

When we returned, I observed that Shikha had removed the hand-rest between their seats. *Slut!* I exclaimed in my mind. I inwardly wished Anjali was present at the scene to make her realize that she was nothing but a conniving little woman taking advantage of Rishabh who could any day get a prettier girl.

Nothing happened between Shikha and Rishabh for the next three days. However, something did happen between Rishabh and Anjali. They fought. I don't know the exact reason, but I guessed that maybe Animesh, being Anjali's batchmate, would have told her about the advances Shikha was making on Rishabh.

⸻

June 4

Despite our best efforts, the countdown timer for our launch had to be extended from 24 to 120 hours. There were several bugs, unsolved errors in codes, in the website and they needed some time to get resolved. We announced the news on our fan page and our followers, who had been eagerly waiting, were quite dismayed. It was our first tryst with extension of deadlines and we blamed it on our inefficient execution for not being able to deliver on time.

The real reason though was that our developers, second-year students, were inept at building a social network. Having no idea about the developmental process, I pressurized them to perform better, with sometimes strict mails like: 'I can't see any development on the website. It's stagnating from where it had been the last day.'

After over five such mails, Animesh freaked out and replied saying, 'Amol, we are working tirelessly every day. You don't understand that to see one little change in the front-end, there has to be hundred lines of codes written in the back-end. It's like making the skeleton before putting the skin. It takes time.'

I gave in. I was a technical imbecile. So was Rishabh. I concentrated on social media and let the web development team take the required time to deliver. Rishabh, in the meanwhile, scheduled several meetings with T-shirt manufacturers, via JustDial or references from people in the industry. He called each one of them at the hostel and they would show us the samples ranging from as cheap as 70 rupees each to the best ones that were around 160 rupees. The aforementioned prices stood only when we bought T-shirts in bulk (greater than 200 tees at least).

I was being exposed to an entirely new industry—the prissy dealers of Delhi who lied with such sky-high confidence that you would have no doubts about their assertion. They promised to offer the most reliable services and the readiness to bargain. However, Rishabh was well-versed with this industry of crooks. He credited his delicate negotiation skills to his father and would courteously win over these dealers by addressing them as Uncles and buttering their egos with namastes and warm greetings, developing a relation with them right from the very beginning. Such was his expertize over his tongue that he, despite being completely insincere, cast a wonderful first impression on every dealer he met. I, on the other hand, was totally opposite. I was direct, at times blunt enough to offend someone.

The art of buttering wasn't exactly in my blood and though I'd started appreciating it after seeing the adeptness with which Rishabh carried out marketing, I didn't try learning it. Having complementary skills was our asset. I prided myself in my strengths instead.

June 5

We were converting some of the quotes into T-shirt designs. As our website was going to be launched on the 10th, we needed to have some designs ready. Armaan, Rishabh,

Shikha, and I spent half an hour in finding out the best quotes by our followers from the fan page. Some of them were super-awesome. We chose five of them and put them in order of the likes they fetched, along with their contributor's name:

1. 'Silence is always misunderstood, especially during vivas.'—Sumit Dugar
2. 'The best way to hate a song is to set it as your morning alarm.'—Mohit Kumar
3. 'To err is human, to Twitter divine.'—Dhruv Jain
4. 'Ass does not mean your butt, it means you.'—Harsh Snehanshu
5. 'Yes, you can read. Now get lost.'—Shweta Pundit

Armaan and Shikha came up with designs that, frankly speaking, didn't suit my taste. They were ordinary, after all both of them were amateurs. Nevertheless, the satisfaction of having something over nothing motivated us to give the website a green signal. By 1 am, after a series of attempts to get the right font and right aesthetics, our mental faculties failed us to conceptualize anything else. And so we decided to retire to our respective rooms. Rishabh, however, decided to carry on with Shikha, adding to my anxiety.

I stayed awake till 6 in the morning before Rishabh arrived. On seeing the lights still on in my room, Rishabh dashed in. He sat on my bed and rested his back against the wall, which implied that he was tired and had a long story to tell. Like a young girl who comes across a secret adult magazine in her parents' almirah, he anxiously spilled the beans without needing any initiation from my side.

'Brother, it was amazing.'

'What? What happened?' I asked curiously.

'Shikha and I kissed last night,' Rishabh said.

I stared at him in silence.

'But she moved away after the brief kiss, saying she felt guilty of cheating on her boyfriend. She said that it didn't feel right,' he continued with faint sarcasm in his tone. 'As you know the kind of scoundrel I am, I kissed her again. Logic, in such situations, is always damaging,'

We chuckled.

'Didn't you go ahead?'

'No, she said that she would need some more time. We talked for an hour after that. She broke into tears, sharing with me stories about how her boyfriend used to ridicule her in front of her friends, how he wanted her to become a housewife when they would get married, and how he threw the birthday cake that she made for him because she didn't comply to make out in the loo the night before.'

'Really? What a desperate guy,' I said.

'One thing—please don't tell anyone about it.'

'Don't worry. The reputation of our start-up is at stake here and I won't say a word to anybody. It'll be known the day you will announce it.'

'I announce what?'

'Your relationship.'

'No, I don't think it's going to work out. It's just a fling.'

I had promised him that I wouldn't tell anyone. And the first thing I did was send a message to Priya. 'Call me. Some chatpat news.'

Chatpat was our code word for gossip. Both of us hailed from small towns, we hadn't been witness to any scandals, flings, or chatpati stories back in our respective homes and that made both of us big gossip-mongers. The word 'chatpat' was second in priority to the word 'urgent'. The prior provoked interest while the latter provoked fear. No wonder, before I could sleep, I got a call. She was again calling stealthily from the loo without her parents' knowledge

'Jerk. Tell me the news. Now, now, now,' she yelled.

I shared the scandalous story with her. She said Oh My God thrice in the process. At first, I thought she couldn't believe what had happened, but like any righteous girl, her disbelief stemmed more from the fact that Rishabh had been an asshole to share his personal stuff with me as he didn't respect Shikha's personal life or interest.

It was not that Rishabh wasn't ethical enough to keep his sudden fling a secret, but the recent turn of events had brought him closer to me in the sense of sharing things, rather than with Anjali or Shikha. To us, we were not discussing a prospective relationship, but a fling with a nymphomaniac employee of ours.

I argued saying that Shikha had been pretty blatant in her approach. I even called her a slut. Priya reprimanded me for using that word. She said that Rishabh was a man-whore instead, for he initiated it. I couldn't agree more.

Sedated by an eventful night, I hung up and dropped off to sleep.

Rishabh had stopped sharing secrets about his most recent love interest with me anymore, which meant that something serious had started brewing between the two. Meanwhile, there was something terrible happening between Anjali and

Rishabh. On two occasions, I observed them fighting loudly at night near the isolated coffee shop. I chose not to intrude.

However, during this time I could see Animesh, our web developer and a batchmate of Anjali's, spending a lot of time with her. Hurrying through our first version launch, I pressurized Animesh to perform, but he would prefer spending the entire night listening to Anjali's emotional sagas instead.

There is nothing worse for an entrepreneur than to see his prime coder falling in love. Coding, though slightly creative, is an utterly analytical process that requires your full concentration. Love, on the other hand, makes you poetic, expressive. What happens when a coder falls in love? He prefers writing love comments in codes more than codes themselves. And this is exactly what happened.

Animesh, a brilliant CS student, had been unacquainted with the fairer sex till then. But suddenly, he found someone who liked spending time with him, sharing stuff about her life, even at the middle of the night. Despite being brilliant at his work, Animesh was stupid when it came to such matters. He failed to realize that he was being used as a dustbin because Anjali's love interest was elsewhere. When his progress in the ongoing project stalled, I knew the reason behind it. I went and talked to Animesh.

When I touched upon the subject of Anjali, he started blushing like a girl. I chose not to go into too much detail and just asked him to focus on work for the time being. I told him that he had all the time in this world to date whoever he wished to later. He was assured. Three days later, he delivered to us the website. It took significant time and motivation from my side to make him come back to normal and to allow his bright mind to stop being emotional and become analytical instead.

We created a great hullabaloo about our website on social media. A lot of interest was generated and we registered a good number of hits. But you can't expect much from a first time coder working with a first time designer and a first time entrepreneur working on his first dynamic website, can you? The product lacked scalability. Adding one more feature required tremendous effort on our part, as we had used a custom template which could not be modified easily. Seeing the inability to motivate the followers on our fan page to use our website, we shifted back to our fan page.

Two days later, Rishabh turned up in my room.

'I have fired Animesh,' he announced.

'What? Why?'

'He doesn't know how to talk,' he said.

'What did he say?'

'Do you want me to repeat the bad things he said about Anjali and me?' Rishabh screamed.

'No, not at all. Your decision, my command.'

He disappeared thereafter. I went to Animesh's room immediately. He chose to remain silent on the issue as well.

A few days later, I observed that Rishabh had stopped talking to Shikha altogether and was accompanied by Anjali most of the time. Bemused, I chose not to poke knowing all the while that the matter involved the love triangle of Rishabh, Anjali, and Animesh.

It was much later that Rishabh told me that Shikha's boyfriend cried for her on Skype from France, melting her heart. Her guilt for having left him made her pull away from Rishabh.

One month later, I met Animesh in the Delhi metro and we started talking. It was then that he opened up. He recounted that he had criticized Rishabh for ruining Anjali's academic life by involving her in the start-up. The argument happened when Animesh told Rishabh that Anjali was a five pointer and until and unless she could focus on her academics, it wouldn't be possible for her to get a good job out of campus, to which Rishabh had lost his temper.

Rishabh had a fraud internship at his father's office in the irrigation department of UP which meant that he didn't have to go to work. Since his work could be managed over the phone, he left for home on June 15.

We were short of a technical guy and we decided that we would run the website as a fan page as long as we didn't have a technical genius on board, which we hoped to find very soon. During this time, one of Rishabh's friends, Tanay, a top-Delhi school passout and a programmer by hobby, joined us. He was smarter than both of us, was a smooth talker, and most importantly, had a car. He joined us to do 'time pass'—as he told us himself—and we listened to him in rapt attention, more because of his suave diction than the content of his talk. Passouts from this particular school are so gifted in influencing with their eloquence that they could sell you your own underwear at a price above the original.

Though Tanay didn't offer much technical help, at least he represented us in various business plan contests and helped us in meeting potential investors. Yes. Two small investors had shown interest in us after they observed our Facebook page and wanted to know more about us. Tanay, Rishabh, and I went to meet them only to realize that they offered us a valuation of only around 20 lakh rupees. We instead chose to lead the venture forward by ourselves before meeting other investors. However, we converted one of them into our mentor, an entrepreneur who had seen the world. Being an IIT-D alumni, he readily agreed to give us free consultation over the phone any time we faced doubts.

Months went by. Other than selling a hundred odd T-shirts, the only other two achievements we had was a stall space in Rendezvous, the annual cultural festival at IIT Delhi, and crossed 10,000 likes on our Facebook page. The very last cultural festival that we would be attending as final year students, was going to be spent not in ogling chics, not in stradlking hand in hand with Priya like I did the last time, but in selling T-shirts instead. Rishabh had estimated around 1000 T-shirts to be sold in the course of four days with a foot fall of around two lakh people. We had a prime location for the stall, thanks to Pratik who was the marketing coordinator.

We had borrowed 80,000 rupees each from our parents, totalling 1.6 lakh rupees, and decided on a manufacturer who would deliver us 1000 one-liner based tees at 110 rupees each, totalling exactly 1.1 lakh rupees. We still had 50,000 rupees left with which we printed lottery cards, stationery, catalogues, borrowed a music system, a mic, and handed over 2,000 rupees each to our six volunteers in advance. We were looking forward to make a profit of a whopping 90,000 rupees in the process by selling our thousand tees at 250 rupees each.

The day of the fest arrived. Anjali, with her booming street play voice, conducted several games at the stall. I remained seated at the stall, turning from a suave entrepreneur to an irritable salesman, while Rishabh went from stall to stalls and networked with other sponsors. Priya arrived to meet me on two occasions but I couldn't give her time, so she went along with Pratik to attend the events. We started with 250 rupees on the first day only to realize that nobody was interested in buying our tees at all. The next day, we slashed down the prices to 200 rupees per tee, so it fetched some takers.

By the last day of the fest, we had managed to sell only 240 T-shirts at 200 rupees each. KK, one of my favorite singers, had come to perform, but I didn't dare to leave my stall. The countdown for the fest to come to an end had begun and desperately, we lowered our prices and kept chanting '500 ka 3' to lure the audience, only to find one or two people coming over. The fest ended for us with the '500 ka 3' finding no takers and we carried the remaining T-shirts, 680 in total, back to our hostel room. We had sold 320 T-shirts at around 200 each, making a revenue of around 64,000 rupees.

Around 86,000 rupees was our loss. Though T-shirts were nonperishable commodities, transporting those huge sacks to any other college seemed like an impossible task.

Nevertheless, we did what we were best at. Boasting. We pretended to have rocked the Rendezvous. We actually had rocked the Rendezvous because now everybody in the campus knew about us and we also received numerous offers to sponsor college fests. Besides all of that, we didn't pay the Rendezvous organizers any money, since we had got the stall through the help of our friend Pratik. Despite incurring a loss of 86,000 rupees, we still proclaimed with pride that we got the stall for free.

On the brink of the loss, a little joy soothed our wounds. We had made it to the top 50 of Asia's Biggest Business-plan

Competition, Eureka, hosted by IIT Bombay, and we had to go to Mumbai in December to attend the mentor meets.

In November, without knowing much about the implications, we registered our company as a Private Limited Company under the Company's Act and robbed our wallets of another 16,000 rupees. A private limited company is a status symbol for entrepreneurs because the existence of a private limited company is eternal. During incorporation, it needs to have at least two Directors and an authorized capital of 1 lakh rupees, which we divided equally between us. Whenever one Director has to leave, one has to appoint another Director in his place and his equity is transferred ('buyout' is the correct term). Thus the company never dies even if the Director wishes to leave. One of the major benefits of a private limited company is that its account and cash flows are annually audited, and therefore, all the investors get a clear idea about where and how their funds are being utilized.

For us, forming a private limited company as students was a way of impressing our investors and showing them that we were ready for a long-term commitment. But the real reason was to polish our resume for campus placements. Yes, we still were quite intent on getting recruited via college as we had realized that it would have become impossible to run a company without money and moreover, after encountering a humongous loss of 86,000 rupees at the fest, we could not convince ourselves of going full time, to say nothing of convincing our parents. Having a secure job assured us of having enough cash to repay our losses and at the same time hire a professional to work for us while we worked for someone else. Stupid thought, as I realize now.

Our company was registered as YourQuote Marketing Private Limited. We added marketing because we believed we were into marketing and moreover, marketing was a broad domain so if later on we desired to enter areas like retail, the company name would allow us to do that. We hosted a big party in its celebration. The only disadvantage was that it took us three months to get it incorporated and we couldn't include it in our CVs.

Did I tell you about my dream to crack the Day 1 of campus placements at IIT Delhi? About Mckinsey & Company?

The Quantum Leap

In IITs, boasting about big placements and even bigger pay packages is considered a status symbol. During the placement, the person who had been your best buddy ever since the first year can suddenly become alienated, solely because he might find a job that pays four times of what you might get, changing his fate from yours in a snap. Like when one arrives at IIT, their AIR determines their status—similarly after placements, the big fat pay package determines one's status. Day 1 of IIT, most often being December 1, is like Judgement Day, a day which everyone, however terrified, looks forward to.

Months are spent consulting seniors on how to make one's resume, how to exaggerate so that no one finds out, how to assure a seat even before companies arrive in campus by kissing asses of your favourite seniors, and if there's no jugaad, then how to ace the interviews by cracking challenging business cases.

I was a published author of a bestseller, an entrepreneur running an online company with no website but a turnover of around 7 lakhs (Okay, I agree that it was much less and I'd exaggerated the figure in my resume.) and a team of around

15 people, none of whom were working at the moment. And perhaps that became a reason why I really wanted to get into McKinsey & Company. I was so fascinated with the great consulting company that I overconfidently asked all my friends to call me on Day 1 to congratulate me. Being a strong believer in the law of attraction, I had put up a chart paper at the centre of my room stating:

Priorities:
1. McKinsey
2. YourQuote
3. Third Novel

Ravi, one of my dear friends from IIT, once asked me why I was placing something that was not even mine as my first priority and I defended my stand by making him understand my passion for business and how McKinsey would become my career launch pad. However, the real reason was that it would make my parents proud of me. My mother would be able to flaunt to all her friends, my bank account would be rich enough to enable my Dad to take voluntary retirement and relax at home, and last but not the least, I would be able to hire people for my venture.

It had a fat pay package of around 12 lakhs per year, which meant that even if I worked twelve hours a day for that company, I could hire three guys at 15,000 rupees per month to build the website. McKinsey is by far the most reputed consulting company ever.

My parents were more excited than me. They were chanting the McKinsey mantra to every kith and kin that they came across, as though I had already been selected.

The reason for their incessant hope was no one but me. My contagious confidence wooed them into thinking that it was made for me.

When McKinsey had come for a pre-placement talk, I had talked to a couple of McKinsey employees and they seemed really interested in my profile—an entrepreneur cum author. One of them clearly stated that I had two spikes in my resume and the chances of being shortlisted were pretty bright. They said that McKinsey looks for passion and determination in the CV, and I couldn't stop smiling as I had plenty of examples to substantiate that.

Almost three months before my placements, I had started preparing for the interviews. Cases, cases, and more cases. My life became a potpourri of mock interviews, guesstimates, puzzles. Priya, YourQuote, and academics became second priority. To my surprise, Priya was quite supportive and understanding.

Almost fifteen days before Judgement Day, shortlists started arriving. BCG, Bain and Company, Booz and Co, and my name was on none. From the shortlist, it seemed that only 8+ pointers had any chance of making it through.

'Son, did any shortlists arrive?' said my father during a phone conversation.

'No,' I hesitantly lied. It hurt me to lie to them.

'Not even for McKinsey?'

'No, it will arrive in three days.'

I was really sad. More than my own rejection, it was the names of Shantanu and Preeti being shortlisted with whom I had practised several cases that became the cause of my anguish. Five other companies released their shortlists for interviews over the next three days. My disappointment climbed the charts as I made it to none of them. My self worth stooped to the nadir. To add to my misery, Preeti made it in all of them and she called me every time to ask about my shortlist, despite knowing that I hadn't made it. I could not face anyone. I was so agonized that I started staying aloof, away from sympathy and pity.

Like always, I was playing click-back-refresh on the placement portal of IIT Delhi. My eyes fell on a particular announcement. It was a list of shortlisted candidates for McKinsey & Company and my name was on it! I decided to update my Facebook status.

McKinsey & Co.—I love you.

Half an hour later, my cellphone started buzzing.

'I have been shortlisted for McKinsey, Mom,' I exclaimed.

'Jai Sainath. Jai Sainath,' she said thanking her favourite God. I checked my status again. It had crossed 20 likes and a dozen of congratulatory messages.

I called Preeti next. To my surprise, she hadn't made it. I expressed my fake sadness and sported a wide grin. I, a 7 pointer, could crack something that Preeti, a 9 pointer, couldn't. After ten days of despair, I could walk with my chest swollen with pride.

I didn't yet tell Priya about it. It had been almost a month since we had last met. She had been very considerate and strengthened my confidence every step of the way. It was time to gift my beloved my time: the only thing that she would appreciate before my credit cards came into existence.

I chose to skip my case practice and go to North Campus to see Priya. Later, I found out from Shantanu that the practice had been called off for Preeti was not in the right mood owing to her rejection; I suspected the reason to be jealousy borne from my getting shortlisted in the best company on campus.

'Hi girlfriend,' I said to Priya on the phone. I was standing right outside her PG and had decided to surprise her with my unexpected arrival.

'Wow, somebody seems to be happy.'

'Why shouldn't I be? After all, I have a girlfriend like... Yu...kta!'

'Jerk. Who's Yukta?'

'Miss World 1999.'

'Oh. I thought there seriously was a girl.'

'What for? A threesome?'

'No dumbass—for finally getting rid of you.'

'How can you get rid of me when I'm standing just outside your PG?'

'Wait. You're kidding, right?'

'Absolutely not.'

She peered down her window, saw me standing on the opposite side of the road in the winter sun, and screamed, 'Oh my God. Wait there. I hate you for surprising me. I'm coming. Where are my jeans?'

'Were you not wearing anything at home?' I asked only to find that the call had been disconnected.

She came running, with a wide beautiful smile that just did it for me. Her eyes were fixated on mine as she ran across the road, missing collision with a bicycle by inches, which made my heart skip a beat. She pounced on me and hugged me like a child.

We were meeting after a month and I couldn't convey in words how delighted I was too finally behold her in my sight.

'How come you turned up all the way to this side of the gdobe?' she said breaking from the embrace.

'It's love that has brought me here, my love,' I said turning cheesy.

'This can't happen. You can't be so nice. Wait a minute… oh my God, you got shortlisted for McKinsey, didn't you?'

What followed was a version of bhangra on the road. To save myself from humiliation in front of the crowd watching us, I stopped her.

'Are you happy for me or the credit cards?' I interrogated.

'Of course, you…r credit cards,' she winked.

We walked our way to the Kamla Nagar market, talking about things that made us smile and imagining my future as a McKinsey employee with a big fat package. The future appeared spectacular.

I returned late at night, checked the placement portal to reaffirm myself that I'd actually made it, and slept peacefully for the last time in my life.

The next few days I completely immersed myself in the preparations. Rishabh, seeing me so focussed about the placement process, took care of the start-up in my absence. Not that he was toiling day and night, as we had nothing spectacular to toil for, but yes, he totally dealt with the T-shirt manufacturers, college orders, and respected my seriousness about McKinsey. Nevertheless, I was still managing the social media of the start-up, which was helping us in the outreach.

Rishabh was not very keen about preparing for placements. He was brainwashed by seniors that students with a low GPA couldn't clear shortlists of reputed companies and therefore didn't apply for many Day 1 companies. With the approaching date, the weather also took a turn for the worse.

⊂⊐

December 1

For the first time in my four years of engineering I took a bath so early in the morning. Other than occasional shivers, slight panting, and a feeble I-can-do-it feeling, I experienced numbness all over. My interview with McKinsey & Company was scheduled for 8 o' clock that morning. Bitten by the cold weather, I rushed to the interview room in my new pinstriped suit.

Other interviewees, some of them my batchmates, were waiting before me already. My interviewer was a Sardarji. He seemed quite scary judging by his walk. He advanced towards me as if he was going to head butt me. I reluctantly advanced towards him. He anticipated the rhythm and that led to a firm handshake. Firmer from my side, just to let him know that I was not scared. Or rather to let me know that I wasn't.

'Hello, I'm Amol.'

'Hi,' I said, waiting for him to continue while we advanced towards the slaughter house.

'Your good name please?' I asked.

'Hmmm,' he said. That's all.

At this point of time, three separate thoughts swayed in my head at the same time.

1. Either he had not heard my question.
2. He could have forgotten his name and was trying to recollect it.
3. He didn't like me asking his good name.

I was lost in his *hmmm*, when he opened the door to the slaughter house. When I saw the insides, my mind went blank. All three thoughts merged into each other.

'Amol, have a seat,' Hmmm said. I was glad to know that he could actually frame sentences.

'Thanks a lot,' I grabbed the opposite chair, the cold seat freezing my bottom.

'So, you're?' Hmmm shot the trigger straightaway. I was startled.

'I am... I am Amol Sabharwal, student of Engineering Physics, 4th year...'

'No, no, stop. I just forgot your name. So Amol, what do you like?' he asked.

Definitely not a creepy guy in the chilly morning! I thought.

'Hmmm...' I said and began thinking in a similar manner to Hmmm. Despite my liking for him, he didn't seem pleased. I continued, 'I like writing. I like business. And, I like people.'

'What's the order of liking?' he asked.

'The reverse. People, business, and writing,' I said. The first big mistake.

'When it's your first choice, why did it come last?'

'I saved the best for the last,' I tried to please him with my wit. He didn't know appreciation.

'Hmmm,' he said. I thought he liked his name too much. His eyes were deadly. 'Okay, so tell me about this YourQuote. com that you've mentioned in your resume?'

'So, YourQuote is my start-up, which I co-founded around six months ago. It caters to people who are good with one liners. As a writer, I realized that there was no platform which promotes the common man's basic creativity of crafting quotable one liners and there was also no way to gain incentives at the grassroot level of creativity that every common man possesses...In this...'

'As I can read here in your CV, you're a novelist too. Interesting!' Hmmm developed some interest. 'Tell me, why are you interested in consulting?'

'Hmmm, consulting is a field which would offer me great insight into the field of business and people, which I'm really passionate about. It would give me a chance to...,' I continued with my best prepared speech.

He looked convinced. Boot-licking, who doesn't like that? That too at the start of the day?

'You're a writer as well as an entrepreneur. And as I can see from your resume, you're making good money too from your venture and I can guess you're getting decent royalties from your book as well. If I'd been at your place, I would have pursued the venture full time. Why don't you?'

I realized one of the gravest mistakes I'd committed while preparing my CV was mentioning the exaggerated turnover of our start-up—7 lakhs in six months' time. What I thought would be the spike in my CV actually became a spike in my ass. 7 lakhs in six months for an online venture with T-shirts as the only product with a profit margin of 30-40 percent meant that soon I would be earning a lot from my venture.

'Sir, as I said that I want to gain experience of the business world,' I uttered, irritably.

'Nothing would give you the experience of the business world more than entrepreneurship. I myself want to be an entrepreneur, but am severely trapped in the job cycle. You are making decent money with the venture. Go ahead.'

I was baffled. I couldn't convince myself. Especially when I had told everyone that McKinsey was my dream company. I couldn't say that what my CV stated was only half the truth, our turnover had zero profit, as whatever we had earned was spent in overheads. There were also those 700 T-shirts lying in my room that had blocked our 1.5 lakh rupees completely.

I had to fight back. Anyhow.

'Sir, I still think joining McKinsey would be more beneficial for me as currently I lack the experience.'

'Amol, we are not looking for candidates who take value from McKinsey. We are looking for someone who can add value to it instead.'

Why are you making it difficult for me? Damn, I can't think of anything.

'I think I can add value. I have the necessary skill set and experience to understand the business intricacies, be a team leader, and solve business problems.'

'Amol, you are contradicting yourself. You just mentioned that you lack experience.'

Damn! It's a stress interview now.

'Anyway, let's do a case,' he said and made sure that he broke down my three months of hard work by giving me his life's most challenging case that required application of game theory and probability which was way beyond my knowledge. Being nervous, I could not come up with anything intelligent in the next few minutes to break the awkward lull between us.

'What would you do if you don't make it in this interview?'

'I'll go full time with my start-up,' I said in an impulse.

'That's what I thought. Thanks for the interview. Wish you all the best with YourQuote.com,' he said.

'Hmmm,' I said in a contemplative tone. I stood up and said, 'It's yourquote.in, not .com,' and came out of the interview room.

∝⊏⊐

I had left the slaughter house, disappointing the executioner. As soon as I came out of the interview room, I found Priya waiting anxiously for me. I had never felt as bad as I did that moment. My cheeks were wet. It was the first time that she had seen me crying. She wrapped me in her arms and broke into sobs. She was crying with me. For me.

We didn't speak at all. I was told by the volunteers there that in case McKinsey wishes to call me for the next round of interview, I would receive a call. Meanwhile, a loud shriek pierced through my ears. One of my batchmates had been given a spot offer in the first round itself. She was jumping with joy. Had I stayed at that place for one more moment, I would have jumped off the third floor balcony. The lull prevailed as I walked till the market just outside the IIT campus and grabbed a seat in a coffee house. I loosened the tie which seemed like a suicide rope tied to my neck.

'Why are you so disappointed? They said they would call you,' Priya said softly.

'Amol, they said...' Priya uttered.

'Will you please shut up?' I screamed, so loudly that the people who were seated nearby turned around to look at what was happening.

'What? What are you looking at?' I screamed irritably at the onlookers.

Priya started sobbing. Her tears did the magic trick. I couldn't stand seeing her cry. I held her hands and apologized.

'If you don't stop crying, I'll start crying too and you know how bad I look when I cry.' Her sobs stopped and a mild smile appeared in its place.

'They have rejected me. Damn the start-up, it screwed me up totally. I should not have mentioned the turnover. It worked against me. It's over.'

'Think positive. They might call you.'

'Priya, I have been rejected fair and square. The partner at the firm himself told me during the interview.'

Just then a call from a random number appeared on my screen. My heartbeat stopped for a while.

'Amol, pick up the phone. It's them,' Priya yelled, 'Amol! Are you listening to me?'

I came back to my senses and picked up the call with wishful anticipation.

'Hi Amol! Preeti this side, I cracked BCG. They just gave me a spot-offer. Also, Shantanu cracked Goldman Sachs. What about you? How did McKinsey go?' I was bereft of hope. Nothing could have been worse than that.

'Congratulations.' It took me immense efforts to fabricate every syllable of that word. I couldn't talk anymore and broke down, so Priya grabbed my phone and uttered, 'Hi Preeti, Amol will talk later. He's not well,' and saved me from the misery.

No phone calls came until dusk. The thought of calling my parents who had been desperately waiting to hear from me killed every piece alive within me. I SMSed my father: 'Sorry

Dad, I couldn't make it. I'll call you at night,' and they were considerate enough to not call me and prod. Though Priya didn't want to leave me alone at that critical juncture, I asked her to leave. I made my way back to the hostel. I wanted to be alone. I wanted to be caged in a shell. I switched off my cellphone and dropped deep down into a sea of depression.

The priorities poster with McKinsey at number 1 was still stuck on my wall and it seemed to mock me. In a fit of rage, I tore it down to pieces and cried like a child.

The walls of Facebook were full of jubilations and felicitations. A record 62 people, most of them from my friend list, had been placed on Day 1, with the maximum package being around 25 lakhs. I closed the website in disgust and retired to sleep, which I knew was not going to come easily that day.

Going Solo

I woke up at 6 o'clock the next morning. I had no companies for the next four days. The early morning sun prompted me to come face to face with the reality of the previous day. As I walked, wrapped in a shawl that was my father's, I observed everything around me. Nothing had changed. The hostel had the same guard, the ground had the same grass, the dogs had the same howl, the sun had the same brightness. It seemed that nobody was even a little bit perturbed by my sorrow. They didn't seem to care at all.

I was too small for them. I was nobody for the world. I was nobody for McKinsey. I was nobody for any of the other companies. Except one that was my own. yourquote.in.

I rushed back to my hostel, opened my laptop, and at exactly 6.30 am, updated my status:

Cracked Day 2: placed at yourquote.in, my dream company

The amount of satisfaction it brought to me was out of this world. I felt enlightened, inspired, and most importantly, happy. I decided to call my parents. When I found my cellphone, I cursed myself. I had forgotten to switch it on.

There were three missed calls from my Dad, two from my Mom, and a dozen from Priya.

I called my Mom and woke her up in the process.

'Son, I have been waiting to speak to you. How are you?'

'I'm fine Mom. Sorry for switching off the phone yesterday.'

'Yes, I got really nervous, thinking whether you had done anything. But then your Dad told me that you had talked to him.'

I hadn't talked to my Dad the day before, but thanked his presence of mind for taking care of my mother's anxiety.

'Oh yes. I had talked to Dad.'

'Son, don't feel sad about McKinsey. Everything happens for a reason. There would be a better company waiting for you,' she counseled me.

'Yes Mom, that's why I called you. I have found a better company.'

'Did you already get placed?'

'Yes mother.'

'Oh God. Jai sainath. Which one is that?' she asked, excitedly.

'My own. YourQuote,' I said ecstatically.

'What are you talking about?' she asked, concerned.

'Yes Mom. I have decided to go full time with my start-up.'

'Are you out of your mind? You are leaving the certain for the uncertain. You know nobody has ever done business in our family before. Do you know how risky is it? What's his name—your partner…'

'Rishabh…'

'Yes, definitely Rishabh—your partner had brainwashed you.'

'Mom, Rishabh doesn't even know about it. And, he's probably going for a job.'

'See how shrewd he is? He wants you to go full time with the start-up while he would benefit from working at two places at the same time.'

'Mom, stop it. He is very nice and supportive. He has not influenced my decision. I want to take my company to greater heights. Think about next year, when I would be coming to recruit students from IIT. How wonderful would that be?'

'But you are going to become a businessman. After a degree from IIT, a businessman—how bad does that sound?'

'Ma, it's not just business. It's called entrepreneurship.'

'A french word doesn't make it sound cool. You are going to sell T-shirts—do you expect IITians to do that? Absolutely not. You are going to sit for the next company that comes in the campus.'

My mother was rigid. I didn't know a way to maneuver around her logic. I gave it my last try.

'Mom, what does Sinha aunty's son do and how much does he earn?'

'He works in some IT company, gets around 6 lakhs.'

'Mom, he passed from NIT Patna and is getting 6 lakhs. Now imagine me getting a similar salary with the next company that comes here. What would you say to Sinha aunty? That even your son, who got 993 rank in the JEE, is doing a similar job. Entrepreneurship is at least better in the sense that you get to tell that your son recruits people for 6 lakhs.'

'But that will take time to happen.'

'But that is not impossible, right Mom? Please. I can't miss the IIT Bombay b-plan contest for placements. I'm going to Mumbai next week.'

'Your father will speak to you regarding this.'

'As you wish,' I said and heaved a huge sigh. My Dad was far more practical than my mother and if given a proper reason, he wouldn't shy away in supporting my unconventional dreams.

It was 9 am. I expectantly opened my Facebook profile hoping to see a flood of likes and congratulatory comments, in awe of my decision to go full time with my fledgling venture. But, as luck would have it, it was the other way round.

1. Are you frigging crazy? Do you have any idea what not having a job means?
2. Happy for you, but I seriously think you should reconsider. There are many other good companies that are still left.
3. yourquote.in—a day 2 company. In your dreams buddy, in your dreams.
4. Bro, please stop being so impulsive. Entrepreneurship is cool in college, but the real world is full of struggles.

I didn't read any further. My friends had given me enough impetus to go ahead and prove them wrong. What I had chosen brought me immense happiness, but they didn't care about my happiness. They instead cared about my ability to earn bread and butter which was fairly practical on their part, but very insensitive towards me.

I went to the YourQuote fan page and initiated a new category, 'Sermon of the Day' and posted the very first sermon that reflected my mood—*Don't let earning for your living stop you from living.*

'Are you sure that you want to go full-time with it?' Priya asked me on the phone.

'One hundred percent.'

And then she said what I would never forget in my life—'I am with you.'

Her four words meant more than the world to me. She was the first person to support me in my decision and her support empowered me like nothing else. For an entrepreneur, the person who shows the first support is the person who truly understands his passion. I was glad that for me, it was Priya and her support which became a testimony to our unwavering understanding.

'I love you,' I admitted, just after the call got cut. The dropped call rendered my utterance more meaningful.

⌁

I was curious about what Rishabh had in mind. He was nowhere to be seen. I went to his room, knocked on his door, and found out that he was sleeping all suited up. I feared he had cracked a Day 1 job, partied all night, and was now sleeping. His selection meant I was going to become a solo entrepreneur. The very thought of being the solo sailor made my feet run cold.

Nervously, I shook him up from his sleep and shrieked, 'Did you crack a job yesterday?'

'Schlumberger,' he muttered in sleep. I was dumbfounded. Schlumberger was one of the best companies on campus with a whopping package of around 22 lakh rupees per annum. My feeling of failure now quadrupled.

'What? You weren't even shortlisted,' I screamed to wake him up.

'They called me just half an hour before and said that there had been some goof up with another guy named Rishabh and it was me who had been shortlisted.'

'Oh, wow. Congratulations.'

'What congratulations! I didn't make it. They raped me in their HR interview.'

'Oh God!' I exclaimed with hidden joy and evident sympathy, 'How could they do that? Damn!'

'Won't you ask about McKinsey?' I said.

'What? Everybody knows that you didn't make it. Chill, there are other good companies,' he said sleepily.

'Like YourQuote.'

'What? What do you mean?'

'I'm going full time with the venture. There is no pressure on you. You sit for the placements, get a job, and support the start-up—financially or by getting business for it. But I am not going to slog 14 hours a day for second-rung companies that are going to come now and pay me peanuts. No offence.'

'Oh man,' he said, now visibly awake, 'Are you really sure?'

'Absolutely man. This is our child. We would make it big.'

'Absolutely,' he grinned. I thanked God for giving me a partner and a friend like Rishabh.

'What about your parents?'

'That's the toughest nut to crack. I'll figure out something.'

'All the best.'

I had to convince my parents. Especially my mother. I could think of just one resort. Writing.

Dear Mother,

I've been fortunate to be the reason for your incomparable happiness since my early childhood. Perhaps that's why you named me Amol—the one who couldn't be compared. It has always been my endeavour to make you proud of me in things that I give my heart and soul into. Lately, I haven't been able to give you that contentment which you had always expected of me. I'm not sorry about it since the truth of the matter is that the thing that I've given my heart and soul has still not borne fruit and is going to take a long time to do so. And you've got to wait, along with me, to celebrate the fruits of my passion.

The road that I've currently chosen is tough, full of prickles and deadly thorns, and has countless possibilities—both heartening and disheartening. It's going to take a lot of time to be able to achieve anything which would make you proud of me, which would enable you to say proudly to your friends that your son is an entrepreneur, that your son pursued something different and made a mark. The road is deadly; it might be possible that in the middle of the journey, I get so bruised that I am not able to carry myself further. Reinforce my faith, if I falter. Because it was you who taught me not to fear mistakes while chasing my dreams. I won't stop at anything.

Believe me mother, when I say that I heartily enjoy what I'm doing, despite knowing the facts that I might not be able to lead a comfortable life for the next two years, that I've become the least prospective bridegroom in consideration for any of the well-off families, that you have to fight the whims of the society which constantly pesters saying that I had been stupid in choosing the road less travelled over the conventional options, that it might ruin my chances of living a life free from hassles, that I might end up being bankrupt if things don't turn out as expected. The good thing is that I'm not scared. The better thing is there is no bad thing, just because of the good thing. I'm ready to take the leap— leap into the unknown just to know where my end lies—across the sky or beneath the ground. I can't promise you success but I can promise you my hard work, and I'll make sure that I leave no stones unturned to bring my dream to perfection.

Coming from your womb, I'm fortunate to be endowed with all your traits—determination, passion, and love—which give me the confidence to trudge through this dangerous path with unmatched vigour and resilience to make the impossible possible. From my end, I can assure you that I wouldn't stop, not until my last breath—to sculpt my passion into a living dream. Please don't worry, and be happy, because I'm happy too.

With love and faith,
Your Son
Amol

As soon as I finished the letter, I realized that my eyes were wet. I reread it a few times and felt that it was the most sincere piece I had ever written. I had always written for others, but this was the first time I had written something for myself.

I sent it to my father and mother separately, messaged them both to check their mails and call me. I shut down the PC, jumped on my bed, and started reading Steve Jobs' biography.

⌁

Fifteen minutes later, my cellphone rang. The screen said 'Mom calling'. I expected a shift in the paradigm. Or maybe a reprimand. In nervous anticipation, I picked up. What would be the first thing you would want to hear when you write a letter explaining what your dream means to you?

Understanding, encouragement, or appreciation? But I didn't get any of those.

I got her tears. I felt so bad. I had made her cry. She was sobbing uncontrollably.

'Mom, please stop crying.'

She didn't seem to listen.

'Mom, please.'

'Why do you have to make me cry? Wasn't your decision enough to worry me?' she croaked, gasping for breath.

'Mom, I just wanted to let Dad and you know about how willing I am to go ahead with my choice.'

'We allowed you to start-up just because we thought it would help you in getting a job. Nobody in our family has ever had anything to do with business before, son.'

'That's why nobody in our family has ever done anything great.' I retorted. I realized I should not have. Mom started crying again.

'Amol, now that you don't want to sit in the placements, come home.' It was my Dad on the phone.

'Dad, but I have my company and I have to go to Mumbai as well, you remember Eureka—Asia's biggest b-plan competition.'

'Go from Dhanbad. Your mother needs you. Also, we need to talk,' my Dad said seriously. I hadn't ever heard him this serious before.

'About what?'

'About your life,' Dad said. I had nothing to say in return. I waited for him to drop the call. He perhaps waited for me. An awkward pause that had a ghastly silence ingrained in every passing moment, prevailed for around half a minute.

'Take care of Mom,' I said and disconnected.

Next morning, amidst all the placement chaos, I sneaked out of my hostel without telling anyone. I was already placed, so it was but natural that I would run off home. I took a flight to Kolkata. Luckily I got a ticket at a reasonable price. Dhanbad was just a four hours' drive from there. During the flight, I immersed myself into Steve Jobs' biography. I was reading the portion where he left University, became a hippie, and travelled across India in search of salvation. I so desperately desired to do the same. There was just one problem—unlike him, I couldn't choose to neglect my parents.

Dhanbad

The call bell was not functioning. I had tried it thrice. I knocked on the door. I was giving them a surprise. It was a Sunday and I expected my father to be at home. After encountering the outburst last night, I was excepting a very cold reception at home.

The door opened and my mother was in front of me. I put up a mild smile to anticipate her reaction and touched her feet. She didn't smile. She didn't say anything. She couldn't, as tears welled up in her eyes and she was back to her previous avatar. She was sobbing, hearing which my Dad turned up. Upon seeing me, a proud smile came up on his face. It was the most reassuring smile I had ever encountered, as if it said to me, 'Son, don't worry. Everything is fine.' I was so glad it came at the right time. He hugged me and greeted me with immense respect. Mom's sobs were over. It appeared that even she was delighted to see me.

It was after six months that I had gone back home.

Mom and Dad very tactfully didn't initiate any unwanted conversations immediately. They left me alone, to freshen up and get acclimatized to the environment. Home was peaceful. The hustle of students, the chatter and nervous discussion of the job aspirants was long gone.

I looked at my room—the room which carried the memories of my most focussed phase of life—preparing for JEE. My parents were so proud of me when I cracked the exam that they didn't whitewash the walls of my room for the last three and half years. They still had the picturesque structure of organic compounds, benzene derivatives, and mathematical proofs. One side of the wall contained quotes which caught my attention. Henry Ford's famous quote: 'Whether you think you can or you think you can't, you are right,' was at the top. I had highlighted it with a fluorescent orange pen. I realized how subtly quotes had crept into my mind back then, much before the idea for YourQuote was born.

I looked at the library. I considered myself lucky to have been born in a home which fostered good habits. Reading, music, art, writing, and gardening. I skimmed through some of the new additions to the library. *Jonathan Livingston Seagull* by Richard Bach was one of them, which I had already read at IIT. It recounted the story of a bird which didn't adhere to the herd mentality and developed a passion for flying, ultimately becoming an outcast but awakened in the end. I wished my Dad had read it.

Mom had prepared a sumptuous lunch: two curries, basmati rice, dal, and my favorite cucumber raita. I realized that coming back home was way better than I'd presumed. Good food should be accompanied by good talk, isn't it? And that's when it started.

'Son, what made you take that decision?' my Dad asked patiently.

'Did Rishabh brainwash you?' my mother asked.

'You keep quiet. Let me talk to him,' Dad reprimanded Mom.

'Dad, I took that decision because I don't want to slog for someone else's dream for 14 hours a day and get paid peanuts for it. With McKinsey it was fine, as the pay was going to be good and I would also have the opportunity to build my reputation for the work. But with other companies that followed Day 1, I would be exploited mercilessly and YourQuote would suffer in the process.'

'Who has brainwashed you?' Mom started again, my Dad calmed her once again.

'How much money are you making with YourQuote?' Dad asked. He was a banker—he knew how the real world worked.

'Nothing at the moment. But if I go full time, I will find a tech guy and get the website designed, after which I'll get investment for it.'

'It's not as easy as you say. Investors won't back you if you don't make money.'

'Dad, that's an old theory. Right now, investors invest in teams and ideas. And you know that my idea is innovative and totally original.'

'That's not true. I have seen a lot of investors in my banking career.'

'Dad, you have no idea. There are angel investors, those who are ready to invest at the idea stage when you don't even have a revenue model in place. You know that Facebook started in 2004. But do you also know that, it didn't have a revenue model even by 2008? That's how it works,' I said defensively. My Dad had no option other than to surrender. He smartly maneuvered the discussion in another direction. Emotional.

'Okay, okay, I get it. But tell me, how would you feel when your friends make 60,000 per month while you will be making only around one-sixth their salary?'

'I will be proud of myself, Dad. I would be earning that 10,000 working for *something* that I love rather than for *someone*.'

'Is Rishabh also leaving his job?' My mother asked. She didn't like Rishabh at all. She thought that Rishabh, being academically less bright than me, wanted me to come down to his level and sell T-shirts.

I knew that he wouldn't. His parents were not going to be as easily convinced as mine. But if I would have told this to my mother, she would have ended my entrepreneurial journey then and there. And so I lied.

'Yes. He left his Schlumberger offer of 22 lakhs.'

'Did he? You said he didn't crack any shortlists.'

'He didn't tell anyone. He left it too, Mom.'

There was a sudden shift in my parents' view about Rishabh. They discovered something that I had months ago—respect for Rishabh.

'Son, you know I was just chatting with your Mama yesterday. He can get you an interview in his company.'

'Mom, no. And, don't start that topic ever again.'

Her face suddenly lost its glow. She was unhappy and I couldn't do anything about it. I had all the more reasons to be unhappier. I went to my room and lay down, contemplating. Start-up is all about passion and as a co-founder, it was my responsibility to instill passion in all my employees, investors, and stakeholders. If I was going to make my parents my first investors, I had to make them invest their trust in me.

'Mom, Dad, are you free tomorrow morning at 8 am?' I had rushed to their room, my face shining in excitement.

'Yes. Why? Where do you want to take us?'

'Nowhere. Just a small meeting in the drawing room.'

'What for?'

'See you tomorrow.'

⊏⊏⊐

I have had terrible experiences with mornings. Most sleep-inducing classes in college were held in the morning, so were the long and boring daily speeches made by our principal in school, and lastly, morning was when the disastrous interview with the Sardarji from Mckinsey happened.

I was not very confident, especially because I hadn't slept well the last night. Impressing Mom and Dad was no easy feat and required immaculate preparation. I had a quick bath and googled how to tie a knot. Yes, I was suiting up. It was going to be my first pitch. Even before my parents had woken up, I had finished the investor's pitch and connected my laptop with the TV in the drawing room. I had even sneaked into the kitchen and prepared chai for them.

Exactly at 8, they came out of their room and were aghast to see me dressed in formals. I escorted them to the sofas in the front, poured down tea in their cups, and began with my pitch.

'Good morning. I welcome you to the elevator pitch of yourquote.in. Elevator pitch derives its name from a short and crisp description about one's business that could be given during an elevator ride. So, here shall we begin.'

'"As you sow, so shall you reap." Ma'am, do you know who said this?'

My mother shook her head to say no.

'Sir, do you?'

My Dad said no as well.

'Neither do I. Neither does anyone in this world. But consider this...' I said, and paused to assess the situation. They were sitting enraptured, with their curious smiles asking me to continue.

'But consider this, sir. How would you have felt had you been the one to coin that proverb and no one gave you the credit for it? You would have felt bad, wouldn't you?'

They nodded their heads in agreement.

'Growth in various social networking sites on the internet is testimony to the surge in creativity in the recent past. But there is a downside to this as well. Every day, creator's copyright is getting lost in massive chunks of data. There was no way to ensure that what you have said today will be credited with your name tomorrow.'

'There *was* no way. But now there is: yourquote.in'.' I continued.

'At YourQuote, you can archive your original quotes, share them with the rest of the world, and claim your credit *forever*.'

I further discussed briefly the three different revenue models that I had in my mind which like any other astute entrepreneur, I am not willing to fully disclosing here. I showed them the scope of the idea and how it had the potential to become as big as Twitter with a little bit of hard work.

'Sir, would you be willing enough to invest in the venture?' I asked my Dad.

'I wouldn't mind,' he said and wished me luck.

My mother had other things on her mind and asked me my favorite question of all, 'Do you want to eat chicken curry at night?' I laughed and put my arms around her and led her to the kitchen. I had won their trust and now, they set me free to make me happy and them proud.

I was sittng comfortably in my room talking to Priya on the phone at night when Mom suddenly made an unexpected entry.

'Hi Mom,' I said nervously. I had managed to disconnect the call just in time.

'What's going on?' she asked, having seen me clung to my cellphone.

'Nothing. I was writing a one-liner about life to post on YourQuote.'

'Interesting. Tell me what you've written,' Mom said.

I started looking at the ceiling first, then awkwardly scanned through the messages in the saved folder. Other than a couple of 'muahhs' and a lot of 'missing you's', there was nothing else in the folder. Just when I thought doomsday had arrived, *phat*, enlightenment!

'Life has two ways. One way leads you to where you want to be. The other leads you to where you need to be. Often, the latter takes you to the prior.'

Mom took two minutes to reflect on what I had said. Impressed, she patted me on the forehead and left my room.

Eureka

I was a runaway. I had broken free from the shackles of placement and while it brought me immense pride, my friends at IIT were not as appreciative. When they figured that I had run back home, they thought that it was a result of my depression from not cracking McKinsey. I wouldn't blame them though. I had never tried explaining to them my side of the story, but their consistent concern and worry had now started bothering me.

When Pratik, who had cracked Royal Bank of Scotland (RBS), called me and suggested I apply to the Day 6+ companies that were visiting campus, I got irritated. I disconnected his call in between and posted an angry status message:

> If you can't see the future that I'm seeing for myself, it doesn't give you the right to say that I'm right or wrong. It just means that you are acting like a dumb and interfering swine.

My friends got angry with me. Not because I didn't pay heed to what they were saying but because I didn't care to explain what was going through my mind. They had every right to get angry. I was still at home. I had to leave for Bombay on 9th December, to meet mentors and prospective investors for YourQuote.

Rishabh, unable to find himself a job, had to choose placements over Eureka under parental pressure. He instead sent Shikha, Armaan and Tanay to Mumbai, to join me.

⌁

My Dad made sure I took a flight to Mumbai. When I insisted on taking a train, he remarked, 'Now that you are the Director of a company, time is of utmost value. Invest in saving your time and make money in the extra time that you get out.'

The moment I set foot on Mumbai soil, it captivated me like no other city had in the past. I took an old premier taxi which drove me from the airport to IIT-Bombay.

As the taxi flew past the skyscrapers of Hiranandani overlooking Powai lake, I was already day dreaming. My desire of earlier making just a successful company was now transformed into a dream of making a billion dollar company. I visualized the top floor of the 30+ storey tower displaying a massive banner saying: YourQuote.

The taxi driver dropped me at Hall 2, a hostel at IIT Bombay, where I was to stay for the next three days. The trio from Delhi had already arrived and greeted me as soon as I entered the hostel. Shikha, in her black one-piece that showed her cleavage, looked especially attractive. I was surprised to find that girls were allowed in the boys' hostel.

We had to prepare for the mentor session the next day, construct our financial model, and figure out a way to impress our mentors with the limited knowledge of what we were doing. But we did none of that. We instead made a grand checklist of places to be covered in the next four days, irrespective of whatever happens in the competition. Being their leader, I chose to be the most indulgent and seconded fun over work.

Juhu, Marine Drive, Nariman Point, the Gateway of India, Bandra Bandstand, Worli Sealink—the list went on. It seemed like we were on vacation. IIT Powai had already sponsored our stay and travel. What more could a man want? The first night, we all were a bit weary from the strenuous journey and decided not to strain ourselves more by travelling.

We sleepily dashed into the early morning session the next day. It was being conducted at the lecture theatre by one of the most prominent lawyer firms in the city—Batra and Associates. As we drowsily cruised through the sessions, we were glad to find that we had more than half of the day at our disposal. We decided that the remaining part of the day would be spent in Mumbai darshan.

We divided ourselves in groups of two, two groups each. Shikha and I were put in a group together.

'Are you single?' I asked her, breaking the silence between us.

'Yes, why?'

'No, was just curious. Haven't heard from Rishabh lately. How did it end?' She knew that I knew about Rishabh and her.

'It wasn't right. In all perspectives. I broke up. Moreover, I found Rishabh very dumb. He is all talk, no substance,' she criticized openly. I was nonplussed. I wondered whether

I should defend my partner who was being bitched by our employee or should I allow her to bitch as he had been her ex? I chose the latter, muting my conscience.

'Why do you say so? He's my partner.'

'Come on. Have you heard him talk about design or creativity?'

'Yes, but again, he's a gifted marketeer.'

'I am not denying that. All I'm saying is I find him dumb.'

'And Kartik—he still has six months left in France, right?'

'Yes,' she said.

'Does he know about what happened between Rishabh and you?' I asked, careful not to exceed my limits.

'No, he is very emotional. I would explain the situation to him when he comes back.'

Day 1 was spent exploring Mumbai and before long it was day 2. After a tiresome first day, we remained asleep till late. Since we had already missed the first mentoring session on Day 2, we rushed back to the college for the second round as soon as we got up.

A bald man, was waiting to assault the four of us. He was an angel investor and a former entrepreneur who had sold his company to Infosys. He was in a terrible mood, as could be seen by his demeanour. He asked all of us to sit around him and began with his torture.

'Who is the founder of the company among you?'

Fearfully, I raised my hand.

'Give me your pitch,' he ordered. I blurted out my sixty seconds elevator pitch that I'd practised one month ago. He didn't seem impressed.

'How much time have you given to the plausibility of the idea?' Baldie asked us.

'Quite a lot. Almost six months.'

'I think you should give it more time. There is no place for such a shitty idea in the market right now. Don't you think so?' Baldie quizzed us.

I got scared. I didn't know how to respond. Armaan was vexed with the criticism and I overheard him whispering a cuss word to Shikha. It set me ablaze, in disgust and anger. I wanted to smash Armaan's face against the table. I just prayed that the mentor's ears weren't sharp enough. Luckily, the mentor didn't seem to notice, so I heaved a sigh of relief. For the next question, Tanay, the smooth talker among us, took the lead.

'Sir, even Coca Cola was not needed at the time it was launched. People were happy with water, but ultimately it created a market for itself, didn't it?'

'Yes, but I don't see any purpose in your idea. It's not a commodity, it's a service. I wonder why anyone would use it,' the mentor said furiously, realizing we were not going to be bogged down so easily. More than 10,000 people are already using our services,' I told him. Our Facebook page had recently crossed the 10,000+ fans mark.

He seemed a little interested. He asked us whether we had any angels on board. We said no. He asked us to send him the business plan. We already had the plan ready and I handed it over to him. Being engineers, the finance portion was all screwed up.

'All these calculations are shit. Meet a CA, get these financial projections sorted out by him, and then forward it to me,' he said and left our table.

The next mentor we met was Mr Jain, a senior entrepreneur who owned a business of bubble wraps. When we discussed our plan with him, he frankly informed us that he had no idea about internet space but really liked our idea. As we probed further, he disclosed that he was a closet poet and our idea could help writers like him get recognition for their creativity. Though he didn't have the necessary profile to invest in us, his encouragement powered our resolve.

After our encouraging talk with Mr Jain came to an end, we got up and walked out to an open hall and saw that journalists from all prominent newspapers like *Mid-Day, DNA,* and the *Times of India* waiting with their cameras and notepads.

But soon we realized that it was PR coverage for Eureka rather than for us, as most of the questions were either, 'How did you find the entire programme?', or 'How was the experience with the mentors?', or 'Why do you like Eureka?'

The four of us were thoroughly disappointed by the turn of events. We decided that we would soothe ourselves by going to Marine Drive, and this time, I would indulge in a beer or two with the rest of the gang as well. By 11, I was really tired and the other two guys were slightly high. They went for a quick walk, leaving Shikha and me behind.

'What happened? You look really tired,' Shikha said.

'Slept in a bad posture last night, so my shoulders have become stiff.'

'Can I help?' she asked and moved her slender fingers near my shoulders.

'What will you do?'

'Give you a massage,' she said, much to my surprise. I kept thinking whether it will be right or wrong to have her massage my shoulders.

If Priya was around, would I have done that? No. I would not have even dared. I thought to myself.

'When I am home, I massage my father's shoulders every day after he returns from office,' she said, making me feel a little relaxed that she didn't have an ulterior motive. I relaxed a little and offered my shoulders at her service. She was good. Really good—unlike Priya who was too delicate to give me a massage.

'You are awesome. Your boyfriend will be one lucky chap,' I complimented.

'Don't talk about my boyfriend.'

'Okay, sorry,' I said after realizing that I might have touched a wrong nerve.

Armaan returned just when Shikha was finishing off with the massage. Tanay wasn't to be seen. Either it was just a co-incidence or they had intentionally thought of not disturbing me during my 'rejuvenation' process. A moment later, upon seeing the wicked smile of Armaan, I realized that things were twisted. I could smell a forthcoming dig.

'How was the massage, sir?' Armaan taunted.

'Do you want it as well?' said Shikha lifting up a nearby book. He was a year junior to her and she treated him like a brother.

'What happened to Tanay?' I asked Armaan while he was busy making ridiculously lecherous noises in response to the shoulder massage that Shikha was now bestowing on him.

'Ah, ou...Tanay is...oh...oh my God...on phone,' Armaan said and ended his speech with, 'Oh fuck!' when Shikha rebuked him and asked him to get lost.

Minutes later, Tanay returned with a gloomy look on his face. Shikha ran to him, concerned like a mother, and asked him what was wrong. The suave, sophisticated, and smooth-talking Tanay crumbled on the ground and started sobbing

After drinking a few sips of water, Tanay finally disclosed to us that his girlfriend had cheated on him. The news shook all of us, even Shikha who, despite being experienced in this field, was at loss of words. My curiosity was quenched and I exhibited a mature indifference. Shikha held his hand.

I swelled with pride as my relationship with Priya had crossed two-and-a-half years without a taint. Thankfully, Shikha cheered Tanay up and he recovered soon enough. Two games of bluff were enough to set things right, temporarily.

I had got up at six in the morning, courtesy an upset stomach. With sleep a distant possibility because of the condition of my stomach, I checked the status of our return tickets online. They were still in waiting. The four of us had to return via the Mumbai-Amritsar mail. An hour later, Tanay's phone buzzed. He talked drowsily on the phone for a few minutes, got up, and told me in his half-asleep state, 'I need to cancel my ticket. My uncle has booked one for me in today's Rajdhani Express.'

'How did he manage to get one for today?'

'He's a judge at the Supreme Court,' he said. His one-line introduction was enough.

'Bro, couldn't you get ours confirmed via your uncle as well?' I asked.

'I can't bother him anymore, you know. He's the Supreme Court judge, for God's sake! Do you realize how senior he is?' I couldn't understand how he could act so selfish all of a sudden.

'My father had told him to do so, not me. I was only informed of it just now,' he exasperatedly said. I chose to not stretch it anymore.

It was the last day of the Eureka mentoring session. There was a grand lunch for all the participants which kept us busy the entire afternoon, despite my upset stomach. At lunch, my cellphone beeped. It was Rishabh's text with an emoticon filled message that said—Got placed, in EWZ. 4.5 lakh package. :)

The four day session had finally come to an end. Thankfully, our tickets got confirmed and we had to bid adieu to Mumbai. A month later, the results of Eureka came out. We failed to make it to the top 8. We were least bothered, relishing the contentment of having enjoyed our stay at Mumbai.

Mishra

Back in college, we were looking at recruiting more people for our company. I first interacted with Mishra during the time Suresh had been dropped from the scene and we were searching for a prospective technical partner. He was referred to me by my batchmate. He had been actively involved in the web development work of the institute, having developed several websites for its cultural festival. However, what bogged my enthusiasm during that time was his keenness to freelance for us rather than coming on board full time as a partner. He wanted regular payment to complete our task within three months. But we wanted someone who could stick with us for a long-term period.

Mishra's full name was Anant Mishra. But he preferred to to be called Mishra Anant instead. When I once asked him about it, he said it just sounds right. I shrugged it off, thinking it was yet another peculiarity of a tech genius.

After struggling for four months to find a tech guy, I approached Mishra once again—this time as a partner rather than a freelancer. We had already made waves in the IIT circuit and I thought it would be a piece of cake to convince him to come on board.

Before initiating the discussion, Rishabh and I formalized our offer.

'What should be his incentive to work with us?' I asked Rishabh.

'Tell him that we will call him our Chief Technical Officer (CTO),' Rishabh said.

'Any share in the equity?'

'Why do you always come down to equity? First let him work, then we will figure out something for him if he turns out to be indispensable.'

We told Mishra that we were students ourselves and from whatever we would earn, we would share with him from time to time. He was like an unpaid executive level employee with perks such as experience, recognition, and free exposure.

With Mishra as our right hand to spearhead technical development, it was time for us to reclaim our lost pride and let the world know that forgoing my placements was a smart decision. For getting the rest of the employees, I came up with a grand recruitment plan along with Rishabh.

It all sprouted in a discussion we had with our Core Team. Thanks to the placement season, we realized how important a start-up experience was for students who had not done much in their four academic years. Working in a start-up would enable them to mention it in their CVs. The idea behind the recruitment was that we would create teams across campuses that would be self functionary, with a manager, preferably a third-year IIT-Delhi student—to ensure smooth functioning.

Shikha created a very catchy poster which said in bold letters: 'YourQuote Mass Recruitment Drive: It's time to spike up your resume'. I marketed it thoroughly on social networking sites and the scheduled date of interviews was kept for February 8. We divided the hiring year-wise and started with hiring 10 third-year students who would hold the position of Business Development Managers (BDMs), so that they would help in subsequent hiring, 15 second-year Business Development Senior Associates (BDSAs), and 30 Business Development Associates (BDAs). Besides, seven people were to be inducted in the Strategy and Content team.

Our strategies worked out well as the already-hired BDMs assisted us in conducting future interviews. It was a sudden status symbol for them as well, for they could now sit on the opposite side of the table and be the interviewer instead of the interviewee. We called Tanay and his articulate friend Sumeet as well to help us look professional as an interview panel. The criterion for selection was simple. Anyone who was eloquent in Hindi or English stood a better chance of selection. However, the criterion was more relaxed for girls as we hired any good-looking girl, who could motivate guys to work. Maintaining a fairly balanced sex-ratio was our bigger concern and when the interviews came to an end, we were happy to observe that we had 15 girls versus 45 guys.

But little did we know what was to come ahead. The mighty team size brought with it its fair share of difficulties. It was so difficult to firstly memorize all the names of the team members and secondly induct them into work, so much so that all other members of core team withdrew from taking responsibility. Even I was one of them, owing to my fear of confrontation. Rishabh, however, took it as a challenge and executed it with great skill and knowhow. He was good with people.

February is a relaxed month for us with no exams for a month and plenty of free time at our disposal. We started training programs for all the 60 hired students. The empty rooms in the isolated blocks which had earlier served as a mating point for college students now became our meeting point. I had the task of educating people about social media, how to use Twitter and Facebook to foster the growth of our brand while Rishabh took on the real deal—educating our juniors about marketing, or The Art of Hot and Cold Calling.

Hot calling implies pitching to a prospective customer who you know is interested. Cold calling is reaching the marketing head of a company via customer care and making them interested in using your product or services. This was precisely the reason why we placed greater importance on articulation while shortlisting.

The first two weeks went really well, with the newly inducted students from myriad departments getting to know each other and enjoying the exposure, the knowhow of how start-ups operate. We were absolutely delighted at how things were proceeding. We had managed to scale from 8 employees to 60 while spending less than 5,000 rupees.

It was February 10 when I finally got time to meet Priya. She had come to IIT to see me. As we walked through the campus hand in hand, I was greeted by around a dozen juniors whom we had newly welcomed in our team.

'Wow, you're famous around here. Is this because of your book?'

'No, it's because of YourQuote,' I said flashing a million dollar grin.

'Wow.'

'Yes.'

'How many girls are there in the team?'

'Fifteen,' I answered.

'Wow, Sabharwal saheb. You are on a roll. Anyone pretty?'

'Umm, two or three. Why?'

'I hope you are not counting that bitch Shikha as pretty?' She remarked. I had told Priya about the rejuvenating shoulder massage that I was offered for free.

'Ha! Still angry about the Mumbai trip?

'If I was with another girl's boyfriend 24/7, wouldn't you have felt bad?'

'No. If I know that you are just friends with that guy, no.'

'It's very easy to say that. Are you really sure?'

'Come on, why are you getting angry with me? I was honest enough to tell you everything,' I said.

'I'm not angry with you. My problem is with her. When she knows that you are committed, how could she even touch you?'

'You know what? You have turned into a psycho. Why did you have to come to meet me when all you want to do is fight?' I was annoyed. She lost her temper. She threw my phone so suddenly at me that my reflexes failed to respond. The phone fell on the ground with a thud, vibrated for a few seconds, and turned off. I was so angry at her then! I picked up my phone from the ground and switched it on. Thankfully, it was still working.

'I'm leaving. Bye,' she said and started walking away from me.

'You're fighting again. Why can't you be cool about these things?'

'I am fighting? You are the one screaming at me for that bitch.'

'I thought somebody was leaving,' I remarked intentionally to hurt her. She left without saying a word. I could see her footsteps racing to reach the main gate. I stood there, near the roundabout, staring at her disappear. When she was out of my sight, my heart whirled and I unconsciously started running. Running after her as fast as I could.

I saw her just at the bus stop outside the campus. She carried a dejected look on her face. She was boarding a crowded bus en route the Hauz Khas metro station. I managed to board the bus just in the nick of time. It was not until we descended at the next bus stop that she saw me. She tried her best to hide the delight at seeing me by turning her face away and walking towards the metro escalator. I caught hold of her hand and pulled her towards me. Grinding her teeth, she said, 'Amol, let go of my hand or I'll scream.'

'I will kiss you right here if you scream.'

'You will be beaten to pulp by the people around.'

'I am ready for it, if I get to kiss you in the process.'

'Jerk,' she said with a hint of smile. We boarded the next bus to IIT and used the isolated block to our service. She was kind enough to not turn me into pulp.

⊏⊏▸

Mishra joined us as a CTO in late January and had promised to deliver our website by March 13, his birthday, as a return gift. It was a very sincere promise from his end and I was designated with the task of keeping track on his activities. I frequented his hostel room often, discussing about prospective functionalities and design, and forbidding him to smoke while I was there.

I didn't like the smell of cigarettes. Not that I was allergic to it, but it just sent me coughing. No wonder, all my smoker friends had stopped counting me as their friend. Mishra, being junior to me, willingly put out the cigarette. I was touched by his readiness to do so.

Mishra belonged to the same state as me—Jharkhand. But unlike me, Mishra had a different lifestyle. Owing to a severe financial crisis at home, he didn't take any money from his parents and paid his own bills. That was the reason he got into web development in the first place.

The work sparked off at a good pace and I could see Mishra reflecting the same zeal we held for the idea. As I worked more and more with him, I realized that he was the ideal guy to be our technical partner. Along with gifted coding skills, he had an astute business sense, a natural penchant for networking, and above all, an impeccable work ethic.

I discussed with Rishabh the possibility of having Mishra as a prospective partner to which he agreed. But ultimately we dismissed the thought because he still had two years of education left and he couldn't have gone full-time with the venture four months later.

⊏⊐

The thing that every college student fears most is having one's parents send them a friend request on Facebook. In February, the fearful moment arrived. My parents had signed up on Facebook and every day, they would like my posts or share them in their profile.

My fear was born from the fact that now I could not share things related to Priya on my profile anymore and I had to monitor the comments that my friends posted. I also had to monitor YourQuote page's content as we had started entertaining adult quotes like: 'The greatest irony of life is that adults suck more than children.' So while I made sure that I posted nothing containing any scandalous or offensive content, they dug older posts of my profile. They got a hint about Priya who had posted some photos of us cozying with each other at a friend's party. They didn't tell me but they interrogated my sister about it. My sister told me that mother had quizzed her whether it was a non-serious relationship between us or whether I was looking at marrying Priya in the long run. I was taken aback, not understanding why my parents were suddenly interested in my ongoing love story.

I wouldn't have faced any inhibitions about telling them about Priya had Priya been as comfortable telling her parents about us. If I had told my parents, their first question would have been: 'Do her parents know? Will they agree?' to which I would have had no answer.

During that period, we were desperate to increase the number of fans on our Facebook fan page as it would have further cemented the wow factor of the brand. Rishabh had taken out time from training the newly recruited juniors in business development to join us in Mishra's room for a discussion on how to increase our Facebook fans. We thought that before the website was up, if we could reach a significant figure of fans, we could easily convince corporates to advertise on our platform. We were already seeing a targeted demographic of 80 percent in the 18-24 years of age, which was seen as a very lucrative segment for advertisers.

Mishra's room had a characteristic smell of cigarette mixed with sweat, which was repugnant at first, but one slowly get used to it. When Rishabh arrived, he immediately got repulsed by it and tactfully led us out in the corridor to carry forth the discussion, which Mishra polluted with his propensity to smoke.

We started with the topic of social media marketing. Ever since Mishra came on board, the discussions were always very practical and technically sound, since he was very well acquainted with technology. Mishra told us how he had discovered a website where you could buy Facebook likes. He said that most brands which had suddenly got over a lakh likes had been buying it. When he showed us the websites that facilitated such 'buying', we were shocked. The Facebook likes were worth 2 rupees each while Twitter followers cost 1 rupee each. We were lured but realized that this wouldn't help, because more than half of the profiles would be fake and wouldn't add any significant value.

After half an hour of brainstorming, we figured out a way wherein our followers could invite their friends on our company's fan page and the one who invited the maximum people would get a prize. Rishabh suggested that we should give a very catchy prize like an iPhone or an iPad to attract more participants. My eyebrows furrowed in disbelief. Here we were with hardly any money at our disposal and had encountered a hefty loss of around 1 lakh rupees barely three months ago, and Rishabh was thinking about gifting a phone worth 30,000 rupees for merely increasing our fan number by a few hundreds? I told them it was a bad idea. Even Mishra seconded me, and from the corner of my eye, I saw Rishabh smiling cunningly in my direction.

'Who is asking you to gift the iPhone?' Rishabh said.

'What do you mean?'

'We will create a fake profile for the winner. Since it'll be a contest where our followers have to mail us, nobody is going to ascertain whether the winner exists in reality or not.'

He looked visibly happy and argued that besides the obvious purpose of creating a buzz about our brand across the social media space, a catchy prize would serve an important purpose of making our well-placed batchmates turn green with envy upon realizing that we are doing great. We had been victims of peer criticism lately, when almost every batchmate of ours cursed us for inducting a large number of juniors and leaving them with no time for other work. At first, the entire concept and the purpose looked brilliant. In fact, it seemed so lucrative and mind-boggling that it had numbed my conscience. But thankfully, Mishra was unmoved.

'I won't give it a green signal. It's unethical. It's dishonest,' he said fearlessly.

'But no one is getting to know,' Rishabh argued.

'We are. And we would always know.'

'But we are cool with it, aren't we?' Rishabh said.

'Not me at least.'

'Neither me. This is not the way to grow as a venture by instilling dishonesty as a core value,' I said.

Rishabh was visibly dejected and asked us to provide him logic to prove our point. There was no logic to it, except that it was morally wrong. When Rishabh persisted, accusing us of lacking business acumen and getting governed by heart instead of brain, I figured out a logical explanation for him. I argued that any of the participants could file an RTI against us and we would be charged with fraud. He retraced, gave in and we agreed. After much arguing, we unanimously agreed to give an iPod Nano to the winner.

We were in the middle of discussing the technicalities of the proposed competition when Rishabh's phone buzzed. He got up and announced that it was a call from Anjali who needed to talk to him urgently. So he excused himself from the meeting, leaving us behind to design the contest. A minute after Rishabh left, there was a knock on the door. It was Rishabh again. He called for Mishra and took him outside with him. I was puzzled by it all but I decided not to say anything at the moment. Mishra returned after a minute and when I asked him what the matter was, he simply smiled and said 'sutta'.

Mishra, despite the fact that he looked naive, courteous and honest, had a twisted side to him. First of all, he was a first-grade pervert. One of his primary incentives for joining YourQuote had been he could add pretty girls who were active on our fan page on his Facebook profile as the CTO of YourQuote. At first, I presumed that he was single. But then he astounded me by saying that he had been in three relationships in the past and was currently dating a girl from Delhi University who had been his classmate from Ranchi.

Curious, I quizzed him about his take on fidelity. He said that he was cool with two-timing a girl and wouldn't mind if his partner two-timed him as well. I was puzzled to note that his stand on relationships and loyalty was in stark contrast to the ethical personality that he projected in business.

On March 1, I left on a ten-day tour to the Andamans with my parents and I handed over the responsibilty of the website to Mishra and Rishabh. I entrusted Rishabh with an additional responsibility of keeping track on Mishra's work and asked him to make sure that by the proposed date, March 13, Mishra's birthday, the website was up and running. Anjali, assisted by one of the recruited juniors, was to take care of social media in my absence.

When I came back to the campus on March 13, a lot had changed.

After dropping off my luggage in my room, I went to see Rishabh. Like always, he was not there. I called his number, but he still didn't pick up. A minute later, I received a message from Anjali's number saying, 'I'm in the cinema hall, will return late. Anything urgent? Rishabh'

Annoyed, I wanted to pour down my anger in my reply. However I chose to write a fake 'Enjoy' instead. I checked the development server—the server where the to-be-launched website was hosted. It was stuck at the same status of development as it had been two weeks ago. I called Mishra, but his number was not reachable. I ran to his hostel room only to find that it was locked. I messaged Rishabh to let me know of Mishra's whereabouts. He replied via Anjali's number saying, 'No idea, have not been in touch with him lately.' It was said with so much callousness and no sense of responsibility that it freaked me out. I didn't reply to him and came back to my room.

As I logged into my mail id, one mail struck my attention. It was from Shikha and Rishabh was copied into the mail.

Dear Amol,
I'm sorry to inform you that I am leaving YourQuote

```
because of some personal reasons. It's unfortunate
that things unfolded in such a way while you were
away. I wish you all the best for YourQuote and hope
you succeed in all your future pursuits.

Regards,
Shikha
```

I was stunned. The mail was four days old. Rishabh, who was copied in the mail, had not replied till then, which confirmed my doubt that it was because of him that our right hand— the only designer of YourQuote—was leaving. I immediately called Shikha and asked her about the mail. She hesitated to talk about it at first but then I played a gimmick 'I know it's about Rishabh. Don't worry, I won't tell him anything.'

Shikha finally opened up. She told me that we were an inexperienced group and there was not much to learn for her. I knew that it could not have been the sole reason for her to leave so suddenly. I pestered her to tell me the truth. She then told me about how uncomfortable she felt in Rishabh's company. Despite their fall-out after the two months fling long back, Rishabh made it impossible for her to maintain a professional relationship between him. She confessed that even though Rishabh had now been seeing Anjali (not officially though), he treated Shikha like his mistress whenever the two were alone.

Realizing that she had spoken too much in front of me, she digressed from the topic and told me that she had got an internship offer at a prominent design agency and would be working there from the summer onwards. Just when she began wishing me well for the future, I abruptly disconnected her call.

I was angry at Rishabh but I couldn't make up my mind about confronting him and charging him for her resignation. What happened between Shikha and him was a private affair and I knew that it would make matters worse if I tried to meddle. I chose to keep mum on the topic until my anger cooled down a little.

For the next few minutes, I stayed in front of my PC, trying to calm my mind by watching useless feeds of useless people in sheer disgust, when suddenly a picture of Mishra with his girlfriend Swati against a backdrop of mountains appeared on the screen. The caption said, 'Celebrating this birthday in the mountains of Shimla…with Swati'. It seemed to be the most disgusting post of all but I still couldn't take my eyes away from it. As it was his birthday, I chose not to spoil his mood and even 'liked' the picture before logging out.

I met Rishabh in his room the next morning. It was the first time my annoyance had given me enough courage to confront him and I began by saying, 'Rishabh, I'm not happy with how things have been managed in the last fifteen days. Why didn't you keep a check on Mishra? We need to understand that he's still an unpaid employee, not a partner, and we can't expect him to work on his own. He needs to be constantly pushed.'

Rishabh replied with an air of indifference saying, 'Fourteen students that we had recruited, our so called "employees", have left YourQuote in the past fifteen days. I was trying to prevent them from leaving and couldn't concentrate on Mishra.'

'And in that process, even Shikha left the team?'

'Yes. It has been very difficult for me to manage everything single-handedly. You don't know how many hours I had to spend to make things right.'

'Did things go right?' I questioned bluntly.

Rishabh was annoyed by this time and got up to leave saying, 'I am going to meet Anjali. She has been offered an internship at the University of Toronto and has to get her passport made.'

'If she has to get passport made, why are you going?' I intentionally chose a hurtful remark. But he had already left by then. Rishabh had placed her above the venture again.

As days passed by, the cracks in our big team started to show. The employees we had recently inducted turned out to be a laidback, confused, and idle lot who had no zeal or attachment to our venture. They did not share the passion for the idea and were in it only to spike up their resumes. The day they would get another similar opportunity, they would drop out. Moreover, we recruited so many people that the exclusivity of being a part of YourQuote had been diluted.

Apart from some T-shirt orders that had been well-executed by Rishabh, no big orders came our way. All the while, we were still waiting for Mishra to come up with the website. We had not been able to establish a connection with Mishra till the 18th when he returned back to the hostel. Both Rishabh and I went to his room. After a formal 'Belated Happy Birthday' wish, I shot him the difficult question: 'When will the website be ready? We are already running three days late from what you'd promised us.' My intonation was a little rude and Rishabh nudged me to choose my words carefully. He took over from me and first inquired about his Shimla trip, cracked a few jokes, and thereafter, very tactfully, brought the topic of work to the fore.

Mishra explained that the work had turned out to be more complicated than what he had presumed earlier and it would take him at least ten days to get it to operate. Owing to our technical illiteracy, we had to agree to extend the deadline and made him promise that this time, there would be no delay.

All our hopes were now concentrated on Mishra who would deliver us the website and make the almost one-year-old idea into a blooming internet venture. But as luck would have it, the plan went haywire yet again. Mishra wasn't reachable for the later part of March and this sent both of us into a state of frenzy. When three days passed by without any contact or mails from him, I approached his girlfriend on Facebook and asked her about him. The news was disastrous—he had contracted typhoid and would be bed-ridden for at least one month.

The entire plan was screwed. Having nothing left to do other than posting 'Quote of the Day' on the fan page and fetching some petty T-shirt orders from third-grade colleges, we chose to take a backseat and finish off our last semester first and then go full-throttle with our venture once Mishra recovered.

⊂⊏

As days passed, there was little that we could do to keep ourselves motivated.

It was during this time that we had applied for a leading business magazine's Young Entrepreneur's Award and were shortlisted in the Top 10. Apparently, they hadn't checked our non-functional website and shortlisted us just on the basis of the idea and revenue figures. Though we couldn't make it to the top 3, we received tremendous media coverage. Just four days after the award, a Mumbai-based newspaper approached us and carried a feature article on us in their reputed daily. The feature carried a big photo of Rishabh and me along with a yellow-bulb representing 'idea' in the background. It was a candid interview where we talked about student entrepreneurship and its challenges.

The coverage had a tremendous effect on our lives. It made my parents proud of me and earned us respect in front of our batchmates and juniors, especially those who had left us midway. More than anything, Rishabh's parents let him forgo his crappy job for the sake of YourQuote.

In less than 24 hours since the publishing of the article, our fan count went up by 500. But we weren't happy. We just cursed Mishra inwardly for not having the website up, otherwise we could have converted all of them into registered users. To motivate Mishra, who had still not recuperated from typhoid completely, we told him that the next time we got a feature offer, he would be a part of it. But before that, he had to launch the website as soon as possible.

During this entire time, one thing remained amiss. My relationship with Priya was going through a rough phase. She had lately been very frustrated with how her life had turned out after graduation. She had got a job at the very same company where Rishabh had been offered employment. It was a knowledge processing outsourcing company named EWZ, which paid her very little.

Rather than acknowledge that she hadn't worked hard in the past three years, she complained about the futility of MBA entrance exams since she hadn't been able to ace them. She complained her course in Economics Honours was useless since the placement committee hadn't assured her a placement at good companies when in fact it was her lacklustre resume which had failed to impress the selectors. Earlier, I would pacify and motivate her. But later, owing to a shortage of time, I started getting miffed with her rants. I would tell her that it was partly her fault as well, and this would lead to a catastrophic outcome. She would explode at me and I would verbally hit back. Things continued like this for some time.

⊏⊂

In the first week of May, 2011, it was announced that all fourth-year students had to vacate their rooms by the tenth of May. I was done with with all my courses and waited for the results of the final semester, which would inform whether I graduated or not.

Rishabh had extended his B.Tech project intentionally so that he could continue living in his inexpensive hostel room for the summer, and at the same time, help Anjali out with shopping before she left for Canada on May 20. My house hunting began and I convinced Mishra to live with me, while Rishabh would join me. Initially, Mishra didn't agree, but when I tempted him with the fact that I would find a furnished home with an AC and allowed him to bring his girlfriend to our den, he couldn't resist.

May in Delhi is nothing short of a furnace. But I had to find a house in Delhi in this very weather. Plus the home had to be within our budget, 2-BHK at least, fully furnished with an AC, near IIT, and with an independent entry, free from interfering landlords.

Faced with the pressure from my hostel warden to vacate the room, I raided the nearby areas. Qutub Institutional Area, Green Park, Safdarjung Enclave, Gautam Nagar, and even Malviya Nagar. Ultimately, I found a house in the interiors of Malviya Nagar that was fully-furnished, inexpensive, and suited us fine.

The locality was one of the worst in Delhi, and other than the fact that it housed an irritable old man, who always pried about our affairs, there was nothing else to bother us. I shifted all my stuff single handedly by three autos, including 680 T-shirts. Once done with the dumping, I heaved a sigh of relief. I had a house and it was to remain mine for the next one day, until Mishra shifted.

Since I was alone at home for the night, I called Priya and asked her to come, which she willingly accepted. We hoped it would help in bringing us closer.

Filled with wild anticipation, I went to buy contraceptives for the first time in my life. I located a shop far away from my place and asked the person behind the counter to give me a packet of Durex condoms. He gave me an orange flavoured one which I wanted to change since I knew Priya didn't like oranges much, but it was too awkward for me to confront the shopkeeper who was looking at me with disdain the minute I entered the shop.

I came back home and hid the packet of condoms in my suitcase. Priya arrived at 8.30 pm and as soon as she removed her scarf and threw it on my bed, we pounced on each other like wild animals. Just when we were in the middle of our passionate encounter, without even moving to second base, my cellphone rang. It was my mother. I went into the next room to talk and by the time I returned, Priya had lost interest. I tried to cajole her into making out, but she got annoyed and left for home. The orange packet remained unopened.

The Rotten Mango

Have you ever observed the life cycle of a mango? It starts as a small flower, turns into a sour and green kachha aam with time, and the first tinge of sweetness arrives as it changes its colour to a bright and beautiful yellow, making it the king of all fruits. However, if you leave that mango hanging there on the tree for some time, it falls down, and sometimes when it doesn't fall, it rots, tumbles, and dies the very same death as any bitter wild fruit. Time is a wicked entity. Whereas at one time, it helps the mango to inch towards its glory, at other times, it takes away its glory with every passing moment.

My relationship with Priya had crossed that moment of glory. It was on its way to getting rotten. We both knew it but none of us acknowledged it. The frequency of fights had become so great that every second day we used to have a break up and every third day, a patch up. The reason behind the entire upheaval was nothing but wicked time. Or rather, the lack of it.

Priya had been an obsessive lover. All throughout her college life, she had nothing but a love affair with me to boast of. She gave her heart and soul to me. While it should have been a matter of pride for me to have such a devoted girlfriend, it somehow always irritated me to see her not use her time for other productive things as well. I used to rebuke her for being idle and clingy, to which she would get offended, leading to disastrous fights between us.

And ever since the start-up came into being, I could never give her the time that she deserved. Initially, she didn't complain, playing the understanding and caring girlfriend. I used to call her at the time of going to bed. Even if she was sleeping, she would wake up and talk to me. But as time moved on, I took her understanding for granted and unknowingly allowed our relationship to go sour.

It was a hot windy night in May when she called me at 11 pm. I was at our Malviya Nagar flat with Mishra, and Rishabh was still at IIT. Night being the most productive time for any start-up guy, I was engrossed with Mishra in designing the landing page of our website, which we had planned to launch at the stroke of midnight. Lost in work, I took a while to pick up her call.

'Hello,' I said, my eyes glued to the laptop screen.

'Amol, I am feeling very lonely,' Priya said. Her tone demanded sympathy.

'Priya, I'll call you in five minutes, I'm stuck with something,' I said instructing Mishra to change the font to Trebuchet.

'But...' Priya said, while I unknowingly disconnected.

Five minutes went by. Ten minutes. The only significant change that happened was that font was changed to Trebuchet. I had got lost in the work, having completely forgotten to call Priya. Half an hour later, as the deadline to launch the landing page neared, my cellphone buzzed.

I angrily uttered to Mishra, 'Damn all the girlfriends in the world. They don't have any work.'

I picked up the call, realized that I had not kept my word of calling her back, and said in a guilt-free voice, 'I'm really sorry, honey. I forgot,' and smiled at Mishra, who looked at me slyly.

'I'm used to all this. Are you still busy?' she inquired, expecting to hear the word *no*.

Now what kind of question was that? Of course I was busy. Had I not been busy, I would have at least remembered my promise of calling her back after five minutes. I thought I had to make it up to her. Leaving Mishra alone for five minutes, I went into the other room along with my laptop.

'Tell me, what's disturbing my child?' I became tender, my voice exhibited motherly warmth.

'Nothing. I am feeling so lonely. I am missing you. It's been almost two weeks since we met. I want a hug. Now, now, now.'

A hug can't be given via a phone. But girlfriends make you bend the rules of science for them. Perhaps, that's why Newton was a misogynist. I decided to betray my loyalty to science and tried to give her a hug through the phone.

'Did you get a hug? I just sent one.'

'Yes, thanks. I love you,' she said. I heaved a sigh of relief. I looked at the time—just twenty minutes were left before midnight. I had to fix the design of the menu bar. In haste, I opened the design in the laptop in front of me and began doodling.

'Amol, I said something,' she muttered, irritably. I got too involved in my work to pay heed to what she was saying, despite the phone being stuck to my ears.

'Amol,' she yelled loudly. I heard her loud and clear this time.

'Yes, sorry,' I said insincerely. Time was running out and I couldn't afford missing the deadline, since we had already made an announcement on all our pages about the basic website launch. It was after a wait of four months that this moment had arrived and I couldn't let anything come in its way.

'I hate you, Amol. You have used me for over a year. Whenever you need me, you call me; and whenever I need you, you are never there. I have asked you for one thing several times, Amol—to give me your complete, undivided attention whenever you talk to me.'

'Hmm,' I said, having not listened carefully to anything that she had said.

'You aren't listening, are you?' she thundered.

I knew that I was trapped. I had two options. Either to face her for the next three hours non-stop, pacify, sympathize, apologize, and make things right. Or else, cut the phone and launch the new design, and once done with the work, call her and face the tsunami. Like any other newbie entrepreneur, I chose the latter.

'Yes, I didn't listen. I don't have time for all this...' I said and realized that she had cut the call midway.

With the call disconnected, I forgot about her, much like any workaholic boyfriend. I immersed myself into designing along with Mishra and managed to launch the new design exactly at midnight, an achievement that required celebration. Mishra brought two bottles of Tuborg from the fridge, and though I hated drinking, I gulped one in to help me take my mind off Priya and what I was to face in sometime. The acrid taste of Tuborg acted like a medicine and induced serenity in my mind.

An hour later, I tried Priya's number. She hadn't slept, as she picked up the call in one ring.

'Hello, I love you,' I said. It was the most insincere 'I love you' that I had ever said until then.

'Amol, we are done. For life,' she said; her voice was cold.

'Yet another break up? I know what you want. Do you want yet another "night" to fix things?'

'Amol, I'm serious.'

'I'm sorry. I had to launch an important element of the website at midnight, that's why I was busy.'

'Then you could have told me that. Why did you have to call me?' she yelled.

'I didn't call you. You called me, both times.'

'That's because you said that you would call me. Bloody liar!' she said in a sharp tone.

'You're a liar. At one point you say that you love me, and a moment later, you say that you hate me. Go to hell,' I retorted, exhausted. I just wanted her to drop the call and leave me alone, for as long as she could.

'You go to hell, asshole. You are the biggest mistake of my life. I never want to see your face again, you bloody bastard,' she said. It was the first time she had cussed at me.

'How dare you abuse my parents? How dare you? I never want to see your face, you whore!' I said and continued, 'You think that you are indispensable. Go to hell! There are a million girls running after me and all of them have something to do in their lives other than feeling lonely in the middle of the night.'

'Ha! Go and try to woo one of those millions. Even that slut Shikha, for all I care. Only when you will try your luck elsewhere, will you realize my worth.'

'You think very highly of yourself. Why don't you ask Mishra what he thinks of you? His revelations will make you realize your worth,' I said, intentionally trying to wound her self respect. No wonder, it hurt her like a sting and she started crying.

Nothing distresses a girl more than being bitched about by her own boyfriend in front of his friends. I had fabricated a hurtful lie, as I had never discussed Priya with anyone. But she believed my lie. I didn't realize what I'd said was so vile and would have devastated her so much that she would stop speaking to me, altogether. I didn't know what to say next.

'It's over. I am never going to speak to you again,' she said, sobbing, and disconnected the call. I was numb. Though I had crossed the limits of disrespect, it didn't make a difference to me. I was unapologetic, indifferent, and cold.

She didn't call me for the next two days. I tried calling her instead, but she rejected it fourteen times, after which she SMSed me saying: 'I am at home. Don't call me. We are done.'

I realized that the mango had rotted and was about to tumble from the tree. Whether it had died or not, had to be known.

Three days later, both Mishra and Rishabh left for their respective homes for a week. I suddenly had a lot of free time at hand. There were no more discussions at home and no meetings scheduled with mentors. The website development was to be managed by Mishra from home and marketing by

Rishabh from his place. I had my share of social media and design to manage, which didn't require much time as posting on social media was barely a two-hour job, while design work was minimal as the functionalities and features had not yet been coded by Mishra.

Anjali was off to Canada for an internship, which actually motivated Rishabh to go and see his parents in Lucknow. After all, he was now an engineer.

Two days without Rishabh, Mishra or Priya by my side, I decided to break the monotony by exploring my contact list to find somebody worthy of spending time with. I went through the contact list twice and during both instances, my eyes got stuck to just one name: Shikha. I decided to try my luck with her and messaged her asking if she wanted to watch a movie with me.

I wasn't sure she would respond as she had quit YourQuote around three months ago, after her experience with Rishabh. Her boyfriend Kartik was also going to return from France since his exchange program had come to an end. Half an hour later, my mobile beeped with an SMS from her. It said 'Sure. Show at 10?' I was pleasantly surprised.

A few hours later, I found her waiting for me outside the movie hall. 'How's Priya?' Shikha asked me after we were done with our initial hellos.

'She's at home. Haven't talked to her for quite some time,' I didn't tell her about the break-up, thinking it would draw unwanted sympathy from her.

'Oh that's why you could go out with me today?' she said good-naturedly.

'No, it's not that. She's not so possessive. She's rather liberal,' I asserted, but my mind questioned the very assertion.

'You know what? I really like Priya. She is smart, understanding, and witty,' she complimented.

The statement went through me like an arrow. Was she being sarcastic? But the sincerity in her voice said otherwise.

'Yeah, she is. How's Kartik? He would have come back by now, isn't it?' I asked, intentionally changing the topic.

'Don't ask about him,' she said, the expression on her face going from happy to that of disgust. I asked her what had happened.

'He came back around a month ago, and since then my life has been hell. On the very first day I met him, I told him everything that happened between Rishabh and me. I told him that I didn't want to be with him anymore. At first I felt guilty of having cheated on him, but then he started abusing me, cussing at me, and finally I lost my mind. I left him and came back to my hostel. He called me and started crying. I was unconcerned. He bugged me for over an hour, after which I convinced him that ending our relation was for his own good. I told him that he deserved someone better. But he disconnected the call.'

'So he understood you? That's nice,' I uttered, reflecting on my own condition at that point of time.

'No, he didn't. For two days, he didn't say a word. But on the third day, he made my life hell. One of the gravest mistakes of my life has been that I allowed him to snap photos of each other in intimate positions. He started blackmailing me that he would spread it in the hostel through LAN if I didn't go back to him. I couldn't tell anyone and he kept torturing me for the next two days, ultimately forcing me to get back together with him.'

'What? You've got back with him?!' I exclaimed, horrified.

'I couldn't think of anything else, I was so damn frightened. You can't imagine what I've been facing for the past few days. He even has a topless picture of me!'

'A topless picture?! Damn, how did you ultimately solve the matter?' I uttered trying to sound sensible, though the voyeur in me wanted to see the picture.

'I got back with him for a week, during which he took full advantage of me. He forced me to get intimate with him, assaulted me, and ...' her voice cracked. Two drops of tears rolled down her face.

Awkwardly, I took her right hand and comforted her by wiping her tears with the other hand. I could not say anything.

'What happened next?' I asked. Her hands still clasped mine.

'Nothing. I felt wasted. I told my parents everything. My father took my phone and I was grounded for one week. As expected, Kartik called on my number but my father warned him not to call me again. He couldn't believe my parents were by my side. Ultimately, seeing his blackmailing would not have the desired effect, he left for good.'

'Huh. Good riddance. It's time for the movie,' I sighed. We had booked the rear seat and entered the cinema hall.

As we sat and the movie began, she leaned against me and kept her head on my shoulders. Her smell was intoxicating and I found it difficult to concentrate on the rest of the movie. I desperately waited for the interval to come and when it did, I made an excuse to go to the loo.

Once I got back, I was normal. I realized that she had removed the divider between our seats.

'I was thinking it's not surprising that Kartik was so obsessed. Even Priya was like that. Obsessed about me,' I said, as I took my seat.

'Was? What do you mean?' she asked.

'We broke up some time ago.'

'Oh, it must be like your regular break-ups.'

'No, not at all. In regular break-ups, you patch up within a day or two. This one is for good. It has gone on for almost two weeks,' I said. I don't know what provoked me to exaggerate five days to two weeks.

She took my hand in hers to comfort me. As the end credits rolled, we walked out, hand in hand, unable to find a topic to chat on. It was half-past midnight. The roads were empty, with only a few autowallahs waiting in the corners.

Since it was late at night, I decided to escort her home. We went to the bunch of autowallahs who seemed like eager dogs waiting to grab a bone.

'Bhaiya, IIT and then back to Malviya Nagar?' I asked.

'200 rupees,' they replied unanimously, which seemed too expensive for my wallet. At that moment, I did the unthinkable. I asked her to come to my place instead.

'If you don't mind, you can stay over at my place. It's right across the street. I would drop you tomorrow morning, when these exorbitant rates would fizzle down a bit.'

'Umm, Rishabh will be there, won't he?'

'No, nobody is there.'

'Not even Mishra?'

'No, all of them have gone home,' I said, hoping she'd say yes.

'I have got an AC as well,' I mentioned out of the blue.

'Okay.'

My heart started thumping as loudly as a jet engine. I contracted a headache too.

⊏⊐

At 1 o'clock in the night, we entered my den.

'Do you want to change? I have got some capris that will fit you,' I asked, handing her a glass of water from the fridge. She nodded and I went and pulled out the capris from my cupboard drawers. She took them from me and went to the loo to change.

I went to the bedroom and switched on the AC. Our inner room had a big double bed, which was so large that it could fit three people. Mishra, Rishabh, and I would sleep on the very same bed in the very same room, since it was the only room with an AC. I didn't know what sleeping arrangement would be the best.

Meanwhile, Shikha came out wearing my three-quarters, which looked too broad on her. Nevertheless, I told her she looked cute.

'Shikha, this is where you are going to sleep,' I said, pointing to the massive bed.

'What about you?'

'I will sleep in the other room.'

'Does that room have an AC?'

'No, but it's okay. I'll manage.'

'Do you consider me a friend?' she suddenly asked me.

'Yes. Why do you ask?'

'Because you are treating me like a guest. Chill Amol, chill.'

'Sure. I just wanted you to be comfortable, that's all.'

'I'm comfortable. And you should be comfortable as well. Sleep here itself. The bed is big enough for the both of us,' she said. I couldn't believe what I was hearing. It delighted as well as scared me at the same time.

'Here's your blanket. The AC makes the room really cold at night. This one's the thickest blanket I have,' I said.

'Thank you. What about your blanket?'

'I will use this bed sheet.'

'What if it gets too cold?'

'Umm, I'll manage.'

'Come inside mine, then. It's big enough to cover two people.'

'Okay,' I said, thoughtfully. She was giving me signs. Very blatant signs. It was an eerie feeling, with no anticipation about what would happen a moment later. My headache had worsened, after the sudden change of temperature due to the air conditioner. I took out a balm and started applying it to my forehead.

'Headache?'

'Yeah, severe.'

'Do you want the shoulder and head massage that I gave you in Mumbai?'

'Sure,' I said gladly. More than the massage, I was happy that I wasn't initiating it—she was.

'Give me the balm. I'll rub it on your shoulders,' she said. I did as instructed.

She began massaging me. Her slender long fingers squirmed against the agitated tissues of my shoulders, the tips of her fingers brushed my scalp, and oozed out every tinge of pain that resided there.

'Take off your shirt,' she ordered.

'What?' I could not believe what I'd heard.

'Yes, take off your shirt. I need to apply the balm on your

shoulders,' she said casually. There was no sign of flirtation from her side. I took off my shirt and lay on her lap.

'Does it feel better now?'

'Yes, thank you. I owe you a treat to repay this debt,' I said, happily.

'I want the treat now.'

'Are you hungry? Wait, I can make maggi for you.'

'No silly, not food. I want the favour, the massage. Now it's your turn.'

'What! I haven't massaged anyone before,' I said, lying. The truth was that I had tried to massage Priya once but she hated it so much that she stopped me in less than two minutes. She called me 'Iron Man' after that, a back-handed compliment for my hands being hard.

'There is a first time for everything. I'll teach you,' she said, as she lay down.

'Where do I massage you? Your head?'

'No, I don't like when someone touches my head. Massage my waist instead,' she uttered. I felt weird. I could feel myself getting aroused.

'How? You'll have to take off your T-shirt for it,' I hesitantly said.

'So ask me to do it. You can't become a good masseur if you're shy. Ask me,' she ordered.

'Shikha, take off your tee,' I faltered, sedating my conscience. She did it in a snap.

There she was, without her tee, in a white bra that held her big bosom, waiting for me to rub my hands against her scintillating waist.

'Sit on my bum, so that you can massage my waist well,' she ordered. I, very meekly, followed her direction but there was a serious problem. The arousal had made me extremely uneasy.

Nevertheless, I began slowly massaging her. After a few minutes, she asked me cover a wider area—from the beginning of her butt line till her bra strap; then it went a step beyond to the entire back as she asked me to unhook her bra, which, though I had experience with, took me six tries to nail.

'I'm done,' I said as I got up from my comfy seat, hoping that she would ask me to hook her bra once again. But she was not in the mood. She turned to face me instead. I don't know why, what, or how, in that moment, I grabbed her hands and sealed my lips on hers. She was taken aback at first, but reciprocated a moment later. As my body settled against hers, Priya's image flashed in my head. But as soon as I remembered her words: 'We are done', they removed every trace of guilt within me. I lifted Shikha's hands up and moved to pull down the three-quarters that she was wearing, only to encounter a resistance. It was her hand.

'No,' she said sternly. And I stopped at once.

I didn't know how and why what happened had happened. I just wanted to make sure that I hadn't, in any way whatsoever, taken advantage of her.

'No, Amol. Don't go there,' I realized that I had tried to go a step further without permission.

'I'm sorry, really sorry. I really like you. I got carried away,' I said, in some way, trying to defend myself.

'No need to be sorry. You can do whatever you want but just answer me one thing—can you promise me your loyalty?'

Frankly speaking, I was sick and tired of the whole concept of relationship. I didn't have frigging time or energy or money or even enthusiasm for it. Inwardly, I knew that when Mishra and Rishabh would return, I would not get time for her at all. Moreover, she was Shikha, Rishabh's ex-fling and YourQuote's ex-employee, and it complicated the situation further.

I didn't want to get into a relationship. Surely not with Shikha.

'I really like you, I have since that trip to Mumbai,' I lied, bitten by the bug of lust, and moved my hands towards the straps of her trousers that didn't encounter any hindrance this time.

We didn't go all the way; she didn't allow me to. After pestering her twice, I surrendered. She had never gone all the way before, not even with Kartik or Rishabh. After her disastrous tryst with Kartik, she had made a promise to her Mom that she would never get physical with any guy till her marriage, a promise that she had however let a little loose for me, just because she trusted me a lot. Interestingly, she liked orange.

She told me, 'You aren't any other guy for me. I have immense trust and faith in you. I can bend the rules for you, but not entirely.'

'I am really not sure how this relationship is going to work since there are so many complications, but I can assure you, I would give my 100 percent to make it work,' I said, even though it was an unsure promise.

The next morning, I dropped her back in an auto. Something that I had never done for Priya.

When I came back, my eyes accidentally fell on a notepad on my desk. I opened it and a rose fell on the ground.

All of a sudden, Priya was all around. Her smell, her smile, her voice, her eyes, her hair, her body. Her thoughts pervaded my very soul. Frightened, I began trembling. *Did I kill her faith?* I pulled out the page that contained a romantic poem she had written for me, shredded that page into pieces, and threw it from the second floor balcony to the ground. As I looked at the small pieces of paper, swaying in the morning breeze racing amongst themselves to first kiss the ground, my body stiffened.

I felt bad. Until bad turned into terrible and I broke down into sobs.

Goodbye, Forever

I didn't talk to anyone the day after. No calls, no chats, no messages, no self-talk. I tried to immerse myself in work, but even work couldn't take my mind off Priya. She was like oxygen for my soul—my own invisible lifeline. I wanted to speak to her but didn't have the courage to do so. I just messaged her asking when she would be back, but she didn't reply.

Before going for a bath in the evening, I sat in front of the mirror and studied myself. My face looked swollen and there were dark circles under my eyes. I couldn't look myself in the eye and turned away from my own image. I then took a towel and went into the bathroom. As drops of cold water kissed my body, which still carried the imprints of my betrayal to Priya, I froze in fear. I started rubbing the water against my body, my hands, my chest, my cheeks, my legs, my face, my neck, my back, trying to erase every evidence of the previous night that had seeped into my life like a dark, permanent scar. No matter how much water I splashed against my body, I had robbed it of the respect it deserved and it was never going to come back again.

Disgusted with myself, I came out after a quick bath. There was a call on my phone. It was from Shikha. I didn't pick it up. But I soon realized I couldn't fix things on my own, so I decided to meet Shikha and try and sort everything out, tell her that things between Priya and me weren't yet over and whatever happened the previous night was a grave mistake on my part.

So I called her up. She insisted on coming over to my place for more massage sessions like the day before, but I didn't trust myself with her anymore. I asked her to wait for me at IIT. My tone was serious.

Half an hour later, I was with her, seated in the middle of the grass field, where there was so little light that our faces couldn't be seen from a distance.

'You look really serious. What happened?'

'I...' I said, struggling to find the right words. My throat was parched and I was almost ready to burst into tears.

'Amol, it's okay. Why are you so sad when I am here?'

How could I tell her that I was sad precisely because she was there.

'I feel really bad for Priya. I feel as though I have cheated on her,' I wailed.

'You broke up with her, didn't you?'

'Yes.'

'Then there is no reason to feel guilty,' she said. Her words comforted me and I felt less guilty.

'Hmm,' I said. My tears had subsided.

'What was yesterday all about?' I asked her.

'We are in a relationship. Do you have any doubts about it?'

'No doubts whatsoever,' I said in a doubtful tone.

For the next half an hour, we discussed about our future together which in reality seemed completely bleak to me. But, at least Shikha succeeded in making one thing clear to me—that Priya and I were not in love.

'Why don't you call Priya and tell her everything?'

'She is at home. Her Mom will ground her if she even finds out that she is seeing a guy. I will tell her when the time is right.'

We went for dinner, hand in hand, chatted about our families, our ambitions, and took utmost delight in bitching about Rishabh. When I received an unexpected message from Priya saying, 'I'm back. What did you want to talk about?', I left for home immediately and asked Shikha not to accompany me until I fixed things with Priya on my own.

Shikha complied after much reluctance. As soon as I reached home, I called Priya.

'Hi, how are you?' she said. Her cordial tone surprised me.

'Hi, I'm fine,' I said formally.

'Why so serious? What did you want to talk about, tell me?' Her curiosity implied that she was expecting a patch-up talk.

'You wanted a break-up. So, let's do it. I want to come tomorrow and return everything that we had exchanged. The letters, gifts—all of it,' I uttered in a hurtful tone.

'What? I have already broken up with you,' she said in anger. 'No need to return the things, you can just burn them.'

I asked for the guitar that I'd gifted her on our first anniversary which she couldn't learn despite my desperate attempts at teaching her. Since I used to make some pocket money to sustain myself by teaching guitar over weekends to some college students, I added, 'I'll use it to teach my students here.'

'Fine, come tomorrow morning,' she said and disconnected the phone before I could get a chance to respond. I realized that I had disappointed her. It affected me a little. But not enough to restrain me from having a deep, guilt-free sleep at night.

Early the next morning, I left for Vishwavidhyalaya. With me, I had taken a big box which contained each and every thing that she had ever gifted me—five red roses that had withered with time, their blackness signifying our decayed relationship, several love letters where Priya signed with a little heart instead of a dot above the 'i' in her name, and two handmade birthday cards that carried funny cartoons depicting the two of us. I chose not to part with the only material thing she had gifted to me—a Fastrack wrist watch, the only one I owned.

As soon as I came out of Vishwavidyalaya metro station, I saw Priya standing at a distance from me. It seemed very bizarre at first. No smiles, no hugs, no handshakes, no tickling, no winks, no blinks, no hand holding—no love.

A guitar pack hung from her shoulder while she looked straight into my eyes.

'Should we go somewhere better?'

'Nothing is open at this time,' she said.

'Let's sit here. I have something to say,' I said pointing towards the steps of the metro station.

'Say, I'm all ears,' she said.

'I am immensely grateful and honoured to have spent the last three years with you. It's unfortunate that we are breaking up despite such a long commitment, but I think it's for the better for both of us,' I said. Words came naturally, as though my fate was speaking through me.

She didn't say a thing. Perhaps, she was heartbroken. Perhaps, she knew it was coming all along. Perhaps, she could not believe that it was the end. Or perhaps, she wanted to say something similar.

'What happened? Are you okay?'

'Yes,' she said, lost in her thoughts.

'If you don't wish to end this relationship, please tell me,' I said, inwardly wishing desperately that she would not utter a thing.

'Nothing. I am fine with it,' she said. I wanted to let out a huge sigh.

'This is what you wanted, right?'

'Yes, I did, for you couldn't care less,' she said, indicating subtly that if I changed my self, things could still be brought on track.

'Hey, let's stop this mudslinging. Let's not end this on a bad note,' I said changing the topic tactfully. Tact had never worked in business for me, but in relationships, it had never failed me.

'Sure,' she said. My heart cried out to me to tell her about Shikha. But my mind wasn't ready. I didn't want her to feel betrayed.

Wait, why did I use the word betrayed? Did I really betray her? We had already broken up before Shikha came into my life, right?

'See, now we are free birds. Rather than us getting irritated of each other because of having different priorities, we should start seeing other people—people who understand us, people who we deserve, people who are like us, people who we want,' I blabbered. I was very happy with myself, the feeling outshining the striking of a very profitable business deal.

'Let's not meet or talk for a few months at all,' she uttered.

'As you wish,' I said and got up to leave. 'Goodbye hug?'

She came towards me and we hugged, I could feel that she didn't want to let me go, but I didn't like that feeling. I held her for a minute, kissed her on the cheek, and mumbled, 'Goodbye, forever. I'll...'

'Don't ruin it,' she said grabbing the packet of gifts I was returning to her. She gave me my stuff quickly in exchange, jumped on the road, and crossed to the other side. I waited, expecting her to turn back towards me and wave like she always did. Instead, she vanished inside her PG, leaving me gaping behind her.

I stood there for the next five minutes, hoping to find her running back towards me with a big smile and asking me to never leave her. She didn't appear.

It was over. I didn't know how I felt; a little sad, a little happy, a little lost. I messaged Shikha to come over to my place on my way back. I needed someone to distract my mind off Priya. I told her about what had happened.

'You look lost,' she said on her arrival and came towards me, placing her hand on my right leg, which firmed its grip with time.

Bloody slut! My mind echoed Priya's opinion of her.

From that very moment on, I let Priya disappear in the past and started taking my fling (or relationship, whatever it was) with Shikha seriously. It was also very beneficial for the venture. She was now working with an ace design company, had started designing professional websites, logos, and book covers, and was charging as much as 30,000 rupees for a week of service. Being close to her, I could utilize her professional services for YourQuote for free, which she wouldn't have agreed to otherwise.

You may think that I was shrewd, but it's a trait that I was proud of. Every bootstrapped entrepreneur is on the lookout for opportunities to get quality work for free. There is nothing wrong with that.

'Ours is a creative venture. We need creative people on board. What Rishabh has done is that he has created a pool of people who are good for nothing and he spends his maximum time managing them, whereas the thing that needs maximum attention—our product—is being sidelined. Tell me, what's the use of marketing if there's no product in place?'

'True. So who's taking care of design at the moment?'

'No one. I mean I am doing it. There is no professional yet.'

'Eeeks, you haven't got a professional yet. No professional, no progress,' she said as though she was the next Vinci. Just fifteen days in a professional company had turned her attitude and made her look at amateurs with contempt.

'I'm not that bad,' I said.

'Every bad designer says that.'

'What does a good designer say?'

'If you're good, you don't have to say anything. Your work speaks for you,' she said.

I gave in. She was both talented and skilled while I was merely 'good'.

'Would you...?' I hesitated to ask for her help, especially after she left the venture.

'Only if I have to deal with you. I don't want to deal with Rishabh,' she said without letting me finish my sentence.

'I understand,' I said, suppressing a loud yes.

'Don't you have to go to work today?'

'I'm at work,' she winked. Her wink reminded me of Priya. I kissed her to get rid of the thought. It worked.

'But there's one thing. I don't want to be exploited by YourQuote again, so I'm not willing to work for free,' she said. It stung me bitterly. For an entrepreneur, even the slightest mention of money by a friend who can otherwise do it for free can impact the relationship. But Shikha was a woman of reason.

'Why? Will you charge fee from me as well? Come on,' I cried, seeking sympathy. I put my head on her shoulders so she could console me.

'I won't charge any fee from you, but I will from YourQuote. I'm doing this work for your company, not just for you. Your company needs to pay me.'

'Why? You know our financial condition is down in the dumps.'

'You need to come out of that situation. If I charge money, you'll be forced to perform with double the current efficiency. And, you guys need to start paying money. When you have to give money to someone, you start taking that person seriously.'

She was right. We had always been stingy in shelling out money. Even when we had money, we chose to spend it on parties rather than hiring professionals for some quick tasks. While we thought that giving money as incentive would increase the expectations of our team members from us, it worked the other way round as most of our team members started feeling exploited by us.

'Okay, if it's about money, then how much?'

'20,000 rupees,' she shocked me with an already made-up figure in her mind.

'What? You are looting us, if that's what your intention is.'

'Be polite. Why should I do your work if that's your opinion about me?' she rebuked. I was irritated. She wasn't like Priya. I could not take her for granted.

'Sorry, I just got carried away. But still, 20,000 rupees is a little too much.'

'For me or for you?'

'For both. I mean you haven't even turned professional. You are just interning with some random design company,' I stated without realizing that my words would hurt her pride.

'I won't work.'

'What? Why? Is it all about money? You have changed Shikha.'

'It's not at all about money. It's about trust.'

Wow, she was talking about trust now, after breaking the trust of every person she was close to. I laughed at the thought of it, but stopped the moment I realized that I was no less than her.

'You don't trust my abilities. There's no point in working with you,' she shot at me.

'I have full trust in your abilities,' I uttered in a reflex.

'Then don't you think that my work deserves 20,000 rupees?'

I was trapped. I just kept thinking whether she had played a trick on me. Unable to think of any counter logic, I gave in.

'I'll discuss it with Rishabh and let you know about our decision.'

The next hour, I was on the phone with Rishabh (who was still in Lucknow), trying to convince him on behalf of my new girlfriend that we should shell out 20,000 rupees to Shikha and get the new User Interface (UI) designed as soon as possible. While he continually asserted that we should discuss it once he was back, I was more than eager to finalize the deal once and for all. Rishabh and I always had our little tussles. While he liked to take more time before coming to a definite conclusion, I liked to go for it just after one discussion. He believed in wasting time and saving money while I believed in exactly the opposite. Neither of us could think alike on any issue.

Owing to my push, Rishabh and I chalked out a deal where we agreed to pay Shikha in four quarterly installments of 5,000 rupees. Shikha happily gave in. It satisfied her professional ego. In turn, she made a stunning outline and wireframe to base our designs on.

The Comeback

One and a half week had passed since Shikha replaced Priya in my life. I hadn't talked to Priya once after the break up. Rishabh and Mishra had just returned to Delhi and I had to be extra cautious to make sure that they didn't suspect anything.

Rishabh and Mishra were both surprised and amused at how Shikha had become so concerned about YourQuote all of a sudden, a company she had angrily left sometime ago. When they tried to confront me about it, I curtly avoided them and said, 'You know I asked her to help design the cover for my second book which is due for release in August. Thanks to that, we have become good friends now and she has agreed to do a bit of freelance work for us.'

Rishabh had ample amount of free time at his disposal since Anjali was off to Toronto. He had slowly begun discussing more and more about the venture with me unlike before when he would keep to himself. I was really astonished at the change in him and gladly allowed him to enter my area—product design. He enthusiastically exhibited his skills on MS Paint and drew the wire frames of the new layouts for all the pages based on our discussion which would also help Shikha in her design work. It was decided that Shikha would join us at our place over the coming weekend for an entire day and we would roll out the new UI simultaneously. Shikha was a little apprehensive about dealing with Rishabh but I comforted her by saying that Rishabh had changed for the better and was putting all his energy into work.

I hadn't mentioned my break up with Priya to anyone. When Rishabh quizzed me if I had had another fight with her, I was dumbstruck. He told me to read her Facebook status which said, 'It's one of those days when the only messages that I receive on phone are from Vodafone.' I calmed myself down and told him, 'Yeah, we broke up a while ago. She has even blocked me from her profile.'

'Ha! What is it like…the nth time? It must be one of your regular break ups.'

'Don't know. I haven't talked to her for over two weeks,' I said and began doodling codes.

'Why don't you go talk to her? Only if you have a peaceful mind will you be able to work efficiently,' Rishabh said. I hmmed in indifference.

⌫

As we had planned, Shikha was to come over to our house early Saturday morning. As soon as I heard the doorbell ring, I excitedly got up to open the door. I was seeing Shikha after a gap of five days since the duo returned. The fact that Rishabh and Mishra were sleeping and I could easily have at least ten to fifteen minutes in the other room with her was enough for me. Lust was the only way I knew how to come out of the regrets of past love.

But the sight that my lustful eyes confronted made me shudder in shock. I felt as if I was facing my worst nightmare ever. Standing at an arm's length was the woman I had least expected to see. She had disheveled hair with dark circles under her eyes. Her lips were as dry as my throat and her wide-open eyes told me that she was in a terrible mood and had come seeking answers from me. I was dumbfounded. I felt busted and having faced the wrath of Priya's temper earlier when we were together, I knew it was going to be one long, painful day.

Thoughts about Shikha—who would land any moment—and Mishra and Rishabh who could be woken up by the racket that might follow, made me sweat with worry. I stood transfixed in front of her. The next moment, she pounced on me and kissed me violently. She took my hand in hers and led me into my house. Once in, she kept kissing me until we were both short of breath. The door was still wide open and I just prayed to God that Shikha wouldn't turn up then and there. Luckily, she didn't.

As I came back to my senses, I looked at her in disgust and could find only one thing to tell her, 'You sick woman. I have not even brushed yet.'

She didn't answer. Meanwhile, Rishabh and Mishra had woken up hearing the commotion outside. Seeing Priya in the house and how hysterical she was, Rishabh and Mishra excused themselves from the house on the pretext of getting milk from a nearby shop. I hurriedly went to the loo and messaged Shikha—'Priya has turned up at my house all of a sudden. Do not come. She is in a very agitated state. I'll try and sort everything out and meet you in the evening.'

She followed with a quick reply saying, 'I have already left for Malviya Nagar. What should I do?'

I was terribly annoyed at her stupidity. I messaged her angrily: 'Do anything that your dumb mind tells you, just don't come here.'

In response, she called me but I cut the phone. She called again, but by this time, I had completely lost my mind. When she called again the third time, I cut her call and wrote her a stern message, 'WHAT THE FUCK DO YOU NOT UNDERSTAND IN MY MESSAGE?'

'Amol, I don't deserve to be treated like this. This won't go on for long,' she messaged back.

'Can't you please wait till the evening? Let me fix things here and I promise I'll call you. Please. I can't pick up your call right now in front of everyone,' I messaged while brushing my teeth.

'So you prefer her over me?' she messaged. She had tested all my patience.

'I'm switching off my phone. Will talk to you in the evening. Bye,' I replied and let out a long sigh. I switched off my cellphone before she could vex me anymore.

I was just stupefied about the way Priya assaulted me a few minutes ago. I came out of the loo—my mouth smelling fresh of peppermint—and looked at Priya. She was standing right across me with a blank face.

'What just occurred was not right. I mean we have broken up. You can't just barge into anyone's home and...' and before I could finish, she attacked me once again. I was too stunned to react.

She pulled my pajamas down and moved her hands inside my vest, her nails scratching my sweaty back. I didn't reciprocate. I didn't know why she was being so reckless. I smelled her mouth for any traces of alcohol, but she didn't smell drunk. She had taken off my vest by then and I was simply in my boxers. She asked me to undress her as well, but I controlled myself from doing so. Besides, I didn't want to.

I pulled up my pajamas and decided to make her sit down and have a conversation like grown ups, but as I parted my lips to say something, she shut them promptly with hers. At once, I grabbed her arms and forcefully made her sit on the bed.

'Priya, stop it. Things are over between us. All this won't help,' I said patiently and went and sat near her. She put her arms around me and rested her face against my bare chest.

'I can't live without you,' she said. Her words were totally unexpected.

'It's okay. Stop crying first,' I said.

'Please don't leave me. Please,' she said and burst into tears.

'I'm here. I'm not going anywhere. We can talk it through,' I said, still unsure whether bringing in the topic of Shikha could prove fruitful or do more harm.

'I don't want to talk. I want you. Promise me that you will never ever leave me.'

'Priya, stop talking like a child...'

'Stop acting smart. Promise me,' she said.

'I still won't have time for you. You deserve someone better.'

'I will change for you. I wasn't very understanding before, but now I will try to be. I know now how difficult it is to do what you are doing, I understand that it requires immense support of your loved ones. I will be there when you need me and I won't ever complain that I'm lonely. Please, don't leave me. We are destined to be together,' she said.

I kept thinking, *Are we really destined to be together? Do I deserve her, especially after all that I have done behind her back?* I didn't know what to say. I wanted to cry with her, cry for what I had done, cry in my inability to erase the past, cry for not having the courage to look into her eyes and admit my mistake. I couldn't see her in such a miserable state. At that moment, even if it would have meant leaving Shikha, I'd have done it.

It was time to let her know the truth. It was time to make her realize that I was not worthy of her. As I looked into her brown eyes, which were inches away from me, I gathered courage to speak, but she kissed me once again. This time, I kissed her back. Unknowingly.

I carried her in my arms and took her to bed. A minute later, we were in another world. I had never felt so close to her before. I even said I love you thrice during that time. Twenty minutes later, she asked me to go and put on some protection. She wanted to go all the way this time. I thought of the pack of Durex lying in my drawer. She asked me where I had kept them and went to retrieve one. While she was gone, I lay on the bed contemplating on how things were getting complicated with every fleeting moment.

After not hearing from Priya for around five minutes, I got a little worried. I went to the other room, thinking she might not have found the pack. I entered the room and found her sitting morbidly next to the open packet of orange-flavoured condoms. At first I couldn't realize what had gone amiss but when I saw the orange-sachets strewn on the ground, I realized that I had been caught.

I could have chosen to lie like my friends, but could not think of a better time to bring up the truth in front of her. Sadly, she didn't give me a chance to speak in my defense.

An extremely loud slap rang out in the room and I went flying to the floor. Neither of us said anything for the next few minutes. She came and sat helplessly on the ground next to me.

I moved near her and disrupted the eerie silence with a meek but sincere sorry. She didn't respond.

Half an hour later, she stood up and went towards the bed. When she came back, she was fully dressed and headed towards the door. I grabbed her hand before she could leave.

'Don't. Please don't go,' I said in a hoarse voice. There was a mirror near the door which showed that my left cheek had turned red with the slap.

'Amol, let go of my hand,' Priya said.

'Don't go,' I persisted.

She started hitting at me with all her might and even tried to strangle me. I fell against the wall, while she tried to choke me with all her force. At first I felt that she was joking, but when I actually started getting asphyxiated, I grabbed her hands and freed myself immediately.

'Are you fucking crazy?' I screamed, panting heavily.

'Who was the whore you fucked? Tell me, who was the whore you fucked?' she screamed at the top of her voice.

'Stop shouting,' I yelled at the same volume and whispered, 'It was Shikha and we didn't.'

'I will kill you if you lie to me.'

'I am not lying. We didn't,' I said. I was still out of breath.

'So who used it then?' she said pointing to the orange sachet.

'I used it. There are other things one can do with it,' I replied annoyingly.

'Despite sleeping around with that slut, you could still dare to touch me with those fingers of yours that would have...you scoundrel!' she yelled and threw whatever she could find around at me—shoes, polish, key chains, hangers, and a plastic chair before dropping down on the ground.

'Are you committed to her?'

'I am. But I don't love her at all.'

'Why did you have to do it?'

'I felt that you would never talk to me.'

'Why could not you tell me before going ahead with her? Wait, when you came to break up with me, it was her, wasn't it?'

I nodded in shame.

'Answer me,' she yelled. 'Can't you break up with her for me?'

I kept mum. My mind was racing through various things. Clearly, Priya was the girl I had ever loved with all my heart. I didn't know whether I still loved her or not. I just knew that I could not see her cry.

'Please answer me. I will never question your answer. Just answer me. I am going home tomorrow anyway for a week's time before joining my job,' Priya said dejectedly and got up.

'Can you tell your parents about us? Now that we have arrived at this juncture of life, I want to make sure of a future before moving forward. If we are to restart our relationship, it's important that both of are secure about never being heartbroken again,' I said.

'If that's what makes you happy, I will,' she said with immense sincerity and left my place.

I had never felt so remorseful before. I cursed myself for letting things get so complicated, for having invited Shikha home that night, for not paying attention to Priya while she was on the phone with me, for my first fight with Priya, and so on. Now when she was ready to face her strongest fear, I was captured by another fear. The fear of another encounter. Shikha.

⊏⊐⊨

When Priya left, I switched on my cellphone. There were twenty missed calls from Shikha and three unread messages.

'Call me as soon as Priya goes,' Shikha's message read. I felt a sudden disenchantment with Shikha, like I wanted to get rid of her from my life that very minute.

'We are going to Noida to see a client. Will come back at night,' the second message said. It was Mishra's and the last message was from Rishabh saying, 'We met Shikha. She cancelled the meet after just two hours. She said she was not well. We had discussed new designs today. She says she will deliver them by Tuesday. Can you convince her to do it by tonight itself?'

'Bloody hypocrite,' I yelled in disgust. She had behaved unprofessionally, having allowed her personal issues with me to affect her professional work. My irritation was at its peak. In that moment of extreme anger, I laid out an elaborate plan of getting rid of her for good. But before everything else, I had to get the work done.

I called her and uttered a fake apology for not having called her. She resisted at first.

'There's good news for you,' I told her.

'What?'

'Everything has been solved. Now, nobody can ever step into our lives again,' I said. I was astonished to see my own falseness, but my conscience supported me because I was doing it for my venture.

'Really? You mean it?'

'Yes. Don't you want to know what happened?'

'No, I don't want to hear about Priya. I'm just glad things are finally over between you two.'

'Mishra and Rishabh won't be here till late and you can stay over on the pretext of work.'

'Wow, I'm coming right away,' she said excitedly and disconnected the call.

⌒

Rishabh and Mishra came back at 10 at night. They were surprised to find Shikha at home.

'Look what we have accomplished in the last few hours,' I said, letting the work to speak for itself. Mishra and Rishabh peered on the screen incisively only to break into a satisfied smile.

'It looks good,' they both echoed like robots. Mishra went into the loo, where he used to smoke and poop at the same time.

I grabbed the plates from Shikha and took them to the washbasin to rinse.

As I returned from the kitchen, I saw that Shikha and Rishabh were missing from the drawing room. I went to the outer room and what I saw stopped me dead in my tracks. Shikha was giving Rishabh a shoulder massage and he, in turn, was moaning in pleasure. When I entered the room, Shikha looked at me helplessly, as if she had been forced to do what she was doing. Rishabh, on seeing me, signalled for me to remain outside and let him enjoy his time with her.

I came out and tried to gather my thoughts. Shikha immediately came running out of the room. I waited for Rishabh to come out as well but he didn't. I asked Shikha

what she was doing back in the room. She said to my disbelief
that Rishabh forced himself upon her and asked her to give
him a massage against her wishes. She hastily explained how
she ran out of the room when he tried to assault her, to which
I remained unperturbed. In that small moment, I came face to
face with the reality that Shikha didn't matter to me at all. I
tried to console her, half-heartedly.

'Do you want to go?' I whispered.

'Not when you are here, I trust you,' she said and sent me
thinking.

'Where am I going to sleep?' she asked, a way for her to
tell me that she was not deterred by the immediate assault
by my able partner, who had by now come out of the room.

'Umm, let me ask Rishabh,' I said.

'The three of us can sleep in the AC room, so we can let
Shikha sleep in the drawing room,' Rishabh suggested.

Shikha looked at Rishabh with piercing eyes and said, 'I
want to sleep in the AC room, please. I don't have problem
in sleeping alongside Mishra or Amol.' 'We can use pillows
as separators, can't we?'

Rishabh face had turned red. He had been humiliated on
his own turf.

'What about Rishabh?' I said, playing the role of her
partner to a T.

'Oh, Rishabh told me that he usually chats with Anjali at
night on Skype, so he can sleep in the drawing room today,'
Shikha taunted and went to the AC room with a victorious
smile. I followed her but was stopped before I could leave the
room.

'Amol, don't you want to work for a while?' Rishabh asked
in all seriousness.

'Yes, that's what I had been doing till now. We can finish the remaining designs in the AC room. Come, sit with us till we retire to bed.'

'No, I'm fine here. Good night,' Rishabh said.

When Mishra came back, he was delighted to find that he was going to be sharing the bed with a girl. We decided that Shikha could sleep along the edge of the bed, Mishra in the middle, and I on the other edge. It was not agreeable to either Shikha or me, but we could not have said a word.

'Mishra, why don't you lie on the edge for a while? We have to work on the design,' Shikha asked Mishra who had by then already dropped his body in the middle of the bed. He pretended not to listen. I rolled him over to one side with great difficulty. He woke up after a while, feigning astonishment at his changed position but when he saw us diligently working, went back to sleep.

We indeed worked for a little while, designing eight out of the total twelve pages which, as Shikha said, would have increased the 'stickiness' of our website ten times the initial figure of zero. A website is completely dependent on how it makes the user feel the first time he logs in. The better it looks, the better will be the user experience, and the more 'sticky' the relationship between the two becomes.

I was extremely happy that my shrewdness had borne good results. Just four more webpages had to be designed after which I could get rid of her forever. Though her involvement as a designer was based on a verbal promise of 20,000 rupees which were to be given to her in four installments, in reality she was pursuing the task only because it allowed her to spend time with me. Had I broken up with her, she would have broken up with YourQuote—no matter what financial incentives we gave her.

At 1 o' clock, tired at last, we went to sleep in the chilly AC breeze, ducked under one blanket that allowed our hands to foray into each other's territory without waking up Mishra.

The next day—a Sunday—didn't turn out as I had imagined it to.

Early in the morning, Shikha received a call from her parents telling her that they were reaching her hostel in two hours. She left before Mishra or Rishabh could wake up. She asked me not to call her during the day as her parents had become suspicious about guys owing to their experience with Kartik and she hadn't told them about me. She assured me that she would return as and when she would get free.

By the time Mishra got up, I had just finished taking a bath and was drying myself with a towel.

'Where is Shikha?' Mishra and Rishabh jointly asked me, ironically for two totally opposite reasons.

'She's gone. Her parents were going to come to her hostel,' I said. While one was disappointed by her departure, the other seemed glad.

My cellphone rang. It was Priya. Curious, I moved out to the balcony.

'When I told my mother about us, she slapped me in front of everyone here in my PG. My father didn't say a word and both of them just left, asking me to never call them. Are you happy now?' she said in anger.

I was speechless. For all our fights, I had always blamed her. We had spent some of the best times with each other and at that moment, I felt like I had let her down. I repeatedly sought her forgiveness, to which she had just one response: 'Are you happy now?'

The burden of remorse in having sinned twice—first by cheating on her and then by being the reason behind her shattered relationship with her parents—trampled my heart. At that moment, I was willing to do whatever it would take to make things right with her.

'I'm really frightened, Amol. I don't want to be alone,' she said.

'Come over,' I said without thinking and disconnected the call.

But no sooner did I put my phone down, I came face to face with the reality of it all. My work held priority and I figured that it wasn't possible for me to break up with Shikha before completing the user interface design. The future of our venture depended on those four webpages that were remaining.

I thought of calling Priya and asking her not to come. But I chose to do something completely else. I called her friend Kamna, who also happened to be a good friend of mine, for help.

'Hi Kamna, this is Amol,' I mumbled.

'Hi Amol, how are you?' she said with no excitement at all.

'Nothing. Things between Priya and me haven't been well lately,' I said trying to seek sympathy.

'I know, you have been seeing Shikha, Rishabh's ex, isn't it?' Kamna plainly said.

I was flabbergasted. Shivers of mortification ran through my body as though I had been caught red-handed. I had taken it for granted that Priya would uphold my privacy, but no.

'Yes, thank you, bye,' I rudely said and dropped the call before she could ask me anything further.

I knew what to do next. The wrath induced a tinge of satisfaction in me as for now I could get the designs made from Shikha before anything happened. I called Priya.

'You don't need to come here,' I commanded.

'But...what happened?' asked Priya.

'I think you prefer to gossip about me and my private life with Kamna rather than coming over and talking to me.'

'What are you saying?'

'I just spoke to Kamna. How does she know about Shikha?'

'Umm...'

'You are one hell of a bitch. You gossip about me behind my back and expect me to believe that you still love me?'

'What else could I have done? You asked me not to speak to you until I confessed everything in front of my parents,' she started crying on the phone.

'That does not justify you talking about my private life with anyone else. Imagine how you would have felt had I talked about our private lives with Rishabh?' I screamed.

'I am sorry Amol, I'm really sorry,' she pleaded and kept crying. It was the most vulnerable I had ever seen her and though it bothered me, I still chose not to comfort her.

⌁

Mulling over the past few days of my life, I came up with a one liner and posted it as the Sermon of the Day quote on our fan page:

In a troubled relationship, never hope for a break up. Let it come as a pleasant surprise.

I looked at the watch. It was 2. I hadn't yet received a call from Shikha. Mishra had translated Shikha's designs into the CSS codes and was waiting for the remaining four designs, and incidentally, the pages remaining were the most important— Profile, Home, Hall of Fame (that was to contain the best original quotes submitted by users), and Leaderboard that was to be used for gamifying the entire experience.

Gamification is an important aspect of any networking venture. It involves an incentive and engagement mechanism that drives the user to participate more. Every networking website subtly or blatantly relies on this aspect. For example, you share on Facebook to get likes, you tweet on Twitter to get retweets and followers and so on.

Getting work done from Shikha was my prerogative, as Rishabh had lost his command on her by his insolent act the previous day and Mishra had to fiddle with codes—or in his words, 'clean' the codes—to make them more scalable, thus easier to manage as the venture grows bigger in terms of size and the number of users.

The way a website is coded is a very important aspect for any internet venture. Rashly coded websites, especially by freelancers off the web and even some professional web development companies, can drastically affect a business while scaling. The codes should follow a proper framework that makes them decipherable to every technical guy that comes on board later. In a venture, it's very important to be quick, but it's more important to be quick with the right process. This was one of the reasons we never hired an agency to build our website and instead waited for the right guy, which we ultimately found in Mishra.

I messaged Shikha to inquire when she would get free. She told me she was already on the way. When I told Rishabh that Shikha was coming over, he told me he had to suddenly attend some follow-up meetings with a couple of clients he had met last week. Mishra chose to stay. I had to somehow push him out as well. It was the much awaited day when I would get the work completed from Shikha and then excuse her from my life forever.

'How long it had been since you met your girlfriend?' I asked Mishra, who had his head stuck to his laptop screen. He seemed taken aback by my sudden concern. He looked around to make sure that I was speaking to him and not anybody else.

'Umm…' he stammered uneasily, 'over a month maybe?'

'Why do you avoid her so much? Fights?'

'No, not fights. She is just really irritating. Calls me every fucking hour,' he said.

'Oh! Why don't you meet her then?'

'Are you crazy? She makes me spend at least a thousand rupees every time,' he said and botched my plan of sending him to meet his girlfriend.

'By the way, you know what?' he said with a wicked smile. 'I'm trying to woo a girl from Click2Closet, the company I'm interning at. She is a real hot Punjabi. I have asked her out on a movie date today evening.'

'Wow,' I said, expressing my genuine delight. 'At what time?'

'5 pm, we are meeting at Saket.'

'Great. Hope she doesn't know that you are already in a relationship,' I said.

'Oh c'mon, obviously. Even I don't know that I am in a relationship,' he winked. I smirked.

Shikha came at around quarter to four. She smelled of lavender and her hair was still wet from taking a bath. Her broad smile shrunk when she saw Mishra in the room with me.

I was glad that Mishra was at home till five because that meant he could assist Shikha in finishing off her work. By the time Mishra got ready, we had completed the remaining designs of the webpages that otherwise would have taken two to three days had Shikha carried them out single handedly. I asked her to mail the designs to me which she readily did, despite no upfront payment, because she trusted me a great deal. When Mishra left after five, I went straight to the point.

'Priya still loves me,' I said plainly.

'Why are you telling me this? Do *you* still love her?' she said.

That was not what I had expected. I didn't know what to say.

'Come on, answer me. Your silence is killing me, Amol,' she shrieked. I expected a slap, but what followed was another story.

'I knew it,' she said. 'I knew it all along.' The shock that she knew it while I didn't boggled me.

'But I also knew that it won't work out between you two, since we are destined to be together,' she said with certainty.

'Who the hell are you to decide?' I screamed.

'Don't shout at me, Amol. I'm not Priya who will take shit from you without saying a word. Treat me with respect.'

'What respect? Fuck respect. Don't talk about respect to me. You screwed up my relationship despite knowing the fact that I was still in love with Priya,' I yelled.

'I didn't screw it up,' she screamed at the top of her voice. 'It was you—you sucker—who initiated and told me that you had broken up with her. You cheated on me at the same time you were cheating on her. It was the day when you came to IIT and cried like a baby that I realized that you were still in love with Priya. What could I have done?'

I was at a loss for words. She was right. It was all my doing.

'Not only this—you have screwed up our beautiful friendship too,' she said.

'Fuck you. Had you been a true friend, you would have tried to solve things between Priya and me rather than getting me to sleep with you, you slut!' I screamed.

'Amol, don't you dare use that word again. And I am going. I have had enough of you. Go and fuck Priya for all I care. I just wish that someday *she* cheats on you. I will never call you again,' she said and got up to leave, expecting me to stop her.

'Even if you call, I will never pick it up,' I said and broke the relationship in a snap. I was beaming with happiness. She was gone, without even making an attempt to make things right.

I opened my laptop, and checked my mailbox. There was just one unread mail titled 'User Interface Designs <3' from Shikha. She had gone without even asking me to pay for the designs that she had just mailed. With her not-so-amiable relation with either of the co-founders, she couldn't bother us about the money anymore. Moreover, since we hadn't signed any agreement for she trusted me so much, YourQuote wasn't liable to pay her for her services.

I went to meet Priya with a red rose hidden in my bag, and left for Gurgaon where she had shifted from Vishwavidyalaya after having resumed her job.

'Do you really love me?' she asked me. We were meeting in one of Gurgaon's many posh malls.

I nodded and kissed her palm to ask for forgiveness. She placed her fingers on my lips and said, 'One needs an apology only when one does not have a heart.' As a reflex, I grabbed her hands and took her to the basement of the mall that was relatively deserted. There, in perfect silence, I knelt down and proposed to her, officially for the first time, with a poem that she had written long back for me.

> Through long years
> Laughter and tears
> I have loved you
> I have lost you
> And again I have found you
> And now, my heart
> And soul are bound to you

I saw her crying tears of joy. I could not believe she was finally back in my life.

No Time For Love

It was late July. Priya was back in my life. Mishra and I had introduced several new engaging features based around the concept of wit on our social media pages where we were receiving immense participation, Rishabh had accelerated his marketing endeavours and we had stopped doing T-shirts altogether since there were already too many players in the market selling the same product.

July saw us meeting many investors and mentors for attaining feedback and the more people we met, the more we realized the value of scale. Scale, in its real sense, is the ability of a business to keep growing in size in terms of revenue, customers, adding more value to the product as time passes, and sometimes being able to tweak the revenue model in later stage without adversely affecting the business.

Good entrepreneurs are always ready to tweak their revenue model to make it more scalable, grow in size, and become more profitable. Size matters! If you are talking about dreams, then certainly it does. Size and scale was the chief reason why Myntra shifted from being a customized merchandize seller to branded merchandize retailer, and also why Flipkart expanded beyond just books.

Upon realizing the evident limiting factor, we began brainstorming for another revenue model and shut down our cumbersome T-shirt business. We delved on our thoughts keeping in mind our two key strengths—creativity and technology. We had a creative pool of around 20,000 people attached on our social media pages and we knew that our new business model would revolve around the creativity of these people. After three hours of discussion, I had a brilliant idea. We could crowdsource creative content such as taglines, brand names, and advertising ideas for corporates, thus accomplishing our basic mission of awarding people for coming up with just one line, together with solving the corporate customer's need at an inexpensive price. The revenue model seemed to be lucrative because it didn't require us dealing with uneducated and unethical manufacturers but highly professional corporates. Moreover, we just needed users to scale up and this one-of-its-kind service where users got rewarded for writing just one line was bound to go viral.

We froze the business model after getting a green signal from our mentors and began working on the contest page where we would hold such a crowdsourcing contest. We scheduled the beta version launch of our website on August 4 and shifted gears.

⌐⊏⊐

In mid-July, Rishabh joined the company full-time and shifted from IIT after finishing his project. It was then that he came face to face with the money crisis that was brewing at our office-cum-home. It is only after coming out of college that one truly becomes an entrepreneur, when one has to pay huge bills, which otherwise were out of picture in dorms with cheap food and stay.

Thankfully, Priya had started earning and was kind enough to sponsor all our dates, but even our dates were so irregular—once in two weeks or so. Maggi was replaced with bread, hotel and movie outings were replaced with occasional sitcoms on laptop, and Rishabh's petrol bill and phone bill for marketing was split into two. Mishra witnessed it all but never offered any financial help, which strengthened our belief that he wanted us to consider him as an employee, rather than a partner. We still hadn't been able to figure out his incentive. Was it exposure? Or experience? Or the challenge of building a social networking website? We didn't know. Mishra went back home on July 17 to spend two weeks with his family.

Not borrowing any money from our parents, we started living life on the edge. We worked our asses off at night and intentionally slept late and woke up to brunch, thus skipping our breakfast, saving around a hundred rupees each morning i.e. 3,000 rupees each month.

⌐⊂

In the last week of July, my sister Saumya, who was four years younger to me, took admission in DU. Though our parents wanted the two of us to stay together, as it would minimize the costs as well as ensure security, I put their wishes on hold saying that the company was my priority.

On the night of July 29, I had gone to meet my sister after setting her up in a PG in South Extension. After settling her into the new hostel, I took her for dinner outside. It was while we were having dinner in a restaurant in South Ex, I received a message from Rishabh asking me to come as late as possible saying that he had called his friend over and she would feel awkward in my company. It was the first personal request from him in days. I agreed to do as he said but was curious to know what was cooking. So I left for home without informing him.

As soon as I reached home, I noticed Rishabh standing at the door talking to someone. It was none other than Shikha!

There could not have been a bigger shock than that. Shikha, the slut who could not wait to pounce on another man after a less-than-a-month old break up. I could just cringe in absolute misery and self pity for having fallen for that bitch.

⌁

August is the month when most colleges reopen in Delhi.

August was also the month when Mishra went back to college after two months with us, the month of Rishabh's unofficial girlfriend Anjali's return from Toronto, and the month when the co-founders of YourQuote scheduled their product launch.

It was our third launch and we planned to make it grand. The first launch had failed because we could not include as much functionality as that available on Facebook. The second failed because we didn't have a sticky UI and users who were addicted to Facebook were not willing to shift. We were hopeful about the third one because of a variety of reasons—we had a sticky UI as promised by Shikha and gamified network and contests that would reward people for coming up with just one line for the first time in the history of internet.

For the contest, Click2Closet—the fashion e-commerce company where Mishra interned—agreed to gift a Fossil watch worth 22,000 rupees to the winner. What more could we have asked for? That was enough to create a buzz.

The launch on 4th was grander than what we had expected and we created a furore in our IIT network. We received floods of congratulatory wishes from juniors, friends, and batchmates who appreciated the concept, the engagement built around our brand, and the UI.

At night, we planned a grand party for all our team members, even the useless ones, at Yo! China in Vasant Vihar followed by a dance-cum-drinks gig at a nearby nightclub. Rishabh was insistent on inviting Shikha as well, saying that she had been instrumental in making the launch a success.

I had invited Priya for the party and bringing the two together didn't seem like the right thing to do. But I couldn't say a word. Rishabh called up Shikha to purposefully invite her in front of me. I stood there helpless, praying to God to either destroy all the mobile phones in the world or take me away from the inevitable. Thankfully, Shikha declined to come.

The party ended with great gusto. Seeing Priya laugh after so long made me cry. How could I have cheated on her? Bleary-eyed, with utmost sincerity and conviction, I resolved that I would never hurt her again. Never.

The next few days were pretty hectic. There was a great difference between the first day traffic that had registered on the site 5000 unique hits to the second day traffic which was merely 700. The statistics deteriorated with every passing day and on the fifth day we received only about 100 unique hits. When we announced on our social media pages that we would not be entertaining quotes on our Facebook page but on the website instead, there was great discord among our users who complained that our website sucked.

I took control of the situation and resolved to make our users see the problems that we were facing. I wrote a very moving letter and posted it on our fan page:

A Note from YourQuote founders

It's always very difficult to accept change—good or bad.

It was around one year four months ago that we started this webpage with a determination to convert our creative idea into a full-fledged business venture. We didn't sit for placements, left the lucrative job offers that our alma mater had to offer us to pursue YQ. Let me tell you that at that point of time, we didn't have a technical team, we didn't have great traction to keep us motivated, and neither did we have any quick way to make money to sustain the venture. We were bootstrapped. We were strugglers.

We lacked a good technical team and we struggled for more than ten months to find out the right guy who had interest and expertize in web development. But our persistence triumphed and we found the right guy. A technical maven who was passionate about our idea. We shared the same dream and we started working on the website. It took us almost four months to build the website from scratch. We revamped the UI, introduced many networking features, and relaunched in August. This time it was different. Traction was on its high. We had about 10,000 page views within just four days.

But we are now facing a grave problem. We are trying to compete with our Facebook page. And everyone knows that comparing the usability of FB with YQ, it would take us another month or so to actually bring adequate features to keep you hooked to us.

We, the founders of YQ, appeal to all our users to kindly embrace us and try to help us grow and prosper with your detailed feedback to perfect the website architecture. We could see many people complain that they preferred the fan page over the website, and understandably so. But do know this that we have been working full time tirelessly for the last one year and have made no money at all—neither for you, nor for us—from the amazing surges of creativity that you people displayed on our fan page. Our FB page didn't allow us a compilation of our individual quotes, a way to compare them with each other, a copyright to be able to market them, an effective way to handle plagiarism, and so on.

We urge you to be a little more patient with us and constantly help us improve.

Sincerely,
Amol Sabharwal
Rishabh Dev
Co-founders, yourquote.in

The letter worked. Around 500 of our active fan page users became our benefactors and started using the website on a daily basis, curating good content and bringing in more people from their network.

Starting off is easy. The difficult part is to sustain growth after establishment. Thanks to Mishra, we had got our first client. The real difficulty appeared a week after we launched our first contest. The submission phase was going to be over and we needed to find another client. Rishabh's marketing mettle was to be tested as we eyed a big player. He hit numerous offices, from a prominent automobile company to one of the most popular beer brands, but without any success. All of them rejected us saying that we were too small a venture to add any value to them.

Frustrated, he asked me to accompany him to IIT to meet some of our team members. After the meeting, we dashed into the Diptea kiosk at the institute and observed its vague tagline 'Diptea can do that!' which neither had any appeal for students nor made any sense to us. The next day, Rishabh went early, determined to find a paying client.

'We would have to do a contest for free again. The famous coffee chain Coffee Every Day is ready, provided we do it for free. They would sponsor the prize though,' Rishabh informed me as soon he returned back home.

'Go for it. Coffee Every Day is the biggest coffee lounge chain in North India. So adding them to our client list would enhance our portfolio and help us in fetching future deals.'

'Right, I have already said a yes to them,' he said, thinking. 'Wait, I have got an idea.'

'What?'

'Why should we wait for future deals? Let's do it now!'

Rishabh contacted all the people whom he had met during his marketing stint and returned with a jubilous smile on his face.

'We have a paying client now: Diptea—10,000 rupees,' he said.

'Wow! How did you manage that?'

'Simple. I told them that Coffee Every Day is doing a campaign to engage the youth of all premium colleges in

India on our website at 20,000 rupees, but since Diptea is our home brand at IIT, we were willing to give them a twenty-five percent discount.'

'But a twenty-five percent discount makes it 15,000 rupees,' I said.

'Yes, and the 5,000 went down in bargaining.'

'Wow.' I was proud of Rishabh; his talent was not just limited to negotiating with rowdy manufacturers but also corporate professionals.

But he wasn't finished at that. Over the course of the next few minutes, I just remained a mute spectator to his genius. He convinced Coffee Every Day to give us 20,000 rupees for the contest with just one simple argument that its competitor Cafe House had agreed to do a contest with us for 18,000 rupees. With brands like Diptea already finalized and having a fan page boasting 20000+ fans, Rishabh's lie about the Cafe House deal had so much conviction and confidence that Coffee Every Day didn't doubt our claim and instead, offered a higher quote than the fictitious 18,000 rupees for the contest, with the contract that we would not do Cafe House's contest for the next one year. Rishabh was more than happy to agree, for there was no Cafe House contest in the first place and said to me, 'Marketing is all about using one client to get other clients, by hook or crook.'

I was so thrilled by whatever I had witnessed that I jumped and hugged Rishabh.

⊏⪽

The coming week was absolutely brilliant. When people saw recognized brands like Diptea and Coffee Every Day on our fledgling portal, they were stunned. Thanks to the big brands and their catchy prizes, even our website started boasting of decent traffic.

During that time, a journalist from *News Today* approached us. She wanted to take our interview. We didn't know whether we were ready or not and decided to discuss the issue with our mentors. One of our mentors advised us not to get carried away with media coverage as they were mere distractions during the growth stage of the company and would take our minds off the imminent task. But when we told him that the interview might help us get investors, he told us to go ahead with it.

The next day, a half page interview carrying Rishabh and my photograph appeared in the newspaper. We were to the point in the interview and did not give too much information away.

A few hours after the interview appeared, we started seeing an unprecedented activity on our website. There was humongous traffic coming in and we couldn't trace the reason behind it. It couldn't have been the small article in the newspaper, could it? Later Pratik called me from his office to congratulate me. He had joined RBS.

'Bro, congratulations. Every person in my office is asking me whether I know you guys or not?'

'Wow, thank you so much. Did they read the newspaper?'

'Newspaper? Which one? No, you guys are on the Yahoo homepage.'

'What!?' I exclaimed.

'Yes, haven't you checked it?' he said.

I logged on Yahoo and there we were—one of the top 50 newsmakers of the day, which said 'IITians launch a site to market wisecracks.'

Numerous calls, messages, and tags followed. My batchmates who had booed us when we left our placements held us in awe now. The cynics had turned into a joke themselves with their lousy and boring-as-hell jobs, and people were now marvelling at our foresight.

People flooded our website, from just two people online in the morning to three hundred online at the same time, when our modest servers crashed. In fact, there were so many posts that day that the website itself went down. We didn't know whether to be happy or sad about it.

Immediately, we proceeded to buy dedicated servers with my Dad's credit card that cost us 16,000 rupees for a month's usage, an expense which we didn't even bother to discuss before purchasing, and Mishra tried to fix the website. The website took full two days to recuperate, data recovery being the sole reason, and two days later, we found that the buzz was lost and our traffic had dropped back to original. Now we couldn't afford to put the website down once again and downgrade it to the basic server, so we let it remain the way it was. In the meanwhile, Mishra tried to find an alternative way to host the website. And he did.

Amazon Cloud infrastructure is very congenial for start-ups as it offers one year of free service for start-up with charges only when your usage exceeds a threshold. After being hosted on the dedicated server for over two weeks and incurring a cost of around 8,000 rupees, we brought our website down for another two days and shifted it to Amazon Cloud server.

With the feature on *News Today* and Yahoo, we just gained 500 users but we lost two weeks of developmental work, 8,000 rupees, and our sleep at night. We could not generate interest among investors, but we did fetch more media attention. A journalist from the *Times of India* approached us the next day but we ignored her.

What all this did do was escalate our self worth. While earlier we presented ourselves meekly in front of our batchmates who were earning a lakh a month, we now went to meet them proudly. I was more carried away with this feeling than Rishabh and I openly criticized my friends for not having enough gumption to trudge the path of their dreams. I started making up derogatory quotes like 'Success means the ability to go to your office in your boxers', 'Ironically, now rats chase CAT!', and 'One doesn't need an MBA to hire other MBAs.'

When some of my friends announced about their selection in IIMs on Facebook and got 200-300 likes for it, I intentionally updated my status with 'I'm going to IIM-A this year, to hire,' and overshadowed each one of them with 450+ likes.

My friends who would earlier complain to me about not giving them ample time were suddenly repulsed by me and stopped hanging out with me altogether. Ravi, my best friend, once hinted subtly to me about my change in behaviour and said, 'You have suddenly changed after college.' I replied without much thinking, 'Yeah, any kind of change is good.' He finished off by saying 'Change is good only when the change is good. Do you…'

I dismissed his statement by whistling and cutting him mid-sentence.

⌁

On August 21, Anjali returned to India. Unlike the time when she had gone to Toronto, this time Rishabh didn't even bother to go and receive her. When she reached the hostel, she called me first. But I knew the real purpose of her call was not to greet me and ask after my well-being but to inquire whether Rishabh was home or not. I disappointed her by telling her that Rishabh was out for a meeting. When Rishabh returned in the evening, I told him that Anjali had returned. He pretended as though he hadn't heard a word. I repeated my sentence but he took offence and snapped at me, remarking, 'I'm not deaf. I heard what you said.'

'Don't you want to meet her?'

'Amol, what I want to do and what I don't want to do with my life is none of your concern. I would be grateful if you mind your own business.'

'Sure, but all I was asking you was to meet an important team member of ours together, not alone,' I said. He didn't respond and went to the balcony to smoke.

The best way to find out about the relation between two people is through Facebook. When I spied a little, I found that Rishabh was neither friends with Shikha nor Anjali. Something must have happened between the three, a mystery I could not trace.

In the evening, Anjali abruptly turned up at our place. She greeted me with a hug and an extravagant smile. She had even brought a gift for me—a University of Toronto mug. I was touched. Rishabh was still working in another room and did not come out, even though I knew he must have heard Anjali's voice. She told me she had come to make things right, which delighted me as I hoped that Rishabh's sour mood would mellow after things were sorted between them. Anjali went into Rishabh's room while I remained seated on the sofa outside, trying my best to eavesdrop on their conversation.

The next fifty minutes were nothing less than a movie. At first I couldn't hear a thing. A few minutes later, I heard mild sobs followed by the sound of someone whispering. It finally ended with what sounded like Anjali's outburst. The door flung open and Anjali came out in a fit of madness and left the house in tears. I ran after her and helped get her an auto, without either of us saying a word.

⊏⊏⊐

One week later, Anjali called me and asked me to get a number of an administrative officer of AIIMS from Rishabh. Worried, I asked Anjali about what was wrong with her health. She told me that the slight childhood accident burn she had on her neck was causing her distress lately and she wanted to get it operated upon through plastic surgery. I wondered the reason behind her sudden decision.

Apparently, Rishabh had a relative working in AIIMS who could make the process faster, which otherwise would have taken months. I asked for the number from Rishabh. Concerned, he asked me if I was alright. I told him that it was Anjali who wanted the number, not me. He smsed the number to me with a blank face, which I passed on to Anjali.

My doubt about Anjali's sudden surgery remained a mystery, until I met Pratik the following day. Pratik, who had been a good friend to Anjali, was aware of most things going on between Rishabh and Anjali.

'Why has she suddenly decided to go for plastic surgery?' I asked Pratik.

'What? Has she? She told me that she would go for one before she joins a job since her parents wanted her to complete

196

her studies first. Wait, has there been a fight between the two of them?'

'Yes, a severe fight.'

'Last year, she had told me that when she had confessed her love to Rishabh, he did not reciprocate, leaving her heartbroken. Thereafter, whenever I asked about her relationship status, she kept telling me that Rishabh won't ever say yes since he wants a "hot" girl.'

'Oh my goodness! She's doing the operation to please Rishabh,' I realized.

The next day when I was logged on to Facebook to type out the next sermon of the day, one particular News Feed caught my eye:

Rishabh Dev is now friends with Anjali Yadav

I smiled. Things seemed to be getting better between the two. Minutes later, Rishabh came out from the bathroom well dressed and informed me that he was going to AIIMS to get an appointment from the doctor for Anjali's operation. I wished him luck. When he was gone, I checked his friend list looking for Shikha's name on it. She was not there. I sighed in relief thinking she was finally out of our lives, YourQuote's life, without charging money for her designs, unless Rishabh paid her privately for her 'services'.

⊏⊐

It had been two months since Priya started working at EWZ. Though her salary was meagre, it allowed her to take care of all the smaller expenses to fulfill her everyday needs.

Initially, though, she hated her work, but with time, she adapted well and started enjoying going to work. The good thing was that her best friend Kamna was a co-employee and to add to the charm, Shardendu, one of my department mates and a good friend, who could make any girl croon 'Aww, so cute', worked in the same department as theirs. Kamna had a big crush on Shardendu right from our fest days almost two years ago when both Kamna and Priya had come over to IIT and I had introduced them to Shendu, as we used to call him. Moreover, Pratik who had been a good friend to both Priya and me, had his RBS office right across EWZ and they would meet every day during lunch hours.

In the last two months, the friendship between the four of them had strengthened and Priya hinted to me one several occasions that Kamna had fallen truly, madly, and deeply in love with Shendu, but nobody knew how Shendu felt. Owing to the corporate nature of her job, another thing had changed in Priya's life—her propensity to drink. She often took a sip or two in their weekend office parties and accompanied Kamna and Shendu to bars and lounges for drink sessions.

A little vexed at her rampant alcoholism, I pleaded to Priya to cut down on her drinking, but she retorted saying, 'Amol, I have never been so free ever. When I was a child, my mother dictated my life. I'm an adult now and earning my own living. So stop trying to be my mother.'

Hurt by her statement, I replied, 'If that's what you feel, you're free to do as you please. All I know is that girls become vulnerable when they are inebriated and guys can easily take advantage.'

'Don't you trust Shendu or Pratik? They are your good friends and are like my brothers,' she said.

'I trust them,' I said thinking, 'but not their friends, who might turn up with them.'

The next night, Priya called me at 2 am and whispered, 'Amol, chatpat news! Wake up. Kamna is making out with Shendu. I can hear them moaning.'

More than voyeuristic delight, it raised an alarm bell in my mind. 'What are you doing at Shendu's place?' I asked her.

'We went to a bar near his place and it was late, so...'

'How drunk are you?'

'Not at all, I just had a breezer. Okay, talk to you later. Gotta go,' she said and hung up.

I tossed and turned on my bed the entire night, concerned.

The next day, I got a call from my mother saying she was going to be visiting me in Delhi for her PhD dissertation. Ever since I was born, her ambitions had taken a backseat. But her love for academics had made her slowly add four degrees to her resume viz. NET, B.Ed, M.Ed, and she was now on the verge of completing her PhD.

She told me she was going to stay with me at our office-cum-flat for a week. When I reluctantly conveyed the matter to Rishabh, he readily complied and said that he had no problem with her staying with us. He anyway used to stay out for 14-16 hours a day and would come only late at night to sleep and again leave early in the morning. The only thing for him to be merry about was the sumptuous morning breakfast that my mother would make for us.

September 4

'Anjali will have her operation day after,' Rishabh said at the breakfast table. My mother had arrived a day earlier and was preparing hot aloo paranthas for us. Even Mishra had come over as it was a Sunday. 'She will be admitted tomorrow evening,' Rishabh added.

'What happened to her?' my mother asked while placing another parantha on my plate. She had previously met Anjali during my convocation.

'Aunty, you might have noticed that she had a slight burn on her neck. She is now getting it reconstructed through plastic surgery. She will be discharged from the hospital by September 8.' Rishabh explained.

'Oh, is there someone from her family coming here?'

'Yes, her father will be arriving shortly,' Rishabh said.

'Where will he be staying?' I asked Rishabh.

'At the hospital for a few days and then he would take up accommodation at some hotel near IIT.'

'Why should he stay at some hotel? He could come here, and until Anjali is completely healed, even bring her here. Why should she lay at her hostel all alone, without anyone to look after her?'

Rishabh's eyes shined with gratitude. The next day Anjali's father arrived. He was very humble and treated me like his own son. After a filling lunch at our place, I took him to AIIMS, where Anjali had been admitted, as Rishabh was already there attending to her and signing off all the paperwork. Late night, when the nurses advised that only one attendant was needed, Rishabh asked her father to return home with me, volunteering to stay at the hospital for the night himself. Anjali's father politely thanked Rishabh for his concern but told him to go home instead.

Rishabh left early morning for the hospital the following day. My mother and I joined him at the hospital shortly after her presentation at JNU got over to a thunderous applause. When we arrived, we were told that the operation had been a success.

We went to see Anjali who had bandages wrapped all across her neck. Interestingly, Rishabh was sitting just next to her with his hands on her forehead, while uncle sat on a chair near the bed. Amused, my mother looked at me with curiosity.

On the way back, my mother quizzed me, 'Are they going to get married soon?' I just chuckled in response.

Anjali was shortly discharged from the hospital and her father went to bring her home. Before she could arrive, my mother took it upon herself to clean the house. I helped her out in the process and cleaned the other rooms.

'Amol, I'm putting all your fresh clothes in your suitcase.'

'Okay Mom,' I shouted from the other room.

'Amol, Amol, Amol, come here,' she squalled. I ran crazily to the other room, thinking that she might have come across a rat.

'What is this in your suitcase?' she interrogated. When I turned my eyes to what she held in her hand, I froze in terror. Embarassed, I grabbed the orange packet from her hand and stood like a statue in front of her.

'Mom, it's not mine. It's Mishra's. He had put it in my suitcase because his father had come over and I forgot to return it to him,' I mumbled a not-so-convincing lie while beads of sweat ran down my face.

'I can't believe you. While we stay a thousand kilometers away, hoping that our son is working hard on his dreams, this is what you people are up to. Shameful!' she chided.

I had never felt so bad in my entire life. All my pursuits had been followed with just one intent in mind—making my parents proud of me. It was the first time my mother's head lowered in shame because of me. Before I could explain or apologize, none of which seemed to set things right, the doorbell rang.

It was Anjali. My mother ran to the door and guided Anjali to one of the rooms. She fed her khichdi with her hands, took her to the loo, and gave her the required medicines from time to time. I was a little jealous of the care my mother was bestowing upon her and I blamed it on my insolence for losing my mother's tenderness that was reserved just for me.

Two days later, my mother got ready to go back to Dhanbad, our hometown, and I went to drop her at the railway station. She didn't speak about the discovery all through the way. Just when the train was about to depart, I touched her feet seeking her blessings and she said, 'You are a young man now. Concentrate your energies on making your life first and then do whatever you want.' I was at a loss for words.

The Birth of a Competitor

The month of September saw slow progress in our venture. We were finding it difficult in getting other corporates interested in our site as our previous clients—Diptea and Coffee Every Day—were not satisfied with our services. We had received only around 250 entries for the contest whereas we had promised them that we would get around 2000+ entries at least. It was a difficult situation for Rishabh who faced rejection after rejection and we had to entertain more barter deals with websites that were popular.

It was during this time that I decided to try my luck in the marketing domain. Being an established author by then, I was well-connected with almost all the other popular authors around. I decided to take the next step in our creative endeavour by crowdsourcing the title of an upcoming book. Since we had closed our doors to the media, the growth was in no way comparable to the one we saw the last month. However, it did get one notable private equity company interested in us.

Purnesh, from Excel Ventures, one of the major International Venture Capital firms that had invested in almost all the Indian entrepreneurial success stories, dropped a mail saying, 'With one promising venture and two bestselling

books at just 22 years of age, you are living my dream.' I
corrected him by telling him that I was just 21 years of age and
would turn 22 in a few days' time.

Purnesh wanted an investment PPT which we didn't
have prepared by then. It sent the three of us thinking about
whether we were ready for investment. We realized that we
weren't ready and asked Purnesh to give us a month's time to
prepare. He told us to have the pitch ready by the first week
of November.

September 18

It was a Sunday, two days before my birthday. We hardly
did any office work on Sundays, as most of the marketing
and outreach work is not possible. But there was something
unusual about that particular Sunday. Right from morning,
I could see Rishabh was up to something fishy. Every time a
call came, he would go to the balcony to attend it.

When I came out after taking a bath, I was greeted by a
bunch of people in the drawing room. Priya, Pratik, Rishabh,
Anjali, Kamna and Shardendu—it seemed like they were
all up to something, but I couldn't fathom what. I couldn't
understand why they were all there until Pratik and Rishabh
lifted me by the legs and asked the others to join them in
giving me birthday bumps!

They had come to celebrate my birthday on Sunday itself
for weekdays were usually busy. I was charmed and thanked
each one of them for planning it.

I asked them whether I could call my sister Saumya as
well, but they reluctantly said, 'You might not want to call

her,' and showed me three bottles of vodka and five cans of beer. Had it not been my birthday, I would have been annoyed at them having brought alcohol. But since they had brought it, they were to drink it, and they had paid for it, it didn't bother me. To my dislike, Priya gulped around six pegs of vodka and because of my friends, I couldn't say a word. Within a few minutes, she was already drunk out of her mind.

All of them left for the drawing room leaving Priya behind with me. She came forward and embraced me, saying, 'Happy birthday, sugar,' and gave me a quick kiss on the lips.

'Thank you for the surprise,' I said.

Anjali came into the room a few minutes later and said, 'Shikha asked me to give you this packet.'

My blood froze at the mere mention of Shikha's name. I put the packet inside the cupboard and thanked Anjali, who left the room. I kept staring at Priya to gauge her reaction.

'Amol, are you still in touch with that bitch?' Priya interrogated sternly.

'Not at all. I have told you this before. Ever since I came back into your life, I have never spoken to her.'

'Let us see what that bitch has sent for you?'

'Leave it. Let's throw it in the dustbin. She doesn't matter to us now, does she?' I argued but she didn't care to listen. She opened the cupboard and unwrapped the gift packet, only to find that it was a Gabriel Garcia Marquez book that Shikha had asked me to read long back.

She looked at me, appalled, and opened the first page that carried a handwritten note, 'To love, from yours truly.' She looked at me in disgust and hurled the book towards me. I didn't bother catching it to show that it meant nothing to me.

'You asshole, you bloody cheated on me,' she screamed and burst into tears.

'Please don't scream. There are other people in the house.'

'Get away from me, you cheat,' she yelled at the top of her voice. Pratik, Anjali, and Shendu came running towards me on hearing the commotion.

'Ask him to get away from me. This scoundrel cheated on me. Ask him to get lost,' she shouted.

'Okay, I'm going. Please don't create a scene anymore,' I said. She threw a photo frame that carried my mother's and my photo at me, which broke into pieces. She then took her bag and rushed outside.

The assault didn't stop there. She called me on her way out and screamed, 'You son of a bitch, how could you cheat on me? Now see what I do to you!'

'Priya, calm down. It was my birthday party and you ruined it. Why did you have to break the photo frame that had my mother's photo?'

'You son of a whore,' she screamed.

'I'm breaking up with you. Go to hell for all I care,' I hanged up the phone in disgust. She kept calling me time and again. Having lost my patience, I switched off my phone.

Two hours later, there were a dozen sorry messages from Priya in my inbox. One of them said, 'I'm sorry for losing my temper. I was drunk. I won't ever drink again and I will make it up to you on your birthday, I promise. Please give me one last chance.'

I softened a bit and replied, 'Okay, but please don't call me till my birthday. I will return to Malviya Nagar on my birthday—the 20th morning.'

September 20

Generally, birthdays in Delhi are lavish parties full of booze, dance, and non-vegetarian food. But me being penniless, I had chosen to make it special in my own way. It was a weekday and Rishabh had gone for some meeting with clients. Priya had taken a day off for me so I invited her and my sister Saumya for a lunch party where I cooked for both of them. Shahi paneer, basmati rice, dal, and salad. Simple fare.

Priya looked surprised at how easily I had let go of the fight between us two days ago and didn't even mention it once to her. After lunch, my sister left for her PG leaving Priya and me behind. Priya sat in front of me, looking at me intently. Her eyes seemed to seek forgiveness.

'Amol,' she came towards me, clasped her hands in mine and said, 'I'm so...'

'Don't...' I said hugging her, 'don't ruin this moment.'

My phone rang all of a sudden and I had to let go of her gentle embrace. It was Shikha and I showed it to Priya. She showed no signs of anger this time and asked me to hand over the phone to her. I reluctantly complied.

'Amol is busy. What do you have to say?' I heard Priya say on the phone. 'Okay, I will convey this to him,.. No, he doesn't want to talk to you...Yes, I'm pretty sure about it.'

I wondered why Shikha had called so suddenly after three months. Did she call to wish me Happy Birthday?

I went and sat on the edge of the bed in my room. There was something sticking out from beneath the mattress. I pulled it out and saw that it was the Marquez book that Shikha had gifted me, ripped apart completely. I pulled the tattered pages out, one by one, and looked at them horrified.

Priya returned from the call with a triumphant smile and on seeing the tattered book in my hand, she immediately grabbed it.

'Why did you have to tear that book apart?' I asked her.

'Because I hate that damn bitch and want to burn everything about her in your life.'

'Then tomorrow you might wish to burn my website down, for it has been designed by her,' I retaliated. She remained silent.

'You always assure me that you have forgiven me about everything, but your actions tell me that you haven't,' I said.

'I have forgiven you, but I haven't forgiven her for spoiling our relationship,' she said.

'Right now, you are spoiling our relationship by bringing things from my past to the fore,' I said and continued with brutal honesty. 'And you know what, she didn't spoil our relationship, I did. I took advantage of her. Look, can we just forget about this and move on for good?'

Priya came forward and hugged me, apologizing for having lost her cool yet again. To ensure that Priya was indeed cool once and for all, I took permission from her to send a sorry message to Shikha, thus redeeming myself of my guilt of using her and assuring Priya that I was loyal to her.

By the end of September, things started moving for us work-wise. The contest section was more or less streamlined—not with big clients like Diptea, but small and medium-sized clients like start-ups and authors instead.

It was during this time that we were shortlisted among the Top 20 for the Global Student Entrepreneur Awards

(GSEA) and it called for one of us to represent the venture at Coimbatore, where they would announce the top 3. As I had applied on behalf of our company, the invitation came in my name. When the matter was brought in front of Rishabh, he asserted that both of us should go for he couldn't afford to miss this marketing opportunity where he could get clients for our contest page. We called the GSEA authorities but they didn't allow the two of us to come. It was not the first difficult situation that we faced, but it was the first situation where our being partners with equal designation and equity failed us. We had two options—either a toss or one of us giving in. A toss seemed too immature to both of us and Rishabh, with his exceptional negotiation skills, convinced me that if he represented us at the contest, it would be more beneficial for the venture.

I chose to remain back at home, doing all the homework like investment PPTs, financial analysis, business plan preparation, etc. The only incentive for me remaining at home was that Priya could stay at my place for a week.

Early October, while Rishabh was away for the GSEA contest, I received an invitation to speak at a Youth to Business Forum organized by a prominent student NGO. I happily accepted the invitation and went to speak at the conclave on October 2 along with Mishra who sat in the audience. I talked about how I had tussled between different choices, societal pressure, and personal ambition and at last chose the road of entrepreneurship. I also highlighted how the imminent future for entrepreneurs is full of struggle that deters many who want to pursue it, but the distant future which an entrepreneur envisions promises the bliss of achievement and financial freedom.

After the talk, there was a question and answer session. Having answered a dozen or so questions till then, I was just about to sit when I noticed that Mishra's hand was raised. I asked him to go ahead and ask his question.

'So you mean to say that people who are employees are not living their life to the fullest?' Mishra asked. It was a tricky question, for even though I believed so, I couldn't say that in front of everyone.

'It all depends on what you aspire for. For people who aspire for security, jobs are best suited. But if you aspire to be the master of your own life, have the talent to run your own venture, start-up now,' I answered, hoping I had succeeded in saving my skin.

'How was it?' I asked Mishra after the show.

'Very inspiring, very moving,' he replied.

October 3-9

Priya had come to stay with me for a few days. On one of these days when she returned from her office she seemed low. I went to the kitchen to make her some tea. When I returned, she was busy on the phone. I thought it was Kamna and started making sensuous noises to tease her. She freaked out and kicked me hard in the shins and disconnected the call hurriedly. 'Don't ever do anything like this when I'm on call with my mother,' she said.

'Oh, when did your mother start speaking with you? You didn't tell me about it,' I asked. She remained silent.

'Answer me.'

'I didn't tell you because my mother had never stopped talking to me.'

'What about your confession to them about me?'

'I never told them about you. I lied to you. It's as simple as that,' she ended and left the house.

I was deeply grieved. I went looking for Rishabh's cigarette packet and found it in one of the kitchen closets. A moment later, I was standing in the balcony, puffing my misery away.

Five cigarettes down, the gruesome memories of the past haunted me. I called her up and questioned, 'How could you have lied to me?'

'I don't know,' she said sleepily and hung up.

I called her again, this time in a better mood.

'Priya, I just realized something.'

'Amol, can we talk about whatever it is later, please?'

'No, listen to me. This will be our last conversation.'

'What?' she said in a nonchalant manner.

'I want to break up with you—not because of the lie, but because I want to be on my own completely. I want to discover things on my own. I don't want to do something *with* someone or *for* someone.'

'If this is because of the fact that I lied to you, then please tell me. I know I can't change that and I can't dare speak with my mother about you even now, because you don't know my mother. She will marry me off immediately if she gets to know about our relationship.'

'But why couldn't you tell this to me earlier?'

'Were you in a mood to listen at that time? It was my only way of having you back in my life. But I can't do anything about it now,' she said in a voice bereft of hope.

'Let's end this misery of lies, betrayal, and what-not,' I said.

'As you wish,' she said plainly.

'You are free to date whoever you wish to, you are free to fall in love with anyone else. I'm not holding you. I'm just taking a break and I won't be dating anyone, I can assure you that. I don't want to get trapped once again,' I added so as to ensure that I didn't hinder her liberty in any sense.

'Okay.'

'You can call me in case you need me for anything, but I won't be calling you for sure,' I said, keeping up my chatter only to vex her some more.

'It's okay, Amol. Now please let me go,' she said.

'You know why I decided to get back with you? Because I couldn't see you so hapless, not because I wanted to be with you,' I kept my panic mode on. I didn't know whether I was trying to convince her or myself by coming up with one logical explanation after another.

This time, she didn't bother to take my shit and ended the call. It was abrupt but I had no option other than to accept it. I had just given her my word that I won't call her. So I didn't. I *couldn't*.

We have had break ups for the silliest reasons in the past— once when I refused to meet her on a lazy Sunday, she broke up with me saying that I didn't love her much; at another time, I broke up with her when she had called one of my relatives 'dumb', which he actually was, but she still hadn't the right, did she? In our first year, I had also broken up on a philosophical reason much like now, where I argued that I didn't deserve to waste my father's hard earned money on her, and should be spending it on my family instead. Though after a day or two, things would always return back to normal, for we were too habitual to each other and couldn't imagine a life where either of us was missing from the equation. Such kind of break ups had been a part of our lives and I inwardly knew that my resolve would weaken soon and I would be back to normal.

October 11

Rishabh had returned from Coimbatore. Unlike what he had promised, he couldn't find any clients for the contest. I didn't quiz him this time. I didn't want to blame him when I didn't know the whole truth.

Rishabh informed me that a TV channel had covered him during the show and a two-minute interview was going to air on TV quite soon. It made me go green with envy.

Rishabh's interview was to appear on October 26 on one of the major news channels. He had never exhibited more pride before as he informed all his friends and even made me post on our fan page for our followers to tune in to the news channel fifteen days in advance and catch him speaking about our venture. On seeing the announcement, my parents called me up to ask why I didn't go to Coimbatore with him and why Rishabh was taking the lead over me. I had no answer for them.

In the afternoon, Mishra dropped in at our place.

'Rishabh, what do I mean to YourQuote?' Mishra said out of the blue.

'What do you mean?' I asked him with curiosity.

'I have been thinking about my place in the team for quite some time now. So am I the co-founder of the venture or not?'

'Ha! Of course you are. Why do you even need to ask this question? Let's get back to work,' Rishabh said.

'Rishabh, don't evade my question,' said Mishra bluntly.

'Okay, tell me what exactly do you want?' We were too stunned to think it through.

'I just want to know my exact incentive. Why should I continue to work with you guys? What's in it for me? Outside, you guys introduce me as the CTO whereas you call yourselves the Co-founder Directors,' he said in an accusatory tone.

'Why are you asking me this now?' I questioned.

'That's because we are working on the project full time and I want my role clearly defined,' he said. 'Without me, there would have been no website in the first place.'

'Tell me what you want,' Rishabh said.

'I have a lot of offers in hand. Click2Closet is offering me a position of CTO. There are other foreign start-ups with a lot more to offer that are interested in hiring me, but since I have been working with you, I give you the right to make me want to stay. I want—in equity and designation— whatever you think is apt for me and I will compare it with other offers I have in hand and decide. I won't stop work in the meanwhile, but I expect you to make your decision fast, at the most by two weeks,' Mishra said.

'Two weeks is too little a time since we are not even prepared for it,' Rishabh argued.

'Two weeks is all I have. By November, I need to have my doubts cleared,' Mishra said and left.

The shock of Mishra's sudden demands was too burdensome to handle alone. Rishabh, who didn't perceive the criticality of the situation, asked me to relax and give Mishra some time to regain his sanity. The attitude of Rishabh in critical HR issues was very laid back, almost like that of a politician. He preferred to let the matter linger for as long as possible before coming to a decision. Rishabh didn't realize that Mishra was being brainwashed by his parents, his elder brother, and more than anyone else, his hostel-mates who hated us for involving him with us. I wanted to offer Mishra an irresistible deal immediately and not waste the next two weeks.

The burden of the upcoming setback was too heavy to carry on my shoulders. I decided to share it with the only person who could lessen my pain. Priya.

'Hi Priya.'

'Hi,' she said. Her tone lacked surprise.

'Mishra has asked us to offer him a lucrative deal otherwise he is threatening to leave us,' I told her.

'Sorry to hear that,' she said insincerely.

'I'm sorry for what I said to you last time, I was out of my mind. I want to get back together with you,' I said as though she was a commodity that I could use when I liked and discard otherwise.

'But I wasn't out of my mind, Amol. I don't want to get back together with you.'

'Come on, what are you still angry about?'

'I am not angry about anything. Much like you had realized something that day, I realized something too.'

'What?'

'That I won't ever be happy with you. All you care about is yourself. You have always taken me for granted,' she said.

'How can you say that? You know how much I care for you.'

'Yes, so much that you left me all alone whenever I was troubled. Whenever you have spoken to me, it has always been about you. Have you ever asked how have

I been? Even now you have called me because you have faced trouble in your life, not because you wanted to know my well being.'

'I have always tried to take care of you, don't say that,' I stammered insincerely.

'Yes, always. Like now, when I am all alone,' she said.

'Are you okay?'

'It's over, Amol. Keep your concern to yourself. You only said that I revived our relationship on a lie, so it is bound to encounter a dead end. Good bye.'

I could not dare to call her back. It was I who was hapless then. A part of me wanted to take the blame for the disaster on myself while the other part tried to shun it off. It was because she allowed me to take her for granted that I could dare to. I came up with a sermon and posted it on our fan page. It said, 'If you will always allow people to use you, get prepared to be treated like a dustbin.'

The next day, Mishra sent us a long mail highlighting his key strengths and explaining why he was indispensable for the company and could add value as a co-founder. His points were quite irrefutable.

```
I joined YourQuote to work for free (even though I
had my own brother's web development company) since
I liked the idea, the team, and was promised to be
made tech co-founder. I'll try to justify myself as
a tech co-founder so that you can take your decision.
A tech co-founder is somebody who:
    • Has belief in the idea
        O  I claim to have the belief.
```

- Can work in a dedicated way
  - Considering the fact that I had no ownership in YourQuote till date, I did what all could have been done by a tech guy single-handedly
  - Can wait patiently for the time when revenue will actually start generating in decent numbers
- Should have the domain knowledge
  - I believe I have a decent amount of domain knowledge, as much as Amol and Rishabh have in their own domains.
- An understanding of the intersection of business and technology decisions
  - I have always helped in strategical decisions from the technology perspective, which means that I am now comfortable enough to understand the business requirements
- Can contribute to finance if required
  - The major portion of online marketing revenue was brought through my personal and business contacts. With my broad technical network, I can continue to do so
  - If required, I'm ready to invest from my side on the business.
- Should have the managing capability
  - Can be verified from the fact that developers/designers I have personally managed are always happy with me just because I know how to interact with them and always consider it important to add value to their learning.

A point raised by Rishabh: what investors would say to hiring me, a student?

Why should my life be dependent on investors (who don't even exist)? Isn't it the authority of present co-founders to choose another one and decide their ownership on mutual discussions and trust basis? Even you guys started while you were students.

Another point raised by Rishabh: We might need a few more technical partners in future.

It's a very justifiable argument that you might meet better persons than me in future. FYI, you will also require a lot more marketing persons and creative heads in future. What does it has to do with the present marketing and creative co-founders?

Let's move on!

I'll always keep YourQuote at top in the list provided there is a reasonable offer for me simply because I love the idea. Waiting for a response at the earliest.

Cheers!

In the next few days, we discussed with various people about the kind of offer that we needed to make to Mishra. Keeping in mind the fact that Mishra had still got one year of his education left which would prevent him from joining the company full-time and the fact that he hadn't contributed anything financially to the venture till date, we figured out an equity of somewhere between 8-10 percent for him. Our decision was given a green signal by all our mentors with some even saying that it was more than what he deserved. We realized how grave a mistake we had done by not hiring him right from the very beginning with 5 percent vested equity over two years. Now that he had proven himself indispensable by not allowing any new techie to come on board, and in the process, his value had increased and he could dictate our terms.

On 25th, exactly two weeks after Mishra initiated the dreaded conversation, we invited him to our place to present our offer to him. He didn't find our offer lucrative enough and argued, 'The company is right now valued at somewhere between 2 to 3 crores. You guys have invested 5 lakhs till now, so that makes around 3 percent equity for your money and you can take 7 percent equity for your idea. So, as far as I think, the rest 90 percent equity needs to be divided equally amongst each one of us, because all three of us are equally indispensable to the company.'

Handing over 30 percent of the company to Mishra! The mere thought sent shivers down our spines. His demands were unrealistic and at some level, even barbaric to us, especially when he knew about our financial conditions, our dependence on him for technology, and our inability to offer him what he desired.

Rishabh had a brainwave at that point of time and he asked Mishra to prove his candidature for a 30 percent co-foundership by working like one over the next one month and if we were satisfied, we would honour his demand. He argued that Mishra had always worked like an employee, with one of us having to always sit on his head to get work done from him.

Mishra went away saying that he would get back to us on mail in a day and left us full of uncertainty.

⊏⊐

On 26th, Rishabh's interview was to be telecast on TV first and would be uploaded on websites of news channels an hour later. Many team members and followers tuned in to the news channel to catch his interview, as advertised by us all across social networks. We didn't have a TV at our place, so we had to wait for an hour. Phone calls started coming soon after the telecast and everyone congratulated him, for he had spoken very confidently. My parents called me to let me know that he had mentioned my name on a number of occasions and had even said I inspired him to take the leap of faith.

I was happy to know he hadn't forgotten about me completely and went to his room to congratulate him for the good work done. He was stuck to his laptop, aghast.

'What happened?'

'Mishra,' he whispered.

I rushed to his laptop with a premonition. There was a mail with the subject: Felicitations.

Congratulations Rishabh and Amol for the interview.

You wanted me to prove my candidature for co-foundership, didn't you? After seeing today's interview, where you could not even mention my name for building the website , I accept the challenge in my own style.

Welcome to the world of talents: Talent Market—the fastest startup ever, an idea in 1 hour and a kick start in 5.

Mishra had gone ahead and started his own company! We were devastated, not because it meant competition, but because a disgraceful employee whom we had invested so much faith in, broke away to become an entrepreneur.

Five hours later, Talent Market was up and running. The site had a countdown timer that said, 'Launching in 30 days, 20 hours, 5 minutes, 12 seconds' and on the team page, Mishra Anant's name shone with his brand new designation. In that disastrous moment, all I could notice was that he had taken the first right step of proclaiming himself as the Founder CEO right from the start.

When we read the about page, we realized how Mishra had copied our ultimate vision of becoming a one-stop creative networking website for all kinds of creativity; because his website Talent Market was to cater to all kinds of talents viz. photography, design, painting, and writing. We realized we had given birth to our competitor!

October 31

Mishra was history. Thankfully, he had let us go with the codes for free after Rishabh literally begged to him to take mercy on our financial condition. Priya had managed to remain single despite my reckless attempts at patching up. I reflected that both of them had left because they thought they were being taken for granted. It was one of the greatest lows in our entrepreneurial lives and my personal life.

The moment demanded great patience and determination from both of us. During this time, Anjali became a part of our household, spending more and more amount of time with Rishabh which didn't go down well with me.

She seemed like an intruder into our house and kept Rishabh away from work by taking up a majority of his time gossiping about personal issues. Once when Anjali stayed over for the night, they took up my room without even asking me if I was okay with it. Thoroughly uncomfortable sleeping in another room, I was counting cracks on the ceiling when loud sounds of moaning made my ears stood up. I instantly gave Priya a call.

'Hello,' she said groggily.

'Chatpat news. I can hear Rishabh and Anjali making out!'

'What, really?'

'Yes. The room is shut, but I can clearly hear what's happening behind closed doors.'

'Wow, good for them,' she said with a marked indifference.

'Yeah. So how have you been?'

'I'm good. Happy after a long time. Don't spoil my mood by talking about a patch up, okay?'

'No, I won't. Why would I? Remember I wanted to be single, and I am now. So I'm happy,' I said .

'Good. You know, I met your friend yesterday.'

'Who?'

'Shendu's best friend, Anirudh Arora,' she said.

Anirudh Arora, plump, extremely fair and tall, was my batchmate. We weren't close friends or anything, but we did talk occasionally for we shared several common interests such as music and writing. He had even recommended me a course in creative writing to hone my skills further. He hailed from an affluent business family and much like me, he shunned a corporate job to pursue his passion for teaching. He taught Physics at a prominent JEE coaching centre of Gurgaon. However, we differed in one aspect completely. He had become a dope addict lately, while I was totally against it.

'Ya, I know him,' I told her.

'He is a very different kind of a guy. Has got great taste in books and sings really well,' she continued.

'Wow, where did you hear him singing?'

'He came over to Shendu's place. We were drinking together.'

'Have you started drinking once again?' I interrogated. I didn't like what I heard.

'Yes, occasionally.'

'Why? Why do you do it? You had promised me you won't.'

'I promised you as a girlfriend, which I am not anymore.'

'No, you promised as a friend.'

'Okay, alright. I won't drink. Now don't nag early in the morning.'

'Good girl,' I said, relieved. 'So, what did you do with Anirudh?'

'We talked till three in the morning while everyone else was sleeping.' Her statement pierced me like a knife because I had sent her two messages last night and she had not replied. She further told me, 'You know what? He said that Shardendu used to like me, until Kamna came into the picture and took him away.'

'Wow,' I said, being grateful to Kamna. 'Did he say something about me?'

'No, nothing at all. He is very chilled out.'

'You are saying as though you have fallen for him.'

'Come on. I just like him,' she said. I didn't know it then but this was going to become her pet dialogue for months to come.

All Hell Broke Loose

I was worried for Priya. I had believed that I loved her so much that her happiness would always make me happy. But now when she was actually happy, I did not like it one bit for I wasn't the reason for her happiness. Someone else had taken my place in her life.

On the work front, our new revenue model had been put in place but we were making very limited money with it. We used to run eight crowdsourcing contests a month, two each week. While we charged 10,000 rupees per contest from many of our clients, we were also entertaining a lot of barter deals that ensured lucrative prizes for our followers and some publicity to keep our followers hooked to our brand. Each of the contests brought us, on an average, 3,000 rupees, totalling 24,000 rupees per month. Subtracting our house rent of 15,000 rupees, we just had 9,000 rupees to run our website, home, and marketing with. I had never seen so much poverty in my entire life. My own little money which I had earned from my books had been spent in the past few months over the security for house rent, brokerage, servers, and buying basic appliances like a washing machine and a refrigerator. I had painted a very vague picture of my life in front of my parents, whom I had told them that I was drawing a salary of 20,000 rupees a month and had sufficient money to run my home with.

During this time, when I found a five hundred rupee note on the side of the bed where Rishabh used to sleep, I shamelessly put it inside my pocket without giving it a second thought. The abject poverty had numbed my conscience completely. Lack of money fostered dishonesty not only in me, but in Rishabh as well. He trapped naïve but rich clients out of nowhere and tricked them into hosting a contest on our website with a fee as high as 30,000 rupees, by showcasing our 20000+ fans on Facebook, instead of a mere 250 active users on our website. In this phase of penury, I could not even ask for financial help from the only person I could—Priya—as I had lost meaning in her life.

While we had completely forgotten about Purnesh of Excel ventures, he approached us on November 7 as he'd promised and asked about our progress. With the stormy entrepreneurial environment that we had encountered in the previous weeks, and right hand Mishra leaving us, all we could do was to beg him for another two weeks' time. He wasn't impressed and we feared that we would not hear from him again, but he gave in. His extension of the deadline meant that this time, we had no other option other than putting our asses on fire and getting the venture up and running within two weeks.

Ever since Mishra left us, Rishabh became more and more authoritative. He designated to me the task of finding a technical co-founder on LinkedIn and other networks. He said, 'Tell anyone you find that we are ready to give him as high as 20 percent equity and a designation of Technical Co-founder,' which I agreed to. A good offer was necessary for getting the right person on board.

There was a sudden shift in paradigm in our stinginess with equity. Whereas we couldn't earlier think of handing over more than 10 percent equity to the person who had built our website from scratch, we were now ready to shell out as high as 20 percent to an untested new person.

Rishabh, in the meanwhile, got involved in outreach and got in touch with people who could connect him to angel investors. We realized that with the kind of progress that we were making without a skilled technical team in place, it would be impossible to scale without money. From a marketing point of view too, we desired investors who could get us big clients. An investor associated with the media and the advertising industry could have added great value, for he could get big media houses and corporate to become our prospective clients.

Rishabh's consistent pressure hindered my creative freedom and I wanted to shift to a new place along with my sister. When I proposed this to Rishabh over mail, he sent a very sentimental reply saying that even his brother was in Gurgaon and his parents had been forcing him to live with him ever since he graduated, but he said that he rejected it for me and our company. Truth be told, he rejected it for himself—so that he could smoke, drink, and sleep with his girlfriend for free.

All the while, I had kept a vindictive watch on Mishra's progress. He was following our procedure of generating social media traction before his website was up, which in my view was bad methodology, as we had seen with our website. He had managed to get 4000 Facebook fans within just two weeks. Rishabh diplomatically won over Mishra by publicizing his venture on our fan page. Thanks to the generosity on our part, Mishra agreed to connect us to the founder of Click2Closet, who he disclosed was interested in investing in us and help us in case of any technical difficulty until we found a tech partner.

November 14

Rishabh and I had been invited to an entrepreneurial seminar at the five-star hotel Surya on Ashram Road. It was a networking lunch and elevator pitch competition organized by a prominent entrepreneurial network. Thanks to Rishabh's connections, we got the passes for free, which otherwise would have cost us 3,000 rupees.

After attending a couple of soporific sessions, I became really hungry. Unlike other days, I had got up 7 am. It was 11.30 am and my stomach was already making explosive sounds. I walked out of the hall and inquired about refreshments from the guard.

'Sir, the refreshments are only for speakers. If you want to have something, you can go to the restaurant on the ground floor,' he said politely.

'That's crazy. When they have an all-day session, shouldn't they have refreshments served along?'

The gatekeeper was not in a mood conversation. Perhaps, he also knew that he earned more than most of us penniless entrepreneurs present there. Annoyed, I left the seminar hall where the so-called young entrepreneurs with pathetic communication skills were presenting elevator pitches of their run-off-the-mill ideas to other entrepreneurs (as no investor was in sight).

Seeing Rishabh engrossed in the pitches, I moved outside without informing him.

I located a small shop outside the hotel which served Pav Bhaji and asked him to give me one.

'Sir, is that your cellphone ringing?' the vendor asked .

'What? Oh yes, it's mine,' I realized and pulled it out, hoping to see Priya's name. The call got cut and I was astonished to see three missed calls. It wasn't Priya, but Rishabh. I grabbed the last piece of paav, gobbled it up, and called him back.

'Hi Rishabh.'

'Where the HELL are you?' Rishabh shouted.

'Just outside, eating.'

'Wow, that's what you have come here for. Truly amazing. Do you have any idea what we have missed?'

'What?'

'An investor from Indian Investors Network was standing right in front of me. I was searching for you all over, but you were nowhere to be found.'

'Why did you not talk to him?' I casually asked.

'I thought we both should talk together. I would have introduced us as IITians, and besides, since you are a bestselling author, it would have completely floored him. Amol, how can you be so casual?' Rishabh yelled.

I didn't respond, marked by a nonchalant indifference and irreverence for everyone present there. 'You should have talked to him. Anyway, where's he now?'

'He's gone.'

'He would have gone for lunch. He'll be back,' I said and cut the call. I tried Priya's number to let out my frustration but she didn't pick up.

Back in the hall, I saw Rishabh interacting with some potential clients. I took out my cards and went to the next stall. Just as I proudly introduced myself as the co-founder of YourQuote, the other guy replied, 'I already talked to your partner, I guess.' The same thing happened at each and every other stall that I went to. Rishabh, being so efficient, had talked to each one of them.

I was mortified. I went to the portico, found an isolated spot, and called Priya again. She picked up this time.

'Priya, why the HELL do you not pick up my calls. Don't you understand that I get worried?' Angered with myself, I vented out at my softest target.

'Amol, talk nicely, otherwise I will never pick up your calls.'

'Are you threatening me? Don't pick up, ever. I will come over to your PG and bang doors. I will create a scene everywhere you go.'

'And I will just cut this call. Goodbye, forever.'

I returned back to Rishabh. He ignored me completely to everyone's notice, left the seminar hall with a group of people he had networked with for lunch. At first I felt bad and even a bit jealous that I had run away at the time I could have networked with people, but when I saw him going to the restaurant of the hotel itself, I got really happy. I saved money, while he was going to spend a lot.

The lunch was over and people started assembling in the seminar hall once again. I was at the Indian Investors Network (IIN) stall, interacting with the counter boy Shadab who was a college student. I saw Rishabh coming towards me and I was now geared up to please him.

'Hi, you know what, he's Shadab. He's going to connect us to Mr Anand, from IIN, in a few minutes,' I proudly exclaimed to Rishabh. He was not amused.

'I already had a talk with Mr Anand during lunch. He hosted us there,' Rishabh informed and started walking away.

'Did he pay for the lunch?' I asked, that being my primary concern.

'No, the sponsors took care of it,' I went green with envy. 'He would recommend us to the IIN monthly presentation to the panel.'

'Wow, but why didn't you take me along?'

'Because food seemed more important to you then,' he taunted and went away.

⌐⊂

Back home, I went to meet Priya for what I told her was to be the last time. She joined me at the Huda City Centre metro station and I made her walk three kilometers till Galleria market with me as I had a lot of things to say.

I thanked her for being a part of my life, for making me whatever I could become in the past three and half years, for inspiring me, for being my support, my honest critic, and listening to my pathetic jokes with a smile. When it was time for me to leave, I hugged her tightly and started wailing, 'Please don't leave me, please. I will die without you.'

As I gathered my senses, I apologized for my impulsive behaviour. She smiled and before I left, I mumbled, 'Can I ask you for one thing, please?'

'Yes, sure.'

'Hug me once,' I asked. And she did. It was the most heartless hug ever.

War with Anjali

November 14

Rishabh and I hadn't spoken a word with each other after that fateful day of the seminar. He would return late at night, much after I had slept. By the time I would get up, he would be long gone. It was on one of those days that I got up and checked my mails. One particular mail from Rishabh caught my eye. Anjali was cc-ed in the mail.

```
Amol,
    We have had enough of our disorganized lives. It's
time we become serious, else, we will never be able
to achieve anything. I'm implementing strict office
hours where we will have to report to each other at
8 am sharp and work till 6 pm in the evening, with a
one-hour break in the afternoon i.e. minimum 9 hours
of work daily.
    I have shared a spreadsheet where we need to report
our work as we keep doing them, so that we can keep
an eye on each other.
Rishabh
```

I appreciated the mail but didn't like the fact that Anjali was cc-ed. Who was she to witness my criticism? A cold war had commenced. Without saying a word, I reported 11.30 am as my starting time on the spreadsheet and Anjali remarked soon enough—So you need to work till 9.30 pm today.

Anjali's comment hurt like a gunshot wound but I chose to remain quiet. In the afternoon, while working, I noticed Rishabh plodding to and fro in the balcony. He had just had a fight with Anjali, who had arrived at our place during lunchtime. The lull that prevailed in the house was ruptured by the screams and ultimately sobs.

Using the same logic, I wrote a mail to Anjali, cc-ing Rishabh.

Dear Anjali,
    I would kindly request you to not disturb the harmony of our place during office hours for your personal matters. Just want you to know that our flat is also our office.
    Please take care of it from the next time.
Amol

A few minutes later, Anjali was sent back to her hostel and Rishabh returned to the drawing room and opened his laptop. His face turned red as soon as he looked at his laptop screen. My mail had hit the bull's eye. Sadistic pleasure, ah! He didn't reciprocate at all till 6 pm after which he left for IIT.

At 7, while I was happily finishing the last task of the day, I received a long sarcastic reply from Anjali.

Dear Amol,

Thank you for your very kind mail. I will certainly not disturb the harmony of your office, which you have certainly maintained to the best of your ability.

When I came today, I didn't come as an employee of YourQuote, I came as a friend of Rishabh's. As far as I think, along with it being YourQuote's office, it is also Rishabh's and your home, both of you having equal ownership of it.

Anyway, I appreciate your frankness and I promise that I will never disrupt 'your' office hours, irrespective of whatever you do at your 'home' at the same time, being the director.

Anjali

I was stunned by the mail. I waited for an hour for Rishabh to come online hoping that he would reply and reprimand Anjali. But he remained passive for more than half an hour. Infuriated, I sent a brutal mail.

Anjali,

I won't be sarcastic with you because it will make matters worse. I just want to be frank with you. I am terribly hurt with your mail and I cannot imagine working in this company if you continue to be working here.

More than my disappointment with you, I am highly let down with Rishabh who chose to remain quiet despite seeing your insolent mail thrown at me in this way.

I don't know if things will ever be right.

Amol

This time, in less than fifteen minutes I received a long hateful mail from Rishabh.

Amol,

   You had no right to ask her to not come. I pay
half the bills as you do. If she had ruined harmony
of the house for the one hour when she had come, then
I can also blame Priya for spoiling the harmony of
the house for an entire week during your birthday,
but I chose to let it go. Moreover, you have no
right to talk about my personal relationship with
Anjali. I don't give anybody the right to abuse my
relationship and if you do it again, you will have
to suffer the consequences.

Regards,

Rishabh

I didn't wait to reply anymore. I had lost hope and I had lost trust in Rishabh. My mind tussled with the choice whether to share my misery and angst with Priya or not. Fearing a nervous breakdown, I gave in and chose to go against my word that I wouldn't call her. I tried her number but she didn't pick up.

I called Pratik, told him that things at YourQuote were getting out of my control and I was forced to contemplate quitting the venture for a job, though my heart was still in my company. Pratik, instead of sympathizing with me, chided me.

'Are you crazy? In this time of recession, how will you manage to find yourself a job? There are a hundred start-ups sprouting every day, and no interviewer pays heed to start-ups until you have raised money. You need to have someone bet money on you to validate your company in front of others' eyes. So, be calm and find an investor instead,' Pratik explained. His advice made sense and I decided to sort things out.

I messaged Rishabh on phone: 'Enough of us wasting time. Let's sort things out and get back to work.' It worked. He returned home late at night and together we went to Saket to chill for a bit, much like the old times.

He asked me if there was anything wrong between Priya and me, and I finally told him that she had dumped me. He consoled me and told me things were going to be alright. We mutually decided that office hours would be religiously adhered to, personal and professional matters would be kept apart, and Anjali was not going to be fired but instead made an assistant to Rishabh in his marketing work.

Fair enough, I thought.

A Date with Investors

November

Entreprenurial Leadership Program (ELP) is a recognized international program which carries out a series of lectures on various important aspects of entrepreneurship. We had applied for it during our initial phase in Delhi back in 2011. Due to the competitive nature of the program, with two layers of shortlisting, it had become a sort of status symbol for newbie entrepreneurs and wannapreneurs. When I failed to clear the second level, it caused a cold rift between us. Ironically, we both had made it to the ELP's first list and they had interviewed us both for the final cut, Rishabh first. Rishabh's interview went on for an hour, while I was interviewed second for just five minutes. They said Rishabh had answered all their queries and proclaimed himself as the one running the company, while he said that I just handled social media as a co-founder. This was the beginning of Rishabh's aspiration to become the prime face of the venture. I didn't say anything to Rishabh about it at first, but when the results arrived, I was heartbroken. I flinched in self-hate for allowing Rishabh to take the lead without asserting control from my side. Rishabh now proudly wrote Fellow, ELP along with Co-founder Director in his team slide, while I was just a Co-founder Director. I accepted my fate.

Being the outgoing person that he was, Rishabh made several friends in ELP and often hung out with them to discuss the b-plan but I never joined him, coming up with random excuses. The truth was that my rejection from ELP had shredded my self-confidence completely.

⌁

On a chilly winter morning on November 16, I was woken up from my sleep very early, shocked to see Priya's name flashing on my cellphone screen. It was after a long time that she had called me. I woke up to her calm and composed voice confessing, 'I don't want to be dishonest with you. That's why this call. I was with Anirudh last night and I kissed him.'

I was too baffled to respond and could just mumble a mild 'Why?'

'I just felt like it. It was platonic—it comforted me somehow.'

'Do you love him?' I whispered, almost speechless.

'No. Not at all. I just like him,' she said. 'I'm sorry. But, as a matter of fact, I'm not really sorry I did it,' she mumbled. My sleep was history now. Having nothing left to speak, I disconnected the call.

In three days, my condition had become so bad that I started smoking four to five cigarettes a day. I was heartbroken not just by Rishabh's sidetracking of me, but by Priya's betrayal as well.

It was her birthday on the 19th and I called her two days prior to tell her not to expect a call from me on her birthday.

'Don't do that to me. I'm not seeing him anymore,' she replied.

'But you have not yet shunned him from your life. Isn't it?'

She didn't respond. As promised, I did not call her. Not once. The entire day passed and I kept getting agitated thinking that she would be with Anirudh. Just when I was about to retire for the day, I received a call from her.

'I am so sorry baby. I have committed a grave mistake. My senses deceived me. I could not see the wrong path I had taken,' she lamented.

I chose not to reciprocate and her sobs filled the silence.

'I waited for your call the entire day, I didn't move out of my house, didn't pick up anybody's call, just because you didn't wish me. I was angry initially, but then I realized that you had been right in not calling me,' she said placidly and continued, 'I didn't deserve your wish.' She burst into tears.

'Happy Birthday. You can't imagine how difficult it was for me to not call you,' I said finally. 'I miss our old times, the old you, the one I fell in love with.'

'I would bring her back, for you. I promise. I'm so sorry,' she whimpered.

'Do you love me?' I asked.

There was silence.

'At present I don't, but I know that if given a chance, I would—truly, madly, and deeply,' she said with an unparalleled conviction.

'Can you do one thing for me? Call Anirudh and tell him that you never want to meet him again,' I asked.

'I have already done that. When he called to wish me, I told him he was the worst person I had come across.'

'What was his response?'

'He asked me why I was saying so. I said because he was a doper and didn't treat me well. He abused me after which I hung up the call.'

'What did the fucker say to you? I will call him and teach him a lesson.'

'Amol, chill. He's history now. Ignore him. Let bygones be bygones and go to sleep.'

But sleep seemed like a distant possibility when my mind was abuzz with a million questions about our future together.

November 20

Our long overdue business PPT for Excel Ventures was still to be finalized and Rishabh took the responsibility on himself to complete it. He asserted that he had got a lot of insights into how to prepare a business plan through ELP and would do justice to it. Rishabh had this innate habit of needlessly delaying anything that he undertook. He could not do anything on time, especially tasks that required deskbound work from him.

In the meanwhile, we started pitching to investors who we had interacted with earlier through mails talking about our progress and vision. Some showed interest, others comfortably ignored.

We got introduced to the CEO of ClickToCloset, who was eager to invest in us. The CEO of the company was an NRI Tamilian named Kartikeya, popularly known as KT.

KT had previously worked in McKinsey & Company for ten years in the US and had returned to India to start-up and get acquainted with the opportunities that shining India had to offer. During his internship, Mishra had mentioned to him about YourQuote, about the fact that we were a Private Limited Company, about the fact that we, the founders, had left our jobs for the start-up and were looking to raise money. On one lazy Friday, Rishabh called excitedly and informed me that KT wanted to meet us. He told me that KT's NRI friend Rajan Biyani wanted to invest in Indian internet start-ups. This was like a godsend opportunity for us—while we were searching for interested investors, an interested investor was looking forward to meet us. The meeting was scheduled at CCD in Nehru Place, Delhi's commercial hub near KT's office. We had been waiting for around 20 minutes.

'Do big guys always arrive late? He said 5, it's almost going to be 5.30,' I complained. No sooner had I uttered the words that a fair skinned man entered CCD in haste and Rishabh stood up to welcome him. It was KT. His impeccable dressing and a Rolex watch on his wrist assured me that our lunch expenses would be taken care of. The two of us ordered the costliest delicacies on the menu, while he was content with just a cup of cappuccino. Once the food arrived, KT came to the point straightaway. 'Who among you two handles the business end?' he sternly asked. Rishabh shyly raised his hand, as though he was going to get ragged.

'I want to know your entire time table. How do you spend your day? Right from the first call that you make to the last mail that you do. Tell me,' KT began. I knew that he had no answer. Highly disorganized, he would begin and end things at his own sweet will.

Rishabh fumbled and then I took over the reins saying, 'Most of the major decisions are taken by a mutual discussion between the two of us.' Rishabh echoed my response. KT, who played the strict cop, was not satisfied. 'Business decisions need to be taken by one person. One person is the CEO, not two. If you are on a call with a client and he offers a final deal, you wouldn't ask him to wait until you two discuss it with each other, would you? Your decision prevails. Who takes that decision?'

'Rishabh,' I said truthfully. He was the only person at that time dealing with clients. I gave him the co-founder status without foreseeing that tomorrow it would place me second in my own venture.

KT wooed us with his smooth talks and asked us about our strategies for the future. We told him that we had hit the gold mine by finding an untapped Search Engine Optimized word (SEO), which had more than 100 million searches on Google every month. That did the trick and got him excited about our idea all the more. He said that he would schedule a meeting with his NRI friend Rajan Biyani at the earliest and prepare us for the angel pitching.

He got a call from someone and left our meeting abruptly, saying that he would call a meeting sometime later. Everything seemed okay until the waiter came towards us with the check, which KT had easily forgotten about and left. We had eaten stuff worth a thousand bucks and it was a huge blow to us. We calmed ourselves by the fact that we might get investment fairly soon.

However, the next meeting never happened. A week later, when Rishabh pursued KT, he came to know that KT was trapped in a police case where his shrewd and greedy partner and COO Jeetendra had bribed police officials to arrest him on the charges of embezzlement of company funds. A month later, Click2Closet, a company that had started doing really well recently, came tumbling down like a pack of cards. KT was going back to the US and he didn't care enough about us to introduce us to Rajan. We were officially screwed.

Priya had returned to my life, silently, slowly. There was so much silence in our lives that I couldn't assess whether she had come back out of her own choice or out of pity for my condition. There were a lot of things that were left unsaid between us. We both needed time to heal, to bring back our old romance. But the thing was I had no time. Work had become tougher and tougher with each passing day.

Ever since Mishra had left, our technical progress had been stalled. Rishabh had delegated to me the responsibility of finding a technical maven for our venture because I had been closely involved with Mishra while he developed the website.

Finding a technical co-founder for an already running bootstrapped venture is more difficult than finding an honest politician in the Indian parliament. Technical wizards, if having an entrepreneurial bent of mind, most often start their own ventures and if they are of the employee bent of mind, they prefer working in companies that pay them well. The only option that I could find after months of search were students, three of whom I had hired on a part time basis at 5,000 rupees per month. Meanwhile, I had also started dabbling with codes, all the while cursing my fate for not having chosen Mishra as the co-founder instead of Rishabh right at the very beginning.

Priya remained patient all the while and never asked for my time. We hardly met and seldom talked. A ghastly silence had crept in our lives like an illegitimate child of our unfaithful love affair. She had stopped hanging out with her friends, stopped picking up their calls, and slowly allowed gloom to paint her life.

Time went on at the slow pace and our work left us no time to repair our relationship.

Second last week of November

Rishabh, with his sluggish work, had failed to deliver an impressive PPT on time. So I had to ultimately make one. We had figured out that we needed around 50 lakh rupees as our first round of investment to make the business climb up the ladder. Our valuation, as determined by our mentors, was around 4-5 crores. Yes! We had co-founded a million dollar company but a million dollar company doesn't become a million dollar company until there's as much money in the bank account. We had to find an investor ready to invest 50 lakhs at 10 percent equity to achieve that. Done with the finances, it was time to get in touch with people who were already interested in us, to get a brief feedback. Purnesh topped that list.

Purnesh liked the presentation but he figured that our current model of crowdsourcing didn't gel well with the Indian audience as the Indian market wasn't ripe. To quote his words, 'To make a crowdsourcing model work, 25,000 users were peanuts and there was no way to get big players interested until we reached a million users within six months.'

He instead suggested we focus on the print merchandize players who could use our content to bring out their specific products and start monetizing whatever little traffic we were getting. No, we didn't have to get involved in the operations, the hassles of manufacturers, but we just needed to outsource those to an established merchandize player. Purnesh had said that if two of Excel's portfolio merchandizing companies get into a strategic tie-up with us, it would befit us to be funded. But, luck didn't favour us, as none of the CEOs found any synergy in YourQuote with their firm.

Purnesh, after a lot of brainstorming, asked us to pitch for a smaller amount in the range of 20 lakhs and get incubated instead, as he said that our revenue model still needed fixing. While that was a sound advice, that also meant that Excel Ventures had lost interest in us and Purnesh was just getting his hand out of the ditch.

Rishabh didn't pay significant heed to what Purnesh said as he believed that IIN was within our reach.

'Amol, remember KT?' Rishabh had called me on phone.

'Obviously. Why?'

'He had said that only one person can be the CEO. I was just talking to my uncle who is an entrepreneur himself. He has asked to finalize the organizational structure before pitching. It's necessary to define CEO of the venture in the investment PPT.'

'Yeah, okay. Let us discuss about it when you come back.'

'What's there to discuss? I'm sitting in the office of an angel investor. I'm editing the team slide. I've changed my designation to the CEO, and you suggest what you want your designation to be.'

I was dumbstruck. It was my company, my bloody company! How could he dare to even claim the position of the CEO?

'It's a big decision. We need to discuss this first. Hell, I need to discuss this,' I said vehemently.

'Okay.'

I was fuming with anger. Equality was the reason why I divided the equity equally in the first place, why I didn't keep the Founder CEO tag for myself right from the very beginning, and bestowed both of us with the same designation. It turned out to be my biggest mistake.

I messaged Rishabh, 'If we have to define CEO-like positions for our company, let's keep it equal—you can be the CMO (Chief Marketing Officer), while I will be the CPO (Chief Product Officer).'

'CMO doesn't suit my position,' he messaged back immediately.

I remained restless for three hours, until he returned.

'Come on, you wanted a discussion, let's have it now,' Rishabh immediately shot me with his blunt question. He seemed irritable.

'CEO would make one of us more visible than other.'

'I had been working tirelessly all through the while, I take business decisions, I steer the growth of the company, I fulfill all the responsibility of a CEO,' Rishabh screamed.

'That's unfair. I don't want to be second to you.'

'Oh c'mon, give me a break. You are even earning from your book, whereas I have to borrow money from my parents to sustain myself on occasions,' Rishabh was almost in tears.

Frustrated, I couldn't say anything.

'Imagine when I go and meet clients, the effect of having CEO written on my business card will be much greater than the designation of a CMO,' he said and went to the other room.

I kept scribbling random gibberish on my laptop, not knowing what to do next. My News Feed on Facebook crushed all my confusion.

Rishabh Dev is now the CEO of yourquote.in

Likes, likes, likes. I was so crushed, so saddened by his sudden action that I couldn't say anything.

This abrupt behaviour or Rishabh had brutally vandalized my independence and our equality. I could observe a change in his attitude right from the very next day. I decided against borrowing any CEO position and chose the designation of Creative Director for myself.

Unable to take the upheaval single-handedly, I called Priya and asked her to come over. I nagged about Rishabh all throughout. She remained quiet and said at last, 'Understanding is the key to a successful relationship. Ignore little fights like this.'

'Would you not feel bad about the fact that someone other than your boyfriend has become the CEO of his own company?'

'Umm, I would be rather proud if that helps his company get bigger. You will always remain a co-founder—nobody can snatch that from you,' she said with an unrealistic serenity in her voice.

I could not tell whether she was on my side or his.

As the days passed, the designation of Creative Director settled in my mind. I didn't fret about it anymore, now that everyone had accepted it. But there was something else that kept bothering me—Rishabh's growing encroachment on my domain. Unable to find interested investors, he focussed all his energies into the management of the venture. He wanted everything organized—next week's posts, the number of hours of work of my interns, the designs of the contests, and so on.

The overhead costs were also quite high due to the three interns that had recently joined us, burning 15,000 rupees per month, coupled with another 25,000 per month on rental, electricity, phones and food and around 2,000 rupees on the server. Desperate for funds, we had said a yes to the IIN presentation on November 28. Meanwhile, we created a database of around 200 investors across India from LinkedIn and Twitter.

On the 27th, I didn't do any significant work for I was busy practising for the presentation the next day and in the process, I had forgotten to update our daily report spreadsheet.

At 5 in the evening, Rishabh, my start-up's CEO, called me.

'Amol, why is your work spreadsheet not updated? What are you busy with?'

'Oh, I was practising for tomorrow's presentation. I'm confident we will nail it tomorrow.'

'Why do you need to compromise your work for that? Moreover, you don't need to practice. Let one of us speak and as I'm the CEO, it's better if I speak.'

'But...' I felt choked and could not utter a single word. With that one sentence, he had alienated me from my venture. I cut the call.

I called Priya. Her phone was busy. I tried once again. It remained busy. Ten minutes later, she called me back.

'Who were you talking to?' I grunted.

'Anirudh. Don't be angry, please.'

'Fuck you! You cheat,' I yelled in helplessness.

'No, nothing like that has happened. I promise.'

'But why do you need to talk to him? Why?'

'Four days ago, he messaged me to ask if I was doing alright.'

'And you bothered to reply!'

'Yes, I was not feeling good about using him the last time.'

'Oh God! Come on, he's my batchmate. If you go around with him, it would totally ruin my friend circle. Anirudh and I have so many mutual friends that it would be humiliating for me if you fall for him.'

'I won't fall for him.'

'But you will continue talking to him, right? Remember when I got back to you, I did that with all my heart; I never ever talked to Shikha thereafter and the only time I did was in front of you.'

She didn't respond.

'What happened to what you'd felt on your birthday? All those feelings were fake, a bunch of lies?'

'Those were the feelings that I had on that particular day. Now, I don't feel that way. Simple.'

'Look, if you don't want to be with me, clearly tell me. I'm so busy nowadays that I would rather be happy doing my work than concentrating on your whereabouts.'

'Frankly speaking, though I have come back to you, I cannot make myself fall in love with you. This doesn't imply that I want to be with Anirudh. I want to be left alone.'

'Okay, just make one promise to me that you would not get into a relationship or be physically involved with anyone until I'm over you completely, which might take three to four months. Okay?'

'Okay.'

'You are a free bird lady, enjoy your life,' I said to which she said a mild thank you.

⊏⊐

In a day, I had let go of two of my most precious possessions—my command over the venture and the woman I loved. The next day, we reached the IIN office in South Ex ten minutes late due to Rishabh's complacent nature.

We were seated in a soundproof room and were surrounded by ten investors, casually dressed, fair skinned Indians with American accents. Rishabh began the PPT introducing himself as the CEO, which automatically shifted their entire focus on him. When I tried to answer a question asked by one of the investors, Rishabh tapped on my knee beneath the table, asking me to stop. I didn't relent, to his disappointment. The presentation seemed to have gone smoothly, and we went home anticipating the outcome. The result was to come in a fortnight.

Two weeks later, IIN responded. Politely, diplomatically, and curtly, they said no, as none of the investors were ready to bet money on us. They wanted run-of-the-mill ideas whose market had already been tested, ideas where their low risk appetite could give them assured returns.

⊏⊐

Mid-December

There is a famous saying about investors and entrepreneurs that when you need money, ask for advice and when you need advice, ask for money.

Despite not being able to generate interest from investors whom we'd talked to earlier we were not deterred. We had tasted the acidic waters of entrepreneurship. We had won awards. We had been covered by major national dailies. We had more than 25 corporate clients, including start-ups, authors, publishing houses, and even a low-budget Bollywood movie, a revenue of more than 13 lakhs, 95 percent of which was fromT-shirts, which we had stopped retailing however. We had a stable product. Most importantly, we were two people with complementary skills from IIT Delhi, the birthplace of the biggest names in the Indian start-up space like Flipkart, Zomato etc.

After IIN rejected us, Rishabh took the list of 200 investors that we had prepared and attacked each one of them with vengeance. Being the CEO of the venture, he took it upon himself to reach out to all the investors through mail. Rishabh proved himself worthy of his position. He skipped his lunch and dinner and didn't get up from his seat until he had sent separate mails to all the investors on the list.

I, despite being one grade below him in designation, sent him a congratulatory mail in appreciation of his diligence. He replied with a mild thanks and a snide comment, 'I set an example of the kind of work I expect from us. Make sure you follow.'

I cursed myself for appreciating him in the first place.

Three days later, while we had received five rejections and twelve out-of-office replies, I was pleasantly surprised to see Purnesh's name on my cellphone screen. We had not sent him our PPT because in his last talk to us, he had asked us to try our luck elsewhere as his Excel Ventures were not interested enough in us.

I picked up his call in great anticipation.

'Hi Purnesh. How have you been?' I said loudly. Rishabh came near me and made me switch the speaker on.

'I'm great Amol. I called you for a reason. When you guys had been in touch with me, why did you have to send mails to other investors without consulting me?' he quizzed. I looked at Rishabh, confused. He looked delighted and hinted incoming money to me.

'I'm really sorry Purnesh. We didn't realize that Excel was interested in us,' I said with a satisfied smile.

'No, Excel is still not interested,' Purnesh said, adding to our confusion. 'It's just that I was your senior, from the same alma mater, and I felt it to be my responsibility to guide you with pros and cons about pitching for investment this season.'

It was the first time we realized the vast storehouse of help that our alma mater was in terms of our prominent and generous alumni. But with the intonation of Purnesh's voice, it seemed that not taking help from our college's resources turned out to be costly for us.

'Season?'

'Yes, December is a bad season. Very few new investments are carried out in this season. Most of the angels right now are on vacation, out of office. When they will come back to work, your mail will be lost in the heap of countless other mails.'

'Oh my God,' I uttered. Rishabh grabbed the phone from me.

'Purnesh, Rishabh this side. What if we send another mail the next month as well?'

'No use. You guys spammed the entire investor belt. You failed to prove your loyalty or interest to any particular investor and thus lost credibility. That's how I got to know about the fact that you spammed, because some of the investors who I know had been discussing about YourQuote with contempt, even on their social networks.'

'Damn!'

What seemed to be Rishabh's diligence turned out to be our biggest mistake. Purnesh continued and said that we had even failed to check with the profile of the investor before mailing; because some retail and real-estate investors, having no synergy with our idea, had received our mails. We were damned. After putting our feet in the entrepreneurial water, we had mistakenly washed them with sulfuric acid.

'What should we do now?' I asked Purnesh.

'Find an incubator. Work hard and be pitch-ready. Make sure your progress in the next three months makes them forget about the spam story.'

This time, when I had the opportunity to charge Rishabh for his casual errors in execution, he decided to flee.

'I urgently need to go to IIT. I have to meet an incubator guy there as well. Meanwhile make sure that the creative posts for the next one week are maintained,' he said and rushed out.

January 2012

The eventful year seemed like it had passed by in a blur. I contrasted my current life with my life a year ago. There were too many changes to count and instead of regretting some things that had gone wrong in the past, I chose to concentrate on the present.

In the course of tireless work, needless discussions, and several battles related to the venture, I had given Priya ample space to do whatever she wanted to do with her life. She used to hang out with Shendu and company, go on out for coffee with Anirudh, go shopping at Zara, the only brand she wore, with Kamna, and spend half of her meagre salary buying dresses in the latest fashion. I didn't accompany her for one more reason—I was financially wretched and it hurt my self respect if she offered to share money for we were not a couple anymore.

Of late the clients we were getting for the contest section of our website were all from barter deals, thus bringing no revenue and making it increasingly different for us to continue with the interns. I had to fire them all, except one. Rishabh was in talks with a start-up incubator which offered 10 lakh rupees for 10 percent equity i.e. a valuation of 1 crore. Our grand valuation of 4-5 crores a few months ago was suddenly pulled down to a mere 1 crore, but even that seemed lucrative at this point. The incubator SproutLabs was run by a noted media group and other than money, it offered office space in Noida for three months, access to renowned mentors, and a demo day, where we could pitch our idea to a panel of prominent investors.

On the 16th, SproutLabs offered us a seven page legal document for our perusal and asked us to decide as soon as possible. When we read through the legal document, we couldn't understand it fully. I forwarded the document to my lawyer uncle. He was not at all happy. He told us that once again the agreement was chopping our wings just before the flight. One of its condition mentioned that SproutLabs would never sell its 10 percent equity thus having a firm hold on the company for the next ten years, with its board members exercising veto power in decisions.

'Amol, they are spending just 10 lakh rupees and gaining the entire control on your company. Don't go ahead with them. If you want only 10-15 lakh rupees, I can find you an investor within just seven days. Most of my clients are multi-millionaires and they would lend you this much money in no time, just on equity, no loans. They have a lot of trust in me,' my uncle told me.

Dazzled by his offer, I mentioned it to Rishabh. He seemed a bit cautious about involving my family member in the venture, but after five minutes of conversation with my uncle, he seemed convinced. We decided to go ahead with it, but before that we had one more thing to wait for. Free money.

January 28

Yes, free money. It was the b-plan competition of IIT Kanpur called Ideas. It promised a big prize money of around 5 lakhs to the top three winners. We had already made it to top 8 of the contest. Being absolutely confident of nailing the biggie, we kept both SproutLabs and my lawyer uncle on hold for some time.

Having been entrepreneurs for two years, we were veterans when compared to the other participants. We had ended up in the top eight teams of the business category thanks to the submission I had sent after hearing from Mishra that he, with his own start-up, TalentMarket, was also participating.

I was seated along with other participants at the Conference Hall at IIT Kanpur. Rishabh had gone to have a smoke. Half an hour later, our presentation was slotted. I skimmed through the slides and got stuck at a point. The slide 10 the contained the team structure.

Rishabh Dev, Co-founder and CEO, ELP fellow
Amol Sabharwal, Co-founder and Creative Director

His designation looked down at me every time I looked at it, as though telling me that I was his subordinate. Being the CEO of a start-up wasn't my ambition at all, but I definitely didn't want to be considered second to Rishabh.

I remembered how earlier, when both of us held the same designation, we always mentioned the team structure, in alphabetical order:

Amol Sabharwal, Co-founder and Director
Rishabh Dev, Co-founder and Director

Why did I succumb to his yelling? Why could I not rebel? Why couldn't I make him realize that it was my venture, that he was a part of it rather than the other way round?

Just then, Rishabh came running towards me and informed me with sadistic delight, 'Mishra's b-plan got smashed by the panel. He projected TalentMarket as a social venture, with the aim of uplifting artisans, which the judges completely disagreed with. Mishra is really disappointed.'

'Oh,' I said without emotion. I was indifferent to Mishra.

'What were you doing? You should have come and interacted with the few people who are already done giving their presentations,' he advised, excitedly.

'I was just revising the PPTs,' I said.

'Oh you don't need to worry,' he said casually. 'I will present all the slides.'

'Why? Why should you speak at every given opportunity? We will speak on alternate slides, like we used to do earlier.'

'Amol, it's not about you or me. It's about the company. Let the CEO speak. If a question is asked in your domain of technology, you can take it heads-on,' he asserted glibly.

'Let the CEO speak' echoed my ears throughout the presentation and I didn't utter a word. Not a single word. I just fixated a plastic smile as my able CEO cruised through the process. During the organization structure slide, he spoke volumes about me being a creative wizard, a bestselling author, while I stood in a corner like a dumb idiot.

When we came out, I saw Mishra smoking outside in the gallery and rushed to him.

'Hi Amol, how was your presentation?' He asked.

'Good. Do you have a cigarette?' I inquired.

'You, and smoking?'

I was so annoyed that I didn't want to utter a word. I just nodded. He lighted my cigarette. I puffed and walked away.

⌐⊨

The bright winter noon was now hidden behind some clouds and I watched the wind rustling through the leaves, caressing the green grass like a mother sways her hand on her child's head. My cigarette burned in ecstasy, nearing its end much faster than I had anticipated. Much like my relationship.

I called Priya. My call was on waiting. She cut the phone and called me back in two minutes.

'Who were you talking to?'

'How is that your concern?' she yelled back.

'So, what did you do yesterday?' I asked.

'Anirudh took me for dinner,' she said. I had stubbed out my cigarette by then.

'Did he take you to his home as well?' I probed, hesitantly.

'No, what kind of a question is that?' She rebuked.

'No, just...I'm sorry,' I faltered. 'So how's he?'

'He's not well; has a severe cold,' she said sneezing.

'You guys got intimate, didn't you? Tell me the truth. That's how you got a cold, isn't it? Did you guys do it?' I erupted.

'Amol, mind your words. I told you that I'm not committed to him. That's all you need to know.'

'Very good, bitch. So you and Anirudh are fuck buddies. Can't you understand that he's not a nice guy? .'

'At least he doesn't abuse me every time he talks to me.'

'Wow, now take his side. Why don't you please all his friends as well—Shendu, and a dozen others?' I hollered and continued, 'You are...'

She had cut the call before I could call her names.

I received a SMS from Priya. 'I don't ever want to talk to you. Good riddance.'

I typed an elaborate hurtful reply to her but deleted the damn thing and chose to remain silent.

⌁

The prize ceremony was supposed to take place in fifty minutes and while Rishabh went with the troop of participants to have something to eat, I got immersed in work. Work acted like a drug for me. It helped me take my mind off every hideous thing in my life. Despite the last three months being an emotional rollercoaster for me, I never neglected work. I remembered one of my lines that I posted on YourQuote, which said: Friends can wait, dreams can't.

I walked out, joined Rishabh and the group, and befriended a couple of participants from Lucknow.

Later, we went for the prize ceremony in the lecture hall. Rishabh got seated in the last row, much like failed backbenchers in classrooms. He was chewing gum as well, his tie was left loose, and his hand held his newly bought smartphone. I went and sat next to him.

'All the remaining ideas are bullshit,' Rishabh said. 'I talked to each one of them. First of all they don't know how to talk and those who do know, have just begun their venture. We are the only ones who have some users, the only ones to have any revenue, and the only ones to have a live product ready.'

I nodded in agreement. We had no competition. Our bank account was going to be flooded with 5 lakh rupees.

We waited patiently as one of the panelists grabbed the mic to announce the results. He appreciated all the ideas, talked at length about the organization he was from—a newly formed start-up incubator by the name of SproutLabs to our shock, and then began unravelling the names of the winners.

First. Second. Third. We waited, we waited, we waited. Until wait betrayed us.

We didn't figure in top 3. We couldn't understand that SproutLabs, the same company which had placed so much faith in us earlier , had ditched us in this contest, perhaps fearing that upon getting the money, we wouldn't join them. While I wanted to run away from the IIT-K campus as soon as possible, Rishabh was intent on taking feedbacks from the mentors as to why we didn't figure in top 3. As he was the CEO, his choice prevailed.

The SproutLab guy carefully avoided us and ran off giving a lame excuse that he had a flight in an hour, when we all knew that Kanpur didn't have an airport. Some of the judges said that we didn't throw much light on the revenue model, while some asserted that they had already discussed about us when Rishabh had spammed every venture capital firm on the planet around a month ago. So our CEO had committed a grave crime, and when I geared up to interrogate him once again, our CEO decided to vent out his frustration by cussing at the panel. I behaved like an employee of my own venture and hmmm-ed all throughout.

We had just one resort left now—my lawyer uncle's millionaire client.

The End

February 2012

February is the month of romance. After burning all the romance from my life, it became the month to romance my start-up, the most crucial month for us. We had to finalize the investor. We had to gain a significant traction to impress the investor. We had to exploit Valentine's Week to grow our user base.

'Should we find a sponsor for the contests that we will be hosting during Valentine week?' I asked Rishabh.

'Let's not find one. Prizes should not be incentive for such non-corporate contests. Our users will start expecting them every time then. Let the number of likes on posts be the incentive,' he said.

'You are right.'

I had thought of a seven days long contest on the website during Valentine Week (February 7-14) where we would ask interesting questions and users would have to come up with a witty one-line answer. Also, we started Valentine tips on our fan page from February 1 in pictorial form which got immensely popular and got 1000+ shares in just two days' time and increased our fan base past 25,000.

Valentine Day Tips:
1. If you are planning to surprise your girlfriend by sending anonymous flowers, keep this fact in mind: you will be the last guess on her mind!
2. Don't buy a teddy for your girl. It will make you feel jealous very soon.
3. If you don't manage to find a Valentine by 13th, you are eligible to join Tiger Sena.

All of those tips garnered spectacular response and kept the site going for a few more days.

On February 1, I had called my lawyer uncle to find an investor for us. He connected us to Darsheel, a young dynamic lawyer from Harvard, who was his partner. Darsheel was an expert in corporate affairs and he knew a lot of senior people in big companies. We had a conference call scheduled with him on the evening of February 2.

But Rishabh was cooking up something else altogether. On February 2, he insisted we go to Noida and check with SproutLabs as well. I went along with him where they completely slammed our idea. Instead of the ready offer initially, they even asked us to return them the offer-sheet. Their argument was that they had been watching our growth in the past five weeks and noticed we were growing at a negligible pace. When we blamed it on having no technical co-founder, they claimed that it lessened our chances. Rishabh tried hard to convince them but to no avail.

'We offer you money to work, we don't offer you money to find someone to work. You are entrepreneurs, not government employees,' they argued.

We had no answer and ultimately returned disappointed. Rishabh yelled on the road, 'There's still time for you to improvize. You have taken over the technical department and you are not delivering.'

I shouted back, 'Why do you keep blaming me all the time? You know the situation.'

'The situation is bad because you have made it bad.'

We didn't speak for a while and returned home. I initiated the conference call with Darsheel.

He had gone through our PPT, which my lawyer uncle had sent to him, and gladly informed us that he found our idea ingenious and thought that with our profile, it could easily interest investors. He promised us to work on our finances and bargain with the investor on our behalf. He asked for two days to find the right guy and in the meanwhile, asked us to prepare our financials. We had the financial forecasts for the IIN pitch ready with us where we had pitched for 50 lakhs, but here the case was different. We were pitching for 20 lakhs and things needed to be recalculated. We needed time.

⌁

While I was busy in Kanpur, there was something else happening on the home front. Late night on February 2, my father called me to inform that my mother needed to see a doctor in Delhi and she had boarded a train for Delhi. I had to go to receive her the next day.

'I am arranging for a leave in the meanwhile, which is quite difficult right now. We are lucky that you run your own company, for you can take a day off as and when possible,' my father said. His statement 'you run your own company' seemed like a tight slap on my face.

Max hospital in Saket is one of the best hospitals in Delhi, right across Malviya Nagar. I had scheduled an appointment with the doctor for the next evening. My parents didn't inform me what the exact problem was and I, completely unaware, thought that it was a minor problem.

February 3

My mother arrived the next day. Owing to the tense environment in our flat, I didn't allow my mother to stay with me at the Malviya Nagar house. I instead forced her to stay in Gurgaon at my aunty's place. In the evening, she consulted a gynaecologist. As I remained seated outside the doctor's chamber, I posted some quotes on YourQuote's fan page and Twitter handle, delegating rest of the day's work to Anjali, whom I'd talked after almost two months' silence and mailed Rishabh (cc-ing Anjali) that I was going to the hospital with my mother.

When my mother came out of the hospital chamber, there was a blank, horrified look on her face. I looked at my aunty, even she seemed crestfallen.

'What happened Mom?'

'The reports suggest I have cervical cancer. They have asked me to do a few blood tests. Only after the operation can we determine whether it's malignant or benign,' she said. I gaped in shock.

'Come on, the reports must be wrong,' I said dismissing her statement.

We went for her blood test. I stood alongside her. The doctor told us to come back the next day for a few more tests. I dropped her at my relative's place in Gurgaon and left for home.

I went back home and found Anjali already there. Neither Rishabh nor she asked me about my mother's health. I called Darsheel for it had been two days since we last spoke. I had turned the speaker on so the other two could hear.

'Amol, congratulations. One of my clients, Mr Mukherjee who works at the executive level position at HUL, is very interested in your venture. He was mightily impressed by your academic background, the IIT degrees, and the idea. He's a great friend of your uncle as well. I think I will be able to convince him to put in 20 lakhs at 10 percent equity, if you give me three more days. In the meanwhile, send me the finance predictions as soon as possible.'

'Okay,' I said. Just when I disconnected the call, Anjali screamed a loud 'yay'. Rishabh seemed delighted too. But my mind was elsewhere.

'My mother is not well. I will have to attend to her in the hospital for a few days.'

'Oh yes, I forgot. How is aunty?' Rishabh asked.

'She's okay right now. The results of her blood tests are due to come tomorrow and only after that we will get to know,' I said.

'Okay. Is she in Gurgaon right now? If the hospital is in Saket, you should have brought her here,' Rishabh said. His generosity touched my heart and I told him that I will bring her the next day.

February 4

As I sat outside the doctor's chamber waiting for the results, three separate feelings of guilt caged me. First, of neglecting my mother when she needed me the most. Second, of pushing Priya away from me especially in times of dire need. And third, of not being able to put my heart and soul into work because I feared that Rishabh would cite my current work later to prove himself superior.

Rishabh had sent me a message asking me about the Valentine Week's contest design. I had delegated the task of designing the special contest webpage to the intern. I called the intern to ask about his progress. He informed me that he hadn't started to work, as he wanted to resign because we didn't pay him well. Furious, I fired him instead.

Just then, my mother came out along with my aunty. There was a serene blankness on her face.

'What happened, Mom? What did the reports say?' I said, concerned.

'They are admitting me on 6th. I will be operated on 8th.'

'Operated for what?'

'Operated for gall stone by laproscopy; my cervix and ovary will be removed as well.'

'Is that necessary?'

'The reports hint towards cancer. The doctor fears that the tissue might be malignant, so the earlier the better,' my aunty explained. I was too scared to respond.

I brought my mother to our flat in Malviya Nagar. The operation cost was around 2 lakh rupees. It was the first time that I cursed my fate of choosing to be an entrepreneur, for I could not offer any financial help.

The End

Without a technical intern, I left my mother at home along with my sister Saumya, who had come over, and went to Mishra's place to get the page designed. Mishra, looking at my hapless face, reluctantly offered me help, making me promise I would invite all my friends on his page for TalentMarket. I hesitantly complied.

Rishabh was at IIT and he gave me a lift back home. For the first day, Rishabh helped me in taking care of her. But my gratefulness was shortlived. On the second day itself, he started finding excuses to stay away from the house and dropped subtle hints that she was not welcome there and was adding to the burden.

February 5

Early morning, I went to receive my father while Rishabh left for IIT. On way, Darsheel called me to ask for the financials. I realized we had forgotten to send it. I profusely apologized and asked him for a day or two. I called Rishabh and asked him whether he had been working on the financials, after all he was the CEO and preparing the financials was his responsibility. He told me he was hoping I would take care of it, as had always been the case. Saying that I wouldn't get time as my parents were over at our place, I asked him to take over. He reluctantly complied.

My father had taken a loan for the operation, making me feel guilty for not being able to pool in during that difficult hour. All through the day, I sat next to my parents who asked me about the future scope of YourQuote. I assured them the future was going to be very bright, now that we had finally got an investor. Rishabh informed me late at night that he

267

would not be coming over and would spend the night at some junior's room in the IIT hostel. He didn't hint whether he had completed the financials or not.

February 6

Early in the morning, we went to the hospital. Now that my Dad had come over, he, along with my sister took care of my mother, while I ran from floor to floor finding nurses, buying medicines, and finalizing the room expenditure, with my father's credit card though.

My output of work in the past four days had been less than 4 hours a day. Valentine week's was yet to be started and I had to launch a contest for it too. I sighed thanking my luck that Rishabh was against having a sponsor this time and I didn't need to be on my toes for the next one week.

It took me three hours of continuous nagging to clear up the advance bills, get the room cleaned and have my mother shifted from the general ward to the single room. I had intentionally chosen a single room for her that had one extra double bed-cum-sofa for two attendants, so that my father and sister could stay along and wouldn't need to stay at my place in Malviya Nagar. It cost 20,000 rupees more than the usual and I kept my father in dark about it.

I was attending my mother at the hospital that night when I got a call from Rishabh who seemed excited. 'Amol, grand news. I have found a sponsor for the contest. It's not giving money, but prizes.'

'But, we decided against any prizes, didn't we?'

'We decided, yes, but now I have found one. Now the contest won't be without a buzz. Isn't this amazing? Whenever you come back, just launch the contests. Details have been mailed,' I was too tired to question him further.

'I will do that once I get back home,' I said and continued, 'What about the financials that Darsheel wanted, did you work on it?' only to find out that he had cut the call by then.

I returned home, leaving my parents and sister at the hospital. As Rishabh had assured, there lay a mail in my inbox but it didn't contain the details of the prizes. The sponsor was a small-scale e-merchandizing company called Gift Shop, and after seeing their website, I realized that Rishabh must have tricked him into the deal. I started working on the contest poster design and fell off to sleep in no time.

February 7

It was Rose Day and the day when we were going to launch our Valentine Week contest. I posted details of the contest on our website saying—Come up with an original and witty pick-up line containing the word 'rose' for your crush and win attractive prizes from Gift Shop.

I left for the hospital thereafter, dropping a mail saying I would return late in the afternoon. It was a resting day for my mother, who was to be operated on 8th morning. Just when I reached the hospital, the doctor arrived and asked my parents to sign a legal document. It was a gruesome document and my Dad assured my mother that it was just a formality. I peered at the document and my feet froze upon seeing what was printed there.

The surgery to be undertaken on February 8 for the patient is one of the most intricate surgeries in medical science. The patient is being informed that it won't be doctor's or hospital's responsibility in case any mishap like a deformity, an infection, or death occurs. Only when the patient and his guardian sign the document, will the doctor perform the surgery.

'Everything will be alright Dad,' I assured him. 'There is so much left to see and take pride. Right now I have just found an investor, and you will see that within the next few years, you will bear witness to my interview with Oprah once I sell YourQuote to Facebook for a billion dollars, our first Sedan, and our bungalow in Dubai. Why do you need to worry?' I allowed him to daydream along with me. He smiled in hope. One of the best things about my parents was that they never belittled my dream.

'Son, we are waiting for the day when your face will appear on the cover of *Time* Magazine, like Mark Zuckerberg,' my father said, taking my dream one notch higher. I smiled.

'Come on, stop day dreaming. Let him focus on his work. We are wasting his time,' my mother scolded my father.

'Come on Mom, how can you even think that being with you is wasting my time?'

In the afternoon, around 2, my aunty arrived at the hospital with a couple of more relatives. I went back to my place to freshen up. My sister accompanied me. Rishabh was not at home as usual. I logged in to check my mail.

There was a mail from Darsheel, who had connected me to Mr Mukherjee, saying he had agreed to invest 20 lakhs at 10 percent equity in our venture and was waiting to receive financial forecasts from us. I jumped in utter joy and screamed a loud 'yes' that scared my sister, who came running towards me. I hugged her and chanted, 'We've finalized an investor for 20 lakhs!.' My sister hugged and picked up her phone to inform Mom and Dad. I stopped her saying that I will tell them in person.

The mail further stated that if Mr Mukherjee is satisfied with the forecasts, he would credit the first quarter of 5 lakh rupees in our bank account by February 13 to allow us to quickly progress. He also asked me to forward the mail to Rishabh, whose email id he didn't have. Darsheel had attached a term sheet which had a drag along clause—it meant that if any of us, the Directors, wanted to quit the venture later, the investor would have the right to quit before him and in such an event, the outgoing Director was liable to return the principal sum invested back to the investor.

As if anyone of us is going to quit now, I thought and smiled to myself. There was an increment in the mail count and I clicked on the inbox.

There was a mail from Rishabh, with the subject: NOT IMPRESSED!

We launched the competition 12 hours late with insufficient information.
1. Exact Prizes should be mentioned. It was discussed with you that we were going to have different prizes for different days.
2. Number of prizes was not mentioned

3. Prizes for one girl, one boy not mentioned
4. Prize pictures are not there.
5. Prize not mentioned on the fan page

Moreover, it was launched very late. People say you should trust your partner with his work. I did that bit he doesn't care for the quality then tell me what should I do?

First you do not share the plan with me. Had I not found a sponsor at the last moment, we'd be doing simple posts on website. I can't do everything on my own. This was your responsibility. You should have discussed the plans the way I do every time by calling you.

I don't believe our team is good. Please wake up before I completely lose trust in the team.
Regards,
Rishabh Dev
CEO, yourquote.in

Earlier, I was stressed. But his mail shot my temper. I couldn't understand how he could be so inconsiderate about my condition. He knew that I was doing duty at the hospital for the past four days, he knew that my mother had not been keeping well, and he knew that despite being so occupied, I had launched the contest. In a huff, I wrote a mail making sure that I didn't play the blame game but politely bring out the evident facts.

I proposed to find a sponsor last week, but that time the idea was ditched. Last night, when I was running with my mother in hospital, you told me you have found a sponsor.
When I asked you for the details of prizes, I was told that everything was there in a mail. I saw Gift

Shop's mail and prizes for specific days and separate prizes for boys and girls was not mentioned. I did what I could do best with the information provided.

Give me the details of all those five points, I will have them rectified.

NOTE: Please avoid these last minute work from next time. No work can be done in haste.

Regards,

Amol Sabharwal

Co-founder and Creative Director, yourquote.in

Pestered, I went for a bath. My sister prepared tea in the meanwhile. I came back, grabbed the cup of tea and once again, sat in front the laptop. There was a new mail. The mail that would change my destiny altogether.

I found a sponsor because without a prize as an incentive, it would not have been possible to gain traction. There has been so less traffic in the past one week owing to your slackness in social media.

It was your mistake that you were not ready with your work beforehand. You should have planned everything beforehand, as your mother's ailment was already known to you.

Your negligence:

1. You didn't share the plan.
2. You didn't have a structure for Valentine's week. You post whatever you wish, without planning. You only know how to write creative things and neglect everything else. You never understand that this is an organization and not your individual property where you can post anything without scrutiny.

If you compare your work with mine, you will realize
that your work is not even 1/4th of mine.

In fact, I have so much doubt about your capabilities
that I'm planning to hire a CMO and then get into the
tech department, learn coding, and build something
good. But you know what, you keep resting on your
comfortable bed and do whatever you feel like, do not
manage, do not organize, do whatever makes you feel
good. When I will need creative one-liners, I will
let you know.

You won't praise me for finding a sponsor when
your ego is being questioned. But you know what? I
can't listen against my self-esteem and dedication
towards my work.
Regards,
Rishabh Dev
CEO, yourquote.in

I couldn't believe what I'd just read. All the while, I believed
that there was at least some mutual respect left that kept
us together but Rishabh, with his previous mail, shredded
every bit of it. I would have cheated on myself had I stayed
even a moment more with him. I kept staring at the mail,
blank and clueless until my sister Saumya, who was sitting
in front of me, quizzed me saying, 'What happened?'

I could not say a word. I turned the laptop's screen towards
her and she went through the mail.

'Oh my God, how dare he write like that to you? Doesn't
he have any manners?'

'I'm quitting YourQuote,' I said in all seriousness.

'What? Are you crazy? You just got an investor.'

'Everything has happened at the right time. I can't work
with a person who doesn't respect me. Moreover, if I quit now,

I will not get tied up with an investor,' I smiled at my fate.

'What would you do then, look for a job?'

'I don't know. When I could sustain myself without money for the past seven months, I can do the same for the next seven as well,' I said with conviction. I realized what entrepreneurship had done to me—it had trounced the fear of uncertainty from my life.

'Don't tell Mom about it now. Her blood pressure will shoot up,' Saumya advised.

Though I had no doubts about my decision, I needed to consult with my father before taking this drastic decision. I had put in his 2.5 lakh rupees into the venture which was going to be lost now.

In the next one hour, I rectified everything that Rishabh had wanted from me in the contest and packed a bunch of my clothes, laptop, and cellphone charger. I would not return to that house for a long time. But before I left, I posted a sermon on the YourQuote fan page:

More than money, more than recognition
More than happiness, more than health
More than friendship, more than love
More than life, more than even your dreams
Care for your self respect!

My parents took my decision better than I had imagined.

'For us, your happiness is all that matters,' my father said.

'What about the *Time* magazine cover?'

'You have quit your venture, not your life. I'm sure you will find a way to fulfill my dream.'

'Come on, stop pressurizing my son. I'm so relieved that now my kids will be able to live together,' Mom said.

In the evening, I drafted my final mail to Rishabh:

```
Dear Rishabh,
    This is to notify you that I'm opting out of my
position of Director of YourQuote Marketing Private
Limited. I expect to be discharged from all the
duties. This decision has been taken after much
thought and consultation with my friends, family,
and mentors.
    In case you don't want to continue the venture
further, kindly let me know, because then I would
want to take it forward.
Regards,
Amol Sabharwal
```

I read my mail twice but still could not decide whether to click on the send button or not. Anxious, I logged into my Facebook account after a gap of almost three days. February 8, Propose Day, held a surprise for me. An extremely unpleasant one though. The very first news feed made me feel suicidal and flushed all my anxiety into a never-ending ocean of grief, fury, and loss. It said:

Priya Singh is in a relationship with Anirudh Arora

This one line was powerful enough for me to block her from my life for good.

Clicking on the send button of my resignation mail never seemed so easy, as I now had yet another reason to run away from Delhi for as long as I could.

Rishabh Speaks

Enough of all that bullshit! He has been feeding you with all kinds of nonsensical stories proclaiming himself to be right and me to be awfully wrong? Well, I tell you that he is the biggest mud-slinger I have ever seen.

I won't allow my vexation with Amol to speak on behalf of me. I'm the business guy, the logical guy who always thinks before acting and I will tell you what exactly was wrong with Amol. If I have to answer in one word, I will say: everything.

Now, I will prove all the things everything accused him of one by one and you will realize why he deserved the mail that he'd got. However, before I begin my monologue, let me inform you that at the time of sending the mail, I had no idea about the intensity of his mother's illness. I just knew that she was not well and was admitted in Max hospital.

When I first met him at IIT, he was one of the most popular boys there. No, don't get me wrong. He didn't secure any of the top ranks, neither had he published his novels back then. He just owned a community on Orkut named IIT-Delhi Entrants 2007 and he promoted networking among most of us newly JEE qualified students.

But when I first encountered him, it was a shock for me. Unlike his cool technical avatar, he was a bloody wimp! He carried this immense fear of girls and it was quite funny when girls whom he had chatted with for hours on internet found out what a chicken he was in the real life. His crooked yellow teeth made him repugnant and his orthodox idealism provoked laughter. A typical small-town smartass. Frankly speaking, I expected somebody suave, somebody articulate in his place. But again, IIT is like a grist mill—the first few years brings evenness and bridges the gaps in the personalities. It even shaped him.

He was my next-door neighbour in our hostel. I didn't realize initially whether it was his desperate attempt to make a mark for himself or to impress others that made him dabble many different things. He got into music, played a dozen of instruments despite not being extraordinary in any of them. He got into photography, shot some snaps, and uploaded them on Orkut followed by Facebook. At times, I felt he was trying too hard and not getting anything in return, which with time provoked sympathy more than contemptuous laughter.

Come the second year and this bashful small-town guy surprises us all by announcing that he had got a girlfriend. Come on, you don't expect such a dumbass to be the first one amongst us to get a girlfriend! Get a life, man. By this time, we were quite good friends and he chose me to be one of the first ones to be introduced to Priya, along with Pratik. Even Pratik agreed with me at that time that she was way too hot for him. We thought she agreed to date him for she wanted to prove her smartness over him by sarcastically taunting him every now and then, inducing some pity for him in my eyes.

I once even asked him whether he was serious about going long term with Priya when he replied with his small town seriousness, 'I will marry her someday.' Only God knows how I restrained my laughter at that time.

There was a remarkable change in him after Priya came into his life. He became more passionate, more confident and thankfully, lost his fear while conversing with-girls. This was the time when I closely observed his passion for writing and him trying to take a leap of faith into the mammoth task of writing a book, which I loved. I was passionately in love with a school friend of mine back then, that's why. She rejected my proposal after making me wait for two months. Yes, Anjali had not arrived by then.

By the third year, with his book published and the fame that followed, he inspired me to blog as well. I wrote a blog on a prank that we played on Pratik and it got pretty famous in the campus—even more famous than Amol's novel—and that's how I got in touch with Anjali, because Pratik was her good friend and the blog was on Pratik, so you get the point!

I think Amol has written a lot of bullshit about Anjali and me. There needs to be some light thrown upon it. Anjali and I are such close friends because we both trust each other completely. That's it. It doesn't imply that we are physically intimate or are going to marry someday. I consider our relationship very sacred and let us stop at that. And regarding everything that she had said to Amol at every occasion, I believe she has done nothing wrong and Amol deserved what he got.

When Amol first disclosed the idea of YourQuote to me, I couldn't exactly get it and was thoroughly skeptical. It was too writer-oriented for me. But when he shared his vision that it could sprout up writers in ordinary people, I could see its scope. Much like Facebook, with its photo-sharing features, has sparked off photography enthusiasts; similarly YourQuote could do the same. Moreover the response on his YourQuote blog had been quite stunning, and since I was an avid follower of his blog, I made my decision quickly. The concept of equal division of equity and designation was what I expected of Amol, because I felt that he was honest and righteous. Today, I don't feel so anymore.

The initial phase was fun. Both of us being competent in our respective fields, we nabbed followers on our facebook page together with T-shirt orders. Amol's creativity was at its pinnacle during this time, when he created amazing content, engaged the followers around our brand with unparalleled dexterity that could have even put social media experts to shame, and built our community from 0 to 14,000 organically in just four months. I admired and valued Amol's creativity and made sure that the hassles of marketing didn't affect him in any way. I rarely shared with him the marketing details, the painstaking negotiations, and the irate customers who treated me like their servants.

During these initial months, I, along with Anjali and others, realized Amol had a short temper. During discussions, he always had something to do—either talk to Priya or post something useless on the fan page. Anjali had nicknamed him 'Mr Ants in his Pants', for he could never sit with us to discuss for long hours. But still, I made sure that he missed none of the strategy discussions. All important points and outcomes were always mailed to him asking for his suggestions, to which we rarely got a reply. With time, I realized two of Amol's most important shortcomings—his inability to read thoroughly and inability to listen. Trust me, you can't make him read anything, until he's thoroughly interested in it. And about listening, you should better ask his girlfriend. Oh sorry, Priya is no more his girlfriend now.

Slowly, Amol's resistance to change came to the front. He was highly disorganized, preferred to be governed by will rather than a set of disciplines. He wanted to do everything on the spot, nothing was pre-planned, which freaked the hell out of me. Somebody needed to tell him that he was not running his proprietary firm but a private limited company. When I chose to be blunt, he got offended as once again, his creative freedom got affected. I had no option other than pulling my hair out and cringing in frustration.

Later on, when Mishra ditched us, he assumed control of the tech department and screwed it completely with such slow work that even a school student could have done better than him. He kept the website for three months, THREE LONG MONTHS, and we observed no progress. He was busy drooling over his love loss, his unrealistic day-dreams that he kept boasting about on Facebook, and his affair with Shikha. Despite being so inefficient and inept, in defense to himself, he dared to question my work—MY WORK—to which any diligent CEO with enough self respect would have lost his mind. I had to show him the reality and I did.

Sometimes I feel that he was too complacent about the fact that his books were selling and he was earning through them that allowed him to take a backseat in the venture, for he didn't experience the kind of struggle that I did. I could see his disenchantment with the company for a long time and I'm happy that whatever decision he took, it has been the best for the company. He had the option to challenge me and uproot me from the Director's position but he didn't do that, because he knew that he was not capable to run this company in any way. He lacks the entrepreneurial spirit.

I'm sure that he would also have pointed out his anguish about my becoming the CEO of the company. I leave it upon you to decide. Had you been in my place, would you have allowed your company to be run by loose hands as his? Could you have allowed your destiny to be dictated by a person who doesn't even care about his own?

I have not hurt him. I have not hurt his self respect. I just showed him the brutal reality that he had been sitting, idling, and crapping all over our dream, rather my dream. And now see how rapidly I will take YourQuote ahead from here, without a limiting factor like him. I have a new resolve now to take this venture to the pinnacle of glory, just because shit happened.

I could just say one thing—dream alone or else get stifled by others.

Death of a Child

February 8

Having slept late, I woke up late on the day of the operation. It was 10 am already. Seeing several missed calls from my family members, I immediately rushed to the hospital. Mom had gone into the operation theatre at 8.30 am and the operation was going to be three hours long after which she would remain unconscious for another two hours.

Dad asked me if I was alright. He wanted to know whether I'd got any reply from Rishabh. I hadn't got one yet. He wanted everything to be sorted out without affecting our friendship, which was impossible, because it was a matter of self respect and nothing could heal a wound on one's self respect, as I witnessed in case of Priya.

My father initiated the topic about what I would do next, to which I flashed a dumb smile. I had no friggin' idea about what I would do next. We all waited in dreadful silence for Mom to arrive. I checked my mail and still there was no response from Rishabh's end. I could understand that it would have been a big blow to him, but I also knew that it was well deserved. He took me for granted, after all.

My mother came out of the operation theatre at 11 am sharp. The smiles on the faces of the doctors assured me that the operation had been successful. The doctor gifted me a bundle of her gall stones in a jar. The cervical tissue had been sent for biopsy and only one hour later would the report come. My father expressed gratitude to the doctors with a tearful smile.

As we waited for her to regain consciousness, I received a mail from Rishabh. It was not the reply to my mail, but instead he reported a bug on the website and rightfully demanded me to fix it. It was similar to the attitude we had shown to Mishra before he ditched us, when we didn't listen to his grievances and asked him to work further. But in my case, it was of no use.

A nurse arrived and informed us that the operation had indeed been undertaken at the right time, because the cervical tissue indeed was turning cancerous. My mother had post-zero stage cancer. The word cancer diffused silence throughout the room. We could just thank God for allowing it to get diagnosed before spreading further.

⌁

An hour later, there was a message in my Facebook inbox. An angry, vindictive, and stupid message by an extremely stupid woman. Anjali Yadav.

I will pray for aunty's good health and will come to see her tomorrow.

    I have removed you from my friend list because the more I see your updates and comments, the more I start hating you. There was a time when I used to admire you a lot for your genuineness and principles, but now all I know is that you have two sides to your personality—a virtual side and a real side.

I know I am wrong in sending this message today, but I couldn't stop myself when I heard some more things about YourQuote and you. Anyway, I hardly matter to you, so you are not losing a friend in your life. I might be wrong in my judgement, but very honestly I want to see the theory of karma work in this case so desperately. Bye.

'Ha!' I laughed out loud breaking the lull. Vehemently, I replied saying, 'No need to come. Thank you from my entire family. There couldn't have been a better time to send this message. Bye.'

I spoke to my lawyer uncle and updated him about my mother's health followed by a quick discussion about my prospects with YourQuote. He insisted on my buying out Rishabh's equity at an escalated price because the new investor Mr Mukherjee was ready to invest in the company. I rejected his suggestion.

By this time, I had made my mind to quit so firmly that I chose to not go ahead. Ever since I sent that resignation mail to Rishabh, I got an outsider perspective to my own startup. Now, I didn't want to continue with YourQuote because of the ghoulish memory it sparked off in my mind.

I chose to call Darsheel thereafter and told him that I had to quit the venture because of my mother's health while Rishabh would continue. I told him that I had full faith in him, which he accepted after initial hiccups and asked, 'Then I should ask for the financials from him, isn't it?'

I connected them over a mail. I responded to the initial mail and assured Rishabh:

```
I don't want to get involved in any mudslinging.
I wouldn't bad-mouth you about anything that has
happened. I will tell all our past and present
employees that I am leaving because of my mother's
bad health. I have talked to Darsheel and the investor
is still ready to invest in the company. You are
requested to send him the financials as soon as
possible, because he had been waiting for them for
quite some time.
```

Rishabh replied immediately, in a slightly arrogant tone.

```
You won't bad-mouth me? What have I done to be bad-
mouthed about?
    Anyway, thanks for making it easier for me to
continue from here. Now see how fast I take this
company forward. Within two months, I would make
it a million dollar company. I have already started
working on the next steps. Just hand over the company
to me and let me take it forward. I will give you a
share of 5 percent from the amount I receive when I
manage to sell the company. Otherwise if you keep
hold of the 50 percent stake of your company, no
investor will be willing to invest.
```

He had a point. I agreed to his condition.

I posted on the group that contained all the team-members—past and new that owing to my mother's bad health, I was quitting the venture, as I was going back home to take care of her.

People were sympathetic towards me but more towards Rishabh, who now had to decide which direction to take the company. Rishabh, contrary to what he had said to me in the mail, sought more sympathy with his comment, 'Should I continue or leave the venture?'

I was the first one to reply, 'Of course you should continue.' People followed up with motivational comments.

⌁

Transferring the directorial rights in a private limited company turned out to a tedious procedure. That's where proprietorships are advantageous. One should never register a venture as a private limited company before investment, as the young guns don't really know whether they will remain together or break apart later on. I let him buy my stake in zero bucks. Knowing each other's financial conditions, I signed on the paper which read that I received 50,000 rupees from Rishabh Dev, Director of YourQuote Marketing Private Limited, without actually receiving the amount.

He nevertheless assured 5 percent later on. I didn't doubt him because Rishabh was a man of his word, but the prospect of a sellout later on seemed improbable. My five days absence had started showing in the quality of YourQuote posts that had deteriorated and my friends, who didn't yet know about my disassociation with the venture, complained.

Five days later, Darsheel called me and said that he was unimpressed by Rishabh as he had still not sent the financials to him. Being a lazy ass when it came to sedentary work, I couldn't expect anything more from Rishabh. I was least bothered and informed Darsheel that he was free to do whatever he wanted.

I announced publicly that I was going home in March, leaving everything that I was a part of. Comments flooded, the number of why's outnumbered the number of likes. I had no answer for it. After humoring them with a response like, 'If I begin answering your why, I would end up writing a book,' I deactivated my account.

Rishabh meanwhile mailed me to not talk about YourQuote on Facebook in any way, as he was in talks with some investors (something that he clearly lied about). I assured him that I had already deactivated my account and wouldn't be activating it for a month at least and reminded him that Darsheel had been waiting for the financials.

My announcement of quitting raised many eyebrows, made many critics of YourQuote smile in joy, made many admirers and followers sad.

Out of all the mails, one stood out. It was from a long lost name in my memory. Shikha.

I am so happy for you that you chose to quit YourQuote. It would help you reach your fullest potential. Rishabh wasn't a nice guy. He wouldn't have allowed anybody creative to flourish there.

Fearing that it might be one of her desperate ways to hook up with me, I chose not to reply to her. I was over my past. I activated my Facebook account and observed Rishabh's last status. It said: Dream alone. Else get stifled by others. Angry, I updated my status with:

You can tolerate
Criticism, taunts and insults

If the person who gives it to you
Matters to you
You can't tolerate
Criticism, taunts and insults
If the person who gives it to you
Doesn't matter to you

Two hours after I updated the status, I received a mail from Rishabh.

Amol,
    I need a public declaration—either in mail, or in your blog/note—containing three points:

1. Rishabh is an able leader and you have full trust in him running the venture
2. You hold the team members of YourQuote in high esteem and you have faith in them
3. You left the venture because of your mother's bad health

It is needed because you are leaving Delhi in a while and will not be accessible (I suppose). I need it as an evidence for an investor/any third party interested in buying us.

I was amused by the confidence with which he could rightfully ask for those three points, none of which were true. He had bad-mouthed me in the entrepreneurial circles, as my fellow entrepreneurs conveyed that he blamed me for shrewdly extricating myself upon realizing that the idea wasn't working, thus hiding the reality that actually it was our team that wasn't. Being sour about the unjust allegation, I chose not to cooperate with him.

I don't understand why you need it all of a sudden. First of all, you haven't kept in touch with Darsheel and he has been complaining to me that he hasn't yet received the financials. Moreover, I would prefer to privately tell the investor the same things than to portray the untruth publicly, because:

1. I don't believe that you are a great leader. Had you been a great leader, you would have managed to prevent your partner from quitting the venture. But you couldn't even utter a mild sorry for your insulting mail.
2. Regarding team members, first of all, let me bust the myth that there is a team. There was just one other person working in our venture for the last three months, Anjali, in whom you very well know how much faith I have.
3. Come on, how dare you ask me to lie publicly about the reason. We both know the reason. If you have forgotten, check the resignation mail once again.

Now that I fearlessly faced him, I realized that I was stronger, more logical and most importantly, right as well. Unlike other times, when seeing his name in my inbox vexed me, this time I waited for his mail to arrive. It arrived, rather soon in just two minutes.

Well done. That's what I could have expected from you. You are unreliable to the core. You claim

that you would keep your account deactivated for a
month and then ten minutes later, you are online
and posting random gibberish. It's ironical that
you are a writer, which should makes you a man of
words, but you aren't a man of your word.

You know what, you left not because of any of the
above reason, but because you know that you don't
deserve to be an entrepreneur. You don't have it in
you.

By not writing a public letter, you are putting
your 5 percent in jeopardy.

His words had stopped affecting me, as though I was insulated
against them. He should have been the one thanking me for
inducting him into entrepreneurship else he would have been
rotting like Priya and her comrades in a shitty company like
EWZ.

I kept my reply simple.

Thank you. Now that you have started stalking me, let
me help you out. I have blocked you. You can breathe
a sigh of relief that now you won't have to read my
random gibberish.

And about the 5 percent, keep it with you. I don't
want it.

Yes, I didn't want anything out of the two years that I
had spent into YourQuote. Not because of my ego, which
definitely was huge but because I knew with Rishabh's
diseased attitude the company would be going nowhere and
die a tragic death.

On February 29, after spending half a month sleeping at
borrowed beds, I went to the Malviya Nagar house for the one

last time and moved all my stuff to a new house in Safdarjung Enclave, where I shifted along with my sister Saumya.

'Have you shifted to your new home?' Mom asked me on the phone a few hours after we had shifted.

'Yes.'

'Did Rishabh say anything to you?

'No.'

'Not even a sorry for what he or Anjali said to you?' Mom persisted.

How could I have told her that she was expecting something totally impossible. Rishabh had never ever apologized for anything that he'd done. I told her that I was coming back home in a day. She ended the conversation with a saying, 'A person who doesn't have the heart to apologize, doesn't have a heart at all.'

Her statement pierced my psyche and Priya's face emerged out of nowhere. I didn't have the courage to apologize to her verbally. I wrote a mail, asking her to forget whatever I'd done or said, for I knew that I didn't deserve to be forgiven, I didn't deserve her. She didn't reply.

Having nothing left or undone and finished with the shifting, I went back to Dhanbad, my hometown to be with my mother for a few days.

Epilogue

June 2012
Dhanbad, Jharkhand

It had been four months since I left Delhi. And, to add to the ongoing banter amongst my friends, relatives and neighbours, I was jobless. My parents, having wrongly trusted me once, were visibly concerned, while I was irritable, reticent, and reserved. I didn't meet anyone during this phase, and did not even come out of my house a single time. Often, I overheard my parents discussing among themselves whether I was in depression, or whether they should take me to see a psychiatrist. They tried hard to talk to me, but I always avoided any conversation that involved questions related to YourQuote, Rishabh, Anjali, or Priya. My secrets were meant to be buried within me. My laptop was my only companion, in front of which I spent countless hours, perhaps the only sign of normalcy that I displayed to my parents.

In mid-March, I was informed that Rishabh had shut down yourquote.in as he couldn't run it solo and got hired by another start-up at an executive position. The news failed to register its effect. It couldn't make me happy, couldn't make me sad. I was indifferent to everything that belonged to my past.

'Are you depressed? Your father and I have been very concerned all the while,' asked my Mom, concerned about my health.

'No, not at all, Mom,' I instantaneously replied.

'So, what have you decided with your life? An IIT degree doesn't look good when it's not brought into use. Why aren't you thinking of a job? Your uncle called yesterday and was saying that Mr Mukherjee, that investor from HUL, could hire you in his company. Do you want me to talk to him?'

I stared into her eyes and questioned, 'Mom, remember when we lived in Patna, I had once very emotionally asked whether you would ever leave me.'

'Yes, I remember. I still wonder what made you ask that question.'

I took out my business card from the drawer, which stated 'Amol Sabharwal, Co-founder and Creative Director, yourquote.in' and crushed it in front of her. She was trying hard to read my mind.

'Do you remember what you had answered?' I asked and threw the card on the ground.

'Yes, … and I realize that I was wrong. Apparently, you left your child, and didn't ever turn back,' she said, pointing to the crushed card on the floor.

'Mom,' I whispered, 'you were not wrong, because…' I made her more puzzled, as I continued, 'I didn't leave my child, I just divorced my partner.'

'What do you mean?'

I took my laptop, maximized the browser, and placed it in front of her. A brand new website with a new domain name, with a suave user interface and the tagline, 'You deserve to be quoted' lay before her wet eyes. She was dumbstruck.

'I just renamed my child, Mom and I'm the father—the founder. This child has no mother, this time.'

I smiled and took her to the bottom of the page, which said, much like the first version of Facebook, ©Amol Sabharwal Production.

Her eyes had become heavy, as she hugged me and said, 'But, it has a grandmother.'

'The last four months, building this was what kept me busy, Mom. And yes, do ask Mr Mukherjee if he still wants to invest in my venture.' I winked at my mother.

My Dad sleepily walked into my room and said, 'Where is my grandson? I just overheard something.'

We both laughed as I introduced my baby to his grandfather. He couldn't believe it at first. He looked at me with his big eyes that had to be assured that he really was awake. When the reality dawned on him, he hugged me and lifted me in his arms.

It was time to cut the umbilical cord. I logged into the website and penned down the first quote there:

In a war where both sides are wrong, the side which loses first, wins.

I re-read the line twice. There was something that didn't seem right. The statement, though the first ever quote in my new website, didn't do what it said. It didn't make me feel like a winner. Not at all. I logged into Facebook, opened my block-list and unblocked two names from there. Priya Singh and Rishabh Dev. I stalked their profiles.

Beneath Rishabh's cover pic that carried his happy face, his designation said 'COO at ApparelFactory followed by 'in a relationship with Anjali Yadav'. He looked happy, he looked satisfied. He didn't look like a loser.

I opened Priya's profile. It was for the first time ever since I last blocked her that I saw her face. She was sitting on Anirudh's lap and they were looking at each other, smiling. Her relationship with Anirudh was four months old now. Clearly it wasn't a rebound relationship. Even she looked happy and for a change I genuinely felt happy for her. I didn't need a cigarette now since I quit.

I read the first quote that I'd posted on my brand new website once again. Again and again, until I allowed my gut feeling to guide me in my venture. I removed it and cut the ribbon with another new quote:

And they lived happily thereafter, without each other.

Acknowledgements

No one deserves more gratitude for this book than my parents, Sudha and S.S. Pathak.

This book is also for my sister Saumya, my choti ma Neetu Pathak, my mentor Ashish Tulsian, and friends who have stood by me like a pillar of strength during my difficult phase—Keshav Agrawal, Ravi Mehta, Akshay Gupta, Sohail Gupta, Abhishek Gupta, Vidhu Garg, Ankit Prashar, Shruti Vajpayee, and Durgesh Nandan.

I am thankful to the extremely professional and prompt team at Random House India, especially Gurveen Chadha and Milee Ashwarya, for giving my story a voice.

A Note on the Author

Harsh Snehanshu is the bestselling author of the Kanav-Tanya trilogy, comprising the novels *Oops! I Fell in Love*, *Ouch! That 'Hearts'*, and *She's Single, I'm Taken*. He is a graduate of IIT Delhi and a former internet entrepreneur. Based in Delhi, Harsh is currently travelling across India writing his fifth book. He is fond of music, photography, and public speaking. You could reach him at:

www.facebook.com/harshsnehanshu1
www.twitter.com/harshsnehanshu
harshsnehanshu@gmail.com